IT IS LONG
AFTER MIDNIGHT...
DO YOU KNOW WHERE
YOUR CHILDREN ARE?

A NIGHTMARE
OF SUSPICION

Gwyn walked over to the canvas swing, her mind registering again that it would have been impossible for Jessica to get out of it without help. It was a baby swing, with material going between the legs, and a smooth wooden bar across the front.

And how long would you say you were in the house, ma'am?

A minute—maybe two. I just went in for a drink and . . .

What kind of drink would that be, ma'am? How many drinks had you had?

Do you always have drinks with lunch?

Why would you leave a two-year-old alone?

Is this a publicity stunt?

Are you going to miraculously find your daughter?

Would you give us the names of all your friends?

Do you have any relatives in the area?

Would you agree to a lie-detector test?

CRY, BABY, CRY

It's every mother's nightmare.

Diamond Books by G. F. Bale

IF THOUGHTS COULD KILL
CRY, BABY, CRY

CRY, BABY, CRY

G. F. BALE

DIAMOND BOOKS, NEW YORK

This novel is a work of fiction. Names, characters, places, and incidents are either the product of the author's imagination, or are used fictitiously, and any resemblance to actual persons, living or dead, events or locales is entirely coincidental.

CRY, BABY, CRY

A Diamond Book / published by arrangement with
the author

PRINTING HISTORY
Diamond edition / January 1992

ISBN: 1-55773-643-X

Diamond Books are published by The Berkley Publishing Group,
200 Madison Avenue, New York, New York 10016.
The name "DIAMOND" and its logo are trademarks
belonging to Charter Communications, Inc.

PRINTED IN THE UNITED STATES OF AMERICA

10 9 8 7 6 5 4 3 2 1

For Brian,
with love

Cry, Baby, Cry,
Put your finger in your eye,
And tell your mother it wasn't I.
—MOTHER GOOSE

CHICAGO, 1962

The child sat in the cold bathwater, shivering. Above her head the terry-cloth curtain moved slightly as the winter air blew in, bringing with it fine siftings of snow that began to gather on the windowsill.

"Momma," she began tentatively. "Momma, can I get out now?"

The woman entered the room and stood looking down at the frail body of the three-year-old. "You were bad this morning. You got cereal all over your clothing," she said tonelessly. "When children are messy, they have to get clean. You will stay in the water until then, do you understand me?"

"But, Momma, it's cold. Please can I get out?" the child asked softly.

The woman's face contorted as she fought for composure. "Why must you always argue with me? I am your mother. You will do as I say." As she spoke her voice began to take on an edge the little girl easily recognized.

1

"I'm sorry, Momma. I will stay in the water. It's okay."

But it was too late. The woman's mind had already clicked over and the child knew it was going to begin again. Terror seized her as strong hands pushed her head under the water and she tried to fill her lungs quickly with air.

CHAPTER ONE

OMAHA, 1992

He cautiously approached the east entrance to the zoo, his cycs darting back and forth for any sign of motion. He had killed the lights and motor a block away, letting the slight incline of the street propel the car noiselessly forward. If anyone showed up he would say the electrical system had blown, and he was merely coasting to a stop.

But he felt confident there would be no eyes watching him. The east entrance to the zoo was rarely used—only for large truck deliveries. The short street was actually more of an alley—overgrown with weeds and large potholes that kept even the police from patrolling the short block. It was perfect.

He rolled slightly past the big iron gates, braked to a stop, and waited. If a patrol car had noticed him, they would come now to investigate. He checked his watch. Five minutes passed before he silently emerged from the car and scanned the area. No one.

Quickly he raised the hood of his car and loosened the distributor wire. If the vehicle was noticed before he returned, he could legitimately plead car trouble. If he saw any activity, he would circle around and approach from the opposite side.

From the side pocket of his jacket he removed a small case of picks, selected one, and deftly opened the padlock attached to the heavy chain holding the large gates together. He slid the chain free and pushed the right side of the gate open.

Returning to his car, he unlocked the trunk and stood for a moment looking down at the blood-stained body of the woman. Somehow he thought she looked better in death than she had in life. At least one thing was sure—she wouldn't be running her fat mouth anymore.

She was heavy, and it was all he could do to lift her from the trunk. This was the dangerous part. If anyone came by now, it would be all over. This thought gave him the energy he needed to quickly hoist her onto his wide-set shoulders, lower the trunk, and slip through the gate. This done, he dropped his load unceremoniously on the ground, pulled the gate closed, and replaced the chain and padlock, being careful not to push the lock all the way down. Anyone coming by would not notice anything amiss.

He checked his watch. Four o'clock. He still had plenty of time before workers who fed the animals arrived, and another two hours before dawn.

It took thirty minutes to get the body to its final destination—longer than he had planned. He was pant-ing heavily from the exertion, but forced himself to jog the half mile back to the entrance.

There was no one in sight. He had made it.

* * *

Gwyn jerked awake, trying to hold on to the dream, to make it real. With the back of her hand she wiped the thin layer of moisture from her face. Jessica had been calling to her, trying to tell her where she was, but Gwyn had not been able to understand her words. Each time when she had almost reached her child, Jessica would disappear and call to her from a different place.

Gwyn threw back the sheets and sat up on the edge of the bed, reaching for her slippers. *It was only a dream. It had no meaning.* She would have liked to have taken some comfort in the idea that her dream was a signal—a hint that she was getting closer to Jessica, but she knew that it was not. She had learned at the early age of four to tell the difference between dreams and psychic revelations. A dream was just that, a dream—something her subconscious wished for or feared, but not that special cognitive awareness that occurred when she was *tuned in* to someone.

Automatically Gwyn glanced at the wreath on the wall. Her best friend Karen had chosen it especially because the heart-shaped form was filled with sprigs of rosemary, for remembrance, and accented with white daisies symbolizing Jessica's innocence. Month after month had passed and the white petals were slowly fading to beige but it would stay on the wall until Jessica was safely back. *My God, had it been nine months?*

Maybe this morning she could pick up something—something that would help her make some sense out of the visions she had been receiving. Something that would at least give her a clue to work from—a starting point. It was always possible. Her psychic ability would sometimes fade slightly and then surge if conditions were right.

Gwyn rose and walked over to the dresser, pushing her long blond hair back from her face. She was oblivious to the striking image staring back at her from the mirror. At five feet seven inches, Gwyn Martin had an almost regal bearing, as well as the kind of beauty most women would kill for. She could have been a high-fashion model, a movie star, or any of the other glamour jobs that incredibly beautiful women tend to gravitate toward, but they had never held any interest for her. She was more than content where she was—hostess of a successful radio talk show dealing with psychic issues. Lord knows she knew her subject well. She sometimes wondered if there was a book on the market even remotely smacking on the paranormal that her father had not either read to her or insisted she read. Most children were raised on Dr. Seuss. She had been raised on Edgar Cayce. Not that she had ever minded. Her fondest memories of childhood were going to the library with her father, coming home and sitting on his lap and reading about the great psychics of the world. So many of them had troubled childhoods, mainly because no one—including they themselves—understood their special gift. Her father had made certain this had not happened to her, and for that Gwyn would be eternally grateful.

Picking up the brush from the dresser, Gwyn began to untangle her mop of golden tresses. "Fat lot of good my *extraordinary* gift is doing me now," she said aloud to the mirror.

Jessica's angelic face smiled up at her from the silver-framed picture amid the clutter on the dresser top. Gwyn picked up the picture and held it to her. *Where are you, my darling? Are you safe? Please be all right. I couldn't bear it if you were not.*

In the red brick colonial house next door, Karen Jackson poured her third cup of coffee, mentally going over her appointments for the day. Karen, at the age of 33, found herself one of *the* foremost buyers for Children's World, a large retail chain selling children and teenage clothing headquartered in Omaha. She had almost a sixth sense about what would appeal to children and teenagers in coming months, and time and again Children's World would corner the market on the latest fad following her suggestions.

At an even five feet and weighing exactly 113 pounds, Karen looked more like one of the young teens frequenting the store than the company's top buyer—a fact not lost on the corporate heads who knew it was time to promote this magical woman to a vice presidency. They worried that Karen's youthful appearance might make it difficult for others to take her seriously. They also worried that if they did not make the move, a rival company would snap her up. Had they bothered to ask Karen *her* wishes, they would have discovered she adored her job as a buyer and had no intention of giving up the extended buying trips across the United States and occasionally overseas. Her salary far eclipsed anything she ever dreamed she would make, her Christmas bonus alone being more than the yearly salary of the average person. No, Karen was perfectly content where she was, and had no designs on a corporate office job.

She glanced at the ornate grandfather clock standing against the east wall of her den. It always gave her enjoyment to look at the heavy mahogany piece, which chimed every fifteen minutes. That alone would drive some people crazy, but its mellow tones were sheer pleasure to Karen's ears. It would always be her most cherished possession. It was one of the first things she had purchased for herself when her salary had finally made it possible to quit scrimping and saving. It brought a smile to her face to remember the movers who had eyed her little one-bedroom apartment suspiciously as they unloaded the clock—not quite believing they had the right address. She had to admit the clock looked better in this house, her home now for the last four years. And when the house next door had gone on the market, Gwyn and Adam purchased it and she then had her best friend next door. It had all seemed so perfect.

Then Jessica vanished. Jessica Lynn—the Lynn named for her, Karen Lynn. Baby Jessie—so bubbly and full of life. Her godchild, her beautiful, loving godchild. Gone. Without a trace. Out of their lives so quickly.

Karen set her coffee cup down on the end table and walked to the window. "Please, God," she whispered. "Please help us find her."

Across town Adam Martin jogged the last few steps to his apartment, unlocked the front door, and collapsed in his favorite easy chair—the only piece of furniture he had taken with him three months ago. He looked around at the remaining furniture and shook his head. Furnished apartments were certainly not decorated with any particular theme in mind—just a hodgepodge of leftover odds and ends the owners probably picked up at garage sales.

Everything he owned, other than a few clothes and this chair, remained at home. He still thought of it as home. Though technically he and Gwyn were separated, he could not quite make himself believe his marriage was over. He looked down at his damp sweatsuit, and memories of Gwyn beside him for their morning run came rushing back. Gwyn, with her long blond hair swinging back and forth in a ponytail as she ran beside him—her quick laughter splitting the early morning air as she teased him when he stopped to rest. Gwyn, prancing around him like a boxer in a ring, taking playful jabs at him, urging him on. He had always considered himself in good shape until he met Gwyn. He lifted weights and occasionally jogged in the park, but when Gwyn entered his life, she was a whirlwind of activity. Running—not jogging—soon became the order of the day, and he found he had to really work to stay up with her, challenging his body every day. He discovered that *high* runners get after a successful workout—that euphoric feeling that comes from nothing else.

Adam hauled himself out of the chair and headed for the bathroom and a hot shower. It seemed like lately he had to force himself to do the most simple, mundane things. Perhaps because life really held no joy for him anymore. He went through the motions like a windup toy. Jessica's face suddenly loomed in his mind, and he felt an almost physical blow to his stomach. He turned

the shower faucet on as hot as he could stand it, then
leaned against the smooth tile and wept unashamedly.

Brent Carlson punched the intercom button, then
remembered the time and realized no one else would be
in the office yet. Ordinarily, he was the last person
to come in, but lately he had not been sleeping well. He
had been up since five, nervous, pacing—his mind
going in a dozen different directions. He thought of
his partner and wondered if he would be able to do any
real work today. Their architectural firm depended
heavily on Adam's brilliant innovative mind. He knew
they would not be even close to the success they were, if
it were not for him. Brent was a good architect—a
solid architect—but Adam was in a league all by
himself.

They had been friends since their days at Princeton.
Then after college, Adam had taken a job with Colbert &
Sons, a prestigious firm in New Jersey. Brent had
come back to Nebraska and started a small business in
Omaha. There was no doubt in his mind, but that Adam
would climb to the top of the ladder quickly. He had the
brains, the flair, and the good looks to succeed at
anything.

Then one day a few years later, Adam had walked into
his office with a smile and said, "Hey, buddy. Got a job
for an old friend?" He had little to say about why he left
Colbert & Sons, other than that they were not ready for
him yet. All of the really plum projects were given to
Hank Colbert's sons, and there was absolutely no way
Adam was ever going to really advance in the firm.

Brent did not care why Adam had left. He was beside

himself with the thought of working with his old friend. He knew his little firm had hit pay dirt. Within six months he had offered Adam a full partnership, and within two years, Adam had married the only woman Brent had ever loved.

CHAPTER TWO

The shrill ringing of the telephone brought Jim Anderson out of a sound sleep. With one hand he felt for the phone amid the clutter on his bedstand, and with the other he groped blindly for his cigarettes. "Yeah? What is it?" he finally managed.

"Captain? I'm sorry to bother you this early, but—"

"Connors? This sure as hell better be good!" He looked at his small alarm clock on the stand through bloodshot eyes. "You know damn well I was at the precinct until four this morning and left word—"

"Captain," Connors interrupted. "Captain, there's been another murder. We aren't sure yet of course, but it looks like it could be the work of the same guy."

Anderson was instantly awake. "Where are you and what do you have?"

Connors spoke swiftly and to the point. "The zoo, sir. The groundskeeper found the body of a woman, about thirty-five years old, in the duck pond when he was making his rounds about thirty minutes ago. We just arrived, but it appears she has been stabbed numerous times—same as the others."

"Shit. That tears it then," Anderson swore quietly into

the phone. "Looks like we have a serial killer on our hands. Are the lab boys there yet?"

"They're on the way."

"All right. Here's what I want you to do. Call Tucker, Petterson, and Bozyk. Have them meet me there in fifteen minutes. Tucker was with me last night, and I told him to take the day off. I think he planned on going by his girlfriend's and might still be there. You'll probably have to beep him. And, Mel—"

"Yeah, Captain?"

"Make sure nothing is disturbed anywhere near that duck pond. Tell the men to stay on concrete or pavement. Maybe we'll get lucky on some prints."

"Right. I'll get right on it."

Anderson replaced the phone and grabbed for his pants and shirt lying on the floor where he had dropped them not quite two hours ago. He looked around at the shambles he had managed to make of the bedroom he and Molly had shared for thirty-five years. Shit. Who was he kidding? The entire house didn't look much different. He searched through a drawer for clean socks, couldn't find any, and grabbed for his dirty ones.

Tonight. Tonight, Molly dear, I will do the washing and straighten up this mess.

He could almost feel her presence. She would be so appalled if she could see the condition of her beloved house—and husband. Damn, he missed her. Right now she would have been in the kitchen making him a thermos of coffee to take with him, and wrapping an egg sandwich for him to eat on the way. She had never complained about his crazy hours—not in all the years they were married. She always insisted he eat breakfast.

Usually they could eat together, but in emergencies, he never left the house empty-handed. He often wondered how she could manage to have something ready for him, no matter how quickly he had to leave.

And who would have thought she would be the first to go? Molly—who never smoked or drank, who took such good care of herself—dead at the age of fifty-seven from a brain tumor.

She had been complaining of headaches for about two months, and Jim had finally insisted she go for a checkup. The doctor had called him at the station and asked him to come to his office. There was a large inoperable tumor at the base of Molly's brain. It had invaded the walls and he was sorry, but there was nothing anyone could do. And after making the rounds of every specialist they could find, they had to accept what Molly's doctor had said. Nothing could be done.

Molly had died three months ago, after almost a year of extreme headaches and seizures. Toward the end she had begged God to take her, and Jim had railed at a God who would allow such suffering.

On the last day of her life, she opened her eyes, smiled at him, and said, "It's almost over, Jim. My pain is gone, and I can see the light. Take care of yourself, my darling. I love you." And she was gone.

Since then, he had immersed himself in work to ward off *his* pain. He spent as little time as possible in their small home. Memories of Molly were everywhere he looked. Her clothes still hung in the closet, her purse still lay on the bureau, and her makeup was still lined up neatly in the medicine chest.

One of these days—

* * *

Gwyn finished dressing and headed for the backyard. As she crossed the patio a flock of starlings rose from her silver maple tree and obliterated the sky for a few moments. She shuddered involuntarily. She hated those large jet-black creatures. They scared away all the pretty little birds and always gave her a feeling of impending doom. For some reason her father's words came back to her from long ago. "One thing you must never do, Gwyn, is try to read something into everyday occurrences. *Everything* does not have some special meaning for you. Many things just happen. They happen to everyone. To try and analyze every event in your life would drive you crazy."

"Daddy, sometimes I think I am already crazy," she'd told him. "Sometimes I think awful things. Then when they come true I worry that I caused them to happen."

"Gwyn Anne Calvert!" he had told her sternly as he wrapped her in his arms. "I don't want to hear such nonsense again. Have you learned nothing from the books we've been reading? A psychic does not *make* things happen. You are not God. You can not control events. You are only able on some occasions to perceive ahead of time that the event will occur. But believe me, darling, it would happen with you or without you. That part is totally out of your hands."

Gwyn smiled as the warm memories of her father surfaced. She pictured him as he was then. A giant of a man—over six feet five inches tall, handsome in a rugged, backwoods way. He was a logger in Oregon— one of the best, his men had told her at the funeral five years ago.

But of course they did not really know Joe Calvert. They did not know the man who had dropped out of school in the sixth grade to help support five younger brothers and sisters after the death of their father. They did not know the man who had learned to use a library in order to help his young daughter who had some myste- rious power he had never heard about. And they did not know the gentle, kind, caring father who raised this daughter all alone after the death of his wife. He took her shopping for frilly little dresses, he braided her hair with extreme precision for a man with rough, worn hands the size of dinner plates, and he was always there for her. Always.

She missed him desperately.

He had died saving the life of another logger. A new man, twenty-eight years old, with three babies at home. He had thrown the man from the path of a falling redwood, but had not been able to escape one of the large branches that crashed down on his own body. Adam had chartered a plane from Omaha, and they were with him constantly the five days he managed to cling to life. When he died, Gwyn thought she would never again feel such a loss or be so devastated.

She had been wrong.

They had purchased the house on Wayne Drive specifically for the safety factor. It was a quiet street, no through traffic to worry about, and lots of old established families. The sort of place a person could put down roots. The house was a large rambling ranch style, which had started out as a small one-bedroom home but had been added to gradually as the previous owners brought their six children into the world. The man had been an excellent carpenter, and Adam had always said you could see his love of his family reflected in the care he took in the remodeling of their homestead. He had passed away five years ago, and since the children were all grown, his wife had wanted to find a small apartment for herself. When she had mentioned this fact to her neighbor, Karen Jackson had immediately called Gwyn. "It's perfect for you," she had assured her. "And it would be so much fun having you both next door."

When Adam and Gwyn went to look at the house, they fell instantly in love with it. It was big and homey, had a fenced-in backyard with good sturdy playground equipment set permanently in cement, and lots of big oak trees and one beautiful silver maple for their future children to climb.

Of course Adam someday planned to design and build a house just for them, but that was in the future, when they had more money and knew more about the type of house they wanted, but until then, he was more than pleased with this home they had found. Even his keen architectural eye could find little fault with this house.

Gwyn walked over to the canvas swing, her mind registering again that it would have been impossible for Jessica to get out of it without help. It was a baby swing, with material going between the legs, and a smooth wooden bar across the front.

And how long would you say you were in the house, ma'am?

A minute—maybe two. I just went in for a drink and . . .

What kind of drink would that be, ma'am? How many drinks had you had?

A Coke! I went in for a Coke. I just walked in the house, opened the refrigerator, got a Coke—a diet Coke—and walked back outside.

There is an empty wine bottle on the kitchen counter. Are you sure you weren't drinking something more than Coke?

No. Of course not. My husband was home for lunch. We had a picnic on the patio and we each had one glass of wine. The bottle was almost empty and we just finished it at lunch, that's all.

Do you always have drinks with lunch?

Why would you leave a two-year-old alone?

Is this a publicity stunt?

Are you going to miraculously find your daughter?

Would you give us the names of all your friends?

Do you have any relatives in the area?

Would you agree to a lie-detector test?

Gwyn shuddered as she remembered the grueling questioning she had been forced to endure. Karen had screamed at the two young policemen, calling them idiots and demanding their badge numbers. She had then marched across the room and phoned Captain Anderson—something Gwyn had not thought to do in all the excitement. Their attitude was markedly different when they finished listening to their captain, and Gwyn took some satisfaction in the knowledge that the two of them would be pounding a beat for a long time.

Still, it galled her. What if she had not known the captain? The extreme distress of having a child missing was bad enough without having the police look at you as if you had caused the disappearance. She knew Captain Anderson had implemented new techniques after that fiasco, and she hoped no other parents would have to go through the grilling she had been forced to sit through.

She looked steadily at the swing, wondering if today would yield anything new. Presently she closed her eyes, letting her long graceful fingers glide over the fabric of the swing. She swayed slightly as the power of her concentration forced all extraneous thoughts from her mind, taking her back in time.

When the mental picture cleared, she could see her child, rocking gently back and forth in the swing, eyes closed.

And there was the woman again—the white-haired woman who kept popping in and out of Gwyn's visions. Her face was lined with wrinkles, but it was a caring, friendly face—a grandmotherly face, with soft blue eyes, old-fashioned wire-rimmed glasses, and framed by a cloud of white, curly hair.

Then the image was gone as rapidly as it had appeared, replaced by swirling water—water that seemed to go on forever, erasing everything else from her mind. It was this image that terrified Gwyn. Why was she picking up such strong images of water, and why did it seem to embody the very essence of evil?

She could feel a tingling sensation move slowly from the base of her neck down her spine. Her hands began to tremble as she tried to force her mind deeper into the vision. It was no use. The water was overpowering.

With a sob Gwyn let go and forced her mind back to the present. It made no sense. *Nothing* about the whole thing made any sense. Who was the woman? What did the water mean? And why was she still able—after nine long months—to continue picking up the same images?

Was Jessica still alive, trying to reach her? Or was she dead, and that was why Gwyn had not been able to locate her? This had happened with her in the past. She could zero in on children if they were alive, but often could not locate them otherwise. Her mind seemed to rebel at the horror of a dead child, and refused to respond.

No. I'm not going to even think such a thing. Jessica is alive. I'm sure of it.

CHAPTER
THREE

Captain Anderson stood looking down at the bloated, wrinkled body of the woman.

"Have we ID'd her yet?" he asked.

"No, sir. We're running a check now through missing persons—should hear shortly."

"What, exactly, do you have so far?"

Detective Jenkins answered swiftly. He knew Anderson wanted answers ticked off tersely and methodically. Facts first, then guesswork. "First, we have a killer who went to great lengths to put this body in the duck pond. He had to carry the body over about twenty feet of rock, throw the body over the fence, then climb over and place it in the water."

"Could he have come in at the pond gate? Picked a lock? Had a key?"

"No, sir," Jenkins answered him as he pointed to a section of the fence. "Right here is where the body was thrown over. There were pieces of the victim's clothing caught on the top of the fence, and probably that's her blood on the cement below where her body fell. We won't know for certain until the lab results are in."

Captain Anderson gazed at the high chain-link fence.

"What would you estimate the weight of the victim at? One-fifty? One-sixty pounds?"

"About that, I'd say. She was tall and her build stocky—not fat, exactly, but a large woman, certainly."

"Could the killer have forced her to climb over the fence, then killed her?"

"No, sir. The body was in the water about three hours, but the woman has been dead at least nine hours, maybe longer."

Anderson shook his head. "Detective Jenkins, you work out with weights, don't you?"

"Yes, sir."

"Take a good look at that woman. Do you think you could lift her up over your head and push her over that fence?"

Jenkins thought a moment.

"No, sir. I don't believe I could. At least not without a great deal of difficulty."

"Do we know how the killer entered the park?"

"Petterson just arrived a few minutes ago. He's rechecking all of the entrances. Our men didn't find anything first time around. We know the zoo was locked at ten last night. The killer either came in before that, or else got in later somehow. If he came in after the zoo was closed, that would mean he had to carry the body at least half a mile. This duck pond is centrally located. It's a long way to any exits or an outside fence."

"How many men do we have combing the area?"

"Six, not counting Petterson and Bozyk. And Tucker should be here any minute."

"Double that. I want every scrap in a half-mile radius

tagged. Tell the men I want everything bagged except
bird shit. Got that?"

"Yes, sir. Can we release the body now?"

"Yeah. But tell the drivers to stay on the sidewalk
when they carry her out of here. We'll surely find some
kind of prints. The killer had to be large and he was
toting a heavy woman. If he stepped off the path at any
point, there should be deep prints. I don't want them
screwed up by sloppy ambulance work—or sloppy
police work."

"Yes, sir," Jenkins answered him. "I'll make certain
they understand."

Anderson walked along the duck pond toward the east
gate. What the hell was going on? Three women in two
months. All in their thirties, all mothers—if this last one
proved to have children—all knifed, and all placed in a
body of water.

The first woman was found in the river that ran by the
mall. Everyone figured it was a mugging. Then, three
weeks later, the body of a second woman was found in a
fountain on the grounds of the Commerce Bank. Only
difference here was the woman wasn't dead when the
killer dumped her in the fountain. The autopsy had
shown the cause of death to be drowning.

There was no link between the first two women, other
than they both had children. The first woman was
thirty-two years old, three children, on welfare, and
had at one time been turned in for suspected child abuse
by her neighbors, although nothing had ever been
proven.

The second woman was thirty-five, middle class,

mother of two, ages ten and four. She was active in school events, taught Sunday school, and was by all accounts a good wife, mother, and member of the community. No hint of child abuse—in fact just the opposite—everyone said she was an excellent mother.

And now this new murder. What would her story turn out to be?

CHICAGO, 1962

The toddler felt the pull on her hair and knew it was over. She came out of the water gasping and choking, trying to shield her face from the harsh slaps she knew were coming, but to no avail.

"Stupid, stupid child!" her mother screamed as she hit her. "Why must you always disobey?"

Tears ran down the reddening face of the three-year-old as she fought for control. When she saw her mother's hand reach for the large bar of lye soap she pulled back yelling, "No, Momma . . . Please." But her words fell on deaf ears as she was yanked by her hair from the tub and pinned on the bathroom floor.

OMAHA, 1992

Gwyn raced around the house gathering up the papers she would need to take in to the radio station. For a moment she stopped and looked at the confusion in the house. There were still dishes in the sink, clothes thrown about, and papers and books everywhere. She really should get someone to come in and clean. At her best she was slightly disorganized, messy, and careless about the house—but since Adam had left, and her mind was so preoccupied with Jessica, she had really let things go. Adam had always helped her so much with the everyday picking up and cleaning. Actually, she had to admit he was much better at it than she was.

Adam liked things orderly. He liked to work in uncluttered surroundings, his papers lined up neatly, his pencils sharpened and in a row. She, on the other hand, worked best when she had her papers and books scattered all around the computer. They had compromised, and the library where Gwyn worked was off-limits to Adam. He could help straighten up any other room in the house, but the library was hers alone. Often he would open the door, look around, and exit shaking his head. It was always with good humor, though. He never once made her think her way was any less perferable than his. They were two different individuals, and certainly their marriage was strong enough to accommodate those differences.

What had happened to them? Why hadn't their marriage been able to survive the disappearance of Jessie? She loved Adam. She needed him now more than ever. Why, then, had she made it impossible for him to stay? She knew she had driven him away. He had reached out to her in his sorrow, and she had not been there for him. She had been so consumed with her need to find Jessica, she had put her husband and her marriage on the back burner.

Was it guilt? Did she feel responsible for that awful

day? Maybe deep down inside she was trying to punish herself for leaving Jessica alone, even for that short time. Or perhaps it was that she had been unable to locate her daughter, and could not stand to see the anguish in Adam's eyes when she failed time and time again.

There had been no harsh words between them when he left. They had talked quietly, emotionlessly, agreeing to a separation. She did not want to lose Adam, but could not find the words to tell him. It was as though all of their emotions and energies had been consumed by the ordeal they had been through.

She remembered him as he was that evening—sitting in his favorite easy chair, head bowed, talking softly. He had needed a haircut. Funny how of all the things, she had noticed and remembered that. His coal-black hair was curling slightly over the collar of his white dress shirt. She had wanted to go to him and hold his head to her, crying out all of her frustrations and misery. But something held her back—perhaps the feeling that Adam was almost at the breaking point himself, and would not be able to continue if she folded.

And so they had parted.

Gwyn took one last quick look around the large, open living room, satisfying herself she had all of the material she would need for today's broadcast. She crossed to the kitchen and then to the utility room that led to the garage. As she entered her car, she shivered slightly. Something was wrong. She couldn't put her finger on the cause of the edginess she was suddenly experiencing, but there was no doubt in her mind that someone she knew was in trouble. She tried to force her mind into the other realm, but nothing came to her. God, she hated it when this happened—and it seemed to be happening more and more lately. What did it mean? For the last two months these waves of extreme dread would come over her, and she felt powerless to halt whatever was coming. She could only hope the apprehension she was feeling did not involve Jessica.

Reluctantly she started her car and backed slowly out of the garage. To her left she could see Karen waving to her as she crossed the short yard separating their two houses. She rolled the window down and waited for her to reach the car before speaking.

"Well, good morning, stranger. When did you get back?"

"Late last night. I would have called, but your lights were out," Karen answered her. "And I was hoping you were getting a decent night's sleep for a change."

"Same as always—off and on." Gwyn sighed.

"Still no word, then?"

"No. Nothing. Last week they found the decomposed body of a child in Columbus and I had to drive over to see if I could make an identification from the clothing."

"How awful for you," Karen said softly as tears filled her eyes. "Did they . . . were you . . . able to rule out that it was Jessica?"

Gwyn smiled ruefully. "Oh, yes. Turned out to be a child about six years old, and a boy at that. Captain Anderson tried to tell me to wait until they had more information, but I couldn't stand sitting around—not knowing—so I went."

"Have you been listening to the news this morning?" Karen asked, steering the conversation to another subject.

"No. Why? Has something happened?"

"Another murder. A woman's body was found in the duck pond at the zoo. She had been knifed, same as the other two."

"Who was she, do they know yet?"

"No," Karen answered. "Her description has been on the news, but as far as I know they don't as yet have an identification. Your station did speculate that this murder points strongly to a serial killer, although they were careful to stipulate the police had not confirmed this."

Gwyn stared down at her hands, coming to a decision. "I suppose I should go see Jim today, then. I didn't go in when the first two women were killed—I was so preoccupied with Jessica, and figured there wasn't much I could do anyway. But if it's a serial killer, maybe I will be able to help. At least I've got to try."

Karen nodded slowly. "Just don't overload yourself. I know how you are—thinking you can solve the world's problems single-handedly. You can't, Gwyn. It will make you crazy if you try. Just do the best you can do, and then let it go."

Gwyn laughed. "You sound like my father. He used to say those very same words to me."

"Well," Karen answered her, "when your father and your best friend give you the same advice, you damn well better heed it, right?"

"Right," Gwyn repeated absentmindedly.

* * *

When Gwyn entered police headquarters, all eyes fastened on her. She was used to the stares, handling them with the easy grace many beautiful women acquire. She felt neither embarrassed nor cheapened by the attention she received from the opposite sex. It was simply a fact of life for her. She had turned heads for as long as she could remember, as had her mother before her. Joe Calvert had entertained his daughter for hours on end with stories about her mother, Anne. "A beauty, Gwyn—inside and out," he would say. "Every man in Oregon was after her, but she chose me!"

Gwyn knew the story by heart. Her parents had met after her mother was chosen Miss Oregon. During her year's reign, she had to make several commercials for Oregon's logging industry, and Joe's camp had been selected for the shoot.

Loggers were all standing around watching as the director tried to make the ineffectual actor playing the part of a lumberjack look convincing. The man was hopeless, and as snickers spread throughout the camp, the director knew he was in trouble. Finally, he yelled, "Cut! Get me a real logger in here." His eyes scanned the crowd and fell on Joe, standing, literally, head and shoulders above the rest.

"You, there—" he pointed. "Come help us out."

Amid yells and clapping from his buddies, he shook his head quickly. "No. Not me! No way!"

At that point, Anne, dressed in a shimmering white evening gown and looking for all the world like the goddess of the forest she was portraying, floated toward Joe. She looked up at him, eyes pleading.

"What is your name?" she asked him in a soft voice.

"Joe," he told her. "Joe Calvert. And I'm a lumber-jack, not an actor."

"Joe, do you know how tall I am?" she asked him unexpectedly.

"Uh . . . no. No I don't," he stammered.

"Well, I'm almost six feet tall," she said in that same soft, lilting voice. "Every time they make me do a commercial with this guy, I end up looking like a giant. You would be so perfect with me."

He gazed at her steadily, becoming lost in her large green eyes.

"Won't you help me out, Joe?" She took his hand, and he capitulated, knowing he could never say no to this beautiful creature.

The commercial was a huge success, even bringing offers of more television work for the tall, handsome lumberjack—who politely declined.

Anne went on to Atlantic City, where she won the swimsuit competition and ended fifth runner-up. Through it all, she kept seeing the gentle face of a logger back home in Oregon.

When she returned, she called the agency that had done the commercial and requested Joe's phone number. They were married six months later.

Gwyn smiled as she remembered the story. She had heard it at least a hundred times, never tiring of it. She wished she had known her mother better, but she had died in an accident when Gwyn was young. Funny though, her father had always managed to keep her alive in their memories.

"Can I help you?" Sergeant Atkins repeated as he

looked down at the stunning blonde in front of his desk.

"Oh, I'm sorry." Gwyn smiled up at him. "Woolgathering I guess. I'm here to see Captain Anderson, if he's in."

Atkins silently cursed the thirty extra pounds around his middle, and the receding hairline he had inherited from his father. Well, what the hell—maybe she was into a little extra girth in her men. Lots of women were these days. Wouldn't hurt to find out.

"Captain Anderson is in a meeting at the present," he said to her. "But he'll be free in a few minutes. How about coming to the back room for a cup of coffee while you wait? I'm due to go on break about now, anyway."

"That would be fine, Sergeant," she answered him. "I could use a cup."

Atkins motioned for one of the other men to take his place, ignoring the smirks from his fellow officers as he came down off the raised platform. He took Gwyn's arm, only then realizing how tall she was. In her heels, she had him beat by at least three inches. Ever the optimist, Atkins could only hope she was into fat, bald, *and* short.

"I don't believe I got your name—uh—to leave for Anderson," Atkins stammered as they headed down the hall toward the coffee room.

"I'm Gwyn Martin," she answered him. "Mrs. Adam Martin, to be precise."

Shit. So she's married, then. "Gwyn Martin. Where have I heard that name before?" he asked her.

"I have a child missing. A little girl named Jessica. She is two years old," she told him. "Actually, she'll be three in about a month. She was two when she disappeared."

Sergeant Atkins looked strange. "Then, that would mean you're that psychic on the radio, right?"

Gwyn smiled warmly at him. "That's correct, Sergeant."

"And don't you sometimes do readings or something for us?" he continued.

"Yes," Gwyn answered, preparing herself for the derision that was bound to come. "Does that bother you, Sergeant Atkins? That I help the police?"

"Uh, well, no, it isn't that. It's just that I don't really believe in that sort of stuff. It's been my experience that psychics come in and take their bows after the police have solved a crime. No offense, ma'am."

Gwyn laughed softly. "No offense taken, Sergeant. I can certainly sympathize with that concept. I've seen it happen too many times myself."

Sergeant Atkins poured her a cup of coffee that, judging from the looks of it, had been perking through the night and early morning. It tasted the same, and it was all Gwyn could do to keep from making a face when she sipped it.

"Uh—I hope it isn't too strong for you," Atkins said. "We all take turns making the coffee, and some of us are better at it than others."

"No, no," Gwyn lied. "It's just fine. Thank you so much for the kind offer. I didn't get any coffee made this morning, so this hits the spot."

"You know," Atkins said, smiling at her. "You aren't at all what I would have expected. I met a psychic once when I worked in California and she was weird—really weird. You aren't like her at all."

"We're all different, Sergeant Atkins," she answered him. "I've met a few *weird* policemen in my day, also. But that doesn't make them all that way, now does it?"

He laughed at her. "No, ma'am. It sure doesn't."

CHAPTER
FOUR

Patrolmen O'Riley and Simms pulled up in front of the shabby wood-frame house on Fourth Street. It looked deserted—windows broken and covered with cardboard, weeds two feet high in the yard, and trash everywhere.

O'Riley checked the address again. "This has to be it."

The woman in the duck pond had been identified by an officer from vice. Her name was Lucy Higgins—a part-time hooker and a full-time jerk. She had beaten her last two raps by giving the judge a song and dance about how she was only doing what she had to do to keep her three young children in food and clothing. She had promised the judge faithfully she would give up that life and get a regular job. According to police records, that was one promise she had not kept.

Simms knocked loudly on the door. From inside they could hear the sound of crying, but no one answered the door.

"We're police," O'Riley yelled. "We have to talk to you. Can you open the door, please?"

Simms turned the knob but it was locked. "Now what? Should we break it down?" He turned to his partner.

"We don't have a search warrant," O'Riley answered him. "It's our ass if anything goes wrong."

"What could go wrong?" Simms said. "The broad is already dead—we aren't exactly looking for evidence to convict her."

"True. But if we find anything in there that points to the killer, we might not be able to use it in court. Anderson will have our hide if we screw this up."

From inside the sound of crying suddenly stopped. "To hell with it," Simms swore. "I'm going in."

He put his shoulder against the door and pushed. The lock snapped surprisingly easily, and the two men pushed the door open and entered. The first thing that hit them was the stench. The odor was a combination of stale cigarettes, booze, and excrement. The house was in shambles—empty food cans scattered among heaping ashtrays and empty bottles of Old Charter.

They heard the crying start again from a back room.

"Jesus!" O'Riley swore as he looked down at the naked baby lying in filth on the bed. "Oh, Jesus. Look at her."

Simms bent over the baby, examining the marks on her body. He knew what the festering sores were. He'd seen enough abuse cases to recognize cigarette burns when he saw them. He looked around for something with which to wrap the baby, and settled on a semiclean man's shirt. Gently he picked the baby up, cuddling her to him.

"Get on the phone. Call Children's Services and tell them we need someone here right away," he said to O'Riley.

There was a flurry of activity and tiny fists started

pelting his legs. "Here, now. Where did you come from?" he said to the small boy attacking him.

O'Riley reached down and picked the boy up. He appeared to be about four years of age and his only clothing was a man's undershirt. By the looks of it, he had been wearing it for weeks. The child was badly bruised about the face, with one eye almost completely swollen shut. His arms and legs bore the same round festering sores as the baby.

"You can't take Nellie," the child said as he twisted, trying to get away. "She's my sister. I have to look after her until Mama gets back."

The two patrolmen exchanged glances.

"Son," O'Riley said tenderly, "I'm afraid we have some bad news for you. Your mother was killed last night. That's what we came here to tell you about. We are policemen, and we're here to help you any way we can. Do you understand?"

The young boy looked at the two men without expression. "She's dead? She isn't coming back anymore?"

"No, son," O'Riley said as he brushed long straight hair away from the child's face. "We're sorry, but she isn't coming back anymore."

The boy looked at him with solemn eyes. "I think my sister needs to see a doctor. Her arm is hurt pretty bad and she cries a lot."

Simms removed the shirt covering the baby and started checking but the boy interrupted, "No. Not that sister. I mean Jenny." He pointed to a door. "It's okay, Jenny. You can come out."

Cautiously a small blond head peered from behind the

door. Enormous pain-filled blue eyes stared back and forth between the two officers. O'Riley put the wiggling boy down. The child went to the door and gently took his sister's hand. As she emerged from behind the door, the officers could see her left arm hanging at a grotesque angle. There was no doubt it was broken and had been left unattended for some time. It was swollen badly and covered with ugly black-and-blue welts.

"Oh, sweet Jesus!" O'Riley swore softly.

He knelt beside the tiny girl. "Don't worry, darling. We'll get help for you right away." He turned to the boy. "Is there a phone here, son?"

The boy shook his head and O'Riley glanced at his partner. "I'll call for an ambulance from the car. And then I'm going to call Children's Services and my wife. These kids are going to need a lot of attention—maybe she can help."

Simms nodded, tight-lipped, unable to trust his voice as he stared at the carnage Lucy Higgins had wrought. *Goddamned bitch! I hope she died slow!*

Jim crossed his office and wrapped Gwyn in an enormous bear hug that he reserved for only a select few.

"Gwyn! How nice to see you!" he said. "You look lovely, as usual."

She took in his rumpled clothing and tired, lined face.

"Thank you, Jim, but I'm afraid I can't say the same for you," she said bluntly. "You look positively dreadful. When was the last time you had a good night's sleep and a balanced meal?"

"It's been a while, I'm afraid." He smiled ruefully. "And this latest murder hasn't helped matters any."

"That's what I'm here about, Jim. Is there anything I can do to help?"

"God bless you, Gwyn. I was hoping that was the reason for your visit. I didn't want to call and ask you to come in—what with Jessie and everything you're going through—but we could use a break in these murders."

Before he met Gwyn, if anyone had told Jim Anderson he would be seeking the help of a psychic to help him solve a case, he would have laughed them out of his office. He had seen how those so-called psychics worked. Detectives would bust their asses solving a case, only to have some psychic call a press conference and claim victory because some tiny detail they had furnished proved correct. Never mind the dozen or so "clues" that had absolutely no bearing on the case at all. Never mind that not one piece of information the psychic gave them helped in the actual solving of the crime.

So when Gwyn Calvert entered his office seven years ago, claiming to be a psychic with information for him, he was more than a little skeptical. He listened to her only because she was a citizen and the Omaha Police Department had recently been making an effort to get locals involved in crime prevention—and maybe also because she was the best-looking young lady he had seen in a while. For whatever reason, he thanked his lucky stars he had listened to her that day.

One of the secretaries from a local bank had been missing for three days. Her car and purse had been found in the bank's parking lot, and family and friends assured the police she was not the sort to have gone off with someone. Her eyeglasses, which she always wore, had been found beside the car, suggesting a scuffle, and medication for high blood pressure was still in her purse. The police had no clues. There had been an exhaustive search in the area, but as yet, no body had been found.

When Gwyn came to see him, she was pleasant, understanding of his concerns, and confident of her information. The victim's brother had asked her to do a reading from his sister's car. She received a clear picture of a man, about forty years old—brown hair, nicely dressed, neat, but rather mousy-looking—almost timid. There was something wrong with one of his hands—a finger missing—maybe two.

"I see," he told her. "You don't happen to have a description of his car or an address, do you?"

She smiled at him warmly, ignoring the sarcasm. "As a matter of fact, I do. He drove a red Ford pickup, and he lives in the country, somewhere west of Highway 6. And there's something else, Captain. I think the woman is still alive. I only get extremely clear pictures if the person is alive. I don't know—my mind sometimes balks when there is death."

Ordinarily he would have dismissed Gwyn as a crank, but there was something about the girl, just in her twenties, which struck him as real. At least she truly believed what she was saying.

He ran a check through Motor Vehicles, narrowed it down to three farmhouses in the area west of Highway 6, and when they arrived at Hank Reynolds's home, the door was opened by a slight, brown-haired man missing two fingers on his left hand. A check of the house found Helen Bateman tied and gagged in an upstairs bedroom. She had been raped and beaten, but was still alive. It had turned into a sensational case when the decomposed bodies of three more women were found buried in Reynolds's cornfield.

Since that time, Gwyn had helped the police on many occasions. She couldn't always give them as much help as she had in the Bateman case, but what she gave them always turned out to be accurate. And perhaps the thing that impressed him the most was her absolute refusal to take any public glory for what she did. Even after she began her highly successful radio show, she refused to discuss her dealings with the police. She would only say she had helped them as much as she could, but would never elaborate. She always made a point of stating it was police work that had solved the crime, not her.

He looked at her, wondering now if she would be able to provide any concrete material in this baffling case. The women were all dead, and so often Gwyn could not help them under those circumstances. Not always, though. Sometimes she could at least give them enough information for a starting point.

"Do you want me to go over the cases with you before we start, Gwyn?" he asked her. "Just a few highlights?"

"I don't think so, Jim," she answered him. "If I have any questions when we're done, we can go over things. Right now I would rather examine the clothing and see if I can pick up any images, if that's all right with you. I need to be at the radio station in about an hour, anyway."

They crossed the lower level to the dual flights of stairs leading to the top floor. Captain Anderson marveled that Gwyn always made this trip without getting winded. It was the biggest complaint of the department, and he secretly felt when it was his time to go, it would be climbing those damn stairs.

He signed the necessary forms to release the boxes of evidence needed, and motioned Gwyn into a small room where they waited for the officer to return with the items.

"We don't have the effects from the latest victim," he said to her. "They won't arrive until later on today or tomorrow, when the medical examiner and our boys are finished with them. Maybe you could come back then?"

"I'd be happy to, Jim. I just hope I'm able to give you some help." She hesitated, averting her eyes that filled unexpectedly with tears. "As you know, I haven't been doing too well lately."

He put his arm around her as he would a child. "I know, Gwyn. And I know just how frustrated you feel. I feel that same frustration. With all the manpower I have at my fingertips, I've not been able to come up with a single piece of evidence on Jessica. Our entire force is still alerted, but we've come up blank every time. It's like Jessie disappeared into thin air. We can only hope she's safe and that one day we'll locate her." He spoke the words mechanically, knowing the odds of Gwyn ever seeing her daughter again were astronomical.

Gwyn's voice broke. "She'll be three years old next month. Whoever took her won't even know it's her birthday."

They could hear the clipped steps of the officer returning. He entered with two medium-sized boxes and sat them down on the table. "Here you go, Captain. I'll be out at the desk if you need anything."

Captain Anderson shut the door behind the officer, crossed to the table, and opened the contents of the first box. It contained a cheap, worn pair of slacks, a torn, water-stained, bloodstained T-shirt, tennis shoes, and, incongruously, a fancy pair of silk underwear.

Gwyn reached for the T-shirt. Closing her eyes, she let her fingers run back and forth over the cotton fabric, feeling the ripped places where the knife had entered. Almost immediately she began to get an image.

"—Yes. I have the victim.

"—She is frightened, trying to get away from a knife.

"—The knife is slashing at her!

"—She raises her arms to try and protect herself.

"—Her arms are cut.

"—Now the knife is plunged deep in her stomach!"

Anderson could feel the hairs rise on the back of his neck. There was no doubt in his mind Gwyn was seeing the attack. The woman had been slashed on the arms where she tried to protect herself, and the fatal wound had been to the stomach. None of those facts had been released to the public.

He spoke softly. "Can you see who's stabbing her, Gwyn? Can you describe him?"

For a few seconds Gwyn did not answer. Then she began again.

"—Yes. I have the assailant.

"—He is a large man—well over six feet tall and muscular.

"—I have the face, now. It is a handsome face, no outstanding features.

"—His hair is brown, eyes blue—or gray. Hard to tell."

Anderson knew his role in these proceedings well. "Look at him closely, Gwyn. Do you see any marks on his arms that would help to identify him?"

Gwyn concentrated. "No, nothing. I'm sorry."

"What is he wearing? Can you describe his clothing for me?"

"Blue—" she began, and then stopped. Suddenly her arms began waving back and forth in the air.

"Water. I see water everywhere. Oh, God, no."

It was the same swirling water she kept seeing when she tried to find Jessica. The same water that seemed to consume her. She forced her mind back to the present and collapsed onto a chair.

"What is it, Gwyn?" Jim said as he grabbed hold of her trembling hands. "Are you okay?"

"The water, Jim. Don't you see?" she babbled incoherently. "The water. It's the same. Oh, God. He's got my baby!"

Jim released her hands and shook her shoulders slightly. "Stop it, Gwyn. You aren't making any sense. Listen to me. The water you are seeing is the water the victims were placed in after they were killed. All three were found in some body of water. That's all you're seeing. It has nothing to do with Jessica."

"No," she insisted. "This is the same. There is some connection. I know it. There is some connection between these murders and my Jessie."

Jim cursed himself for letting Gwyn go through with this. It was obvious she was in no frame of mind to give them an accurate reading. He should have realized the impact all this would have on her now.

He spoke to her gently. "Let's quit for now, Gwyn. We can try it another day if you wish, but for now you've had enough." He began putting the items back in the cardboard box.

Gwyn jumped from the chair. "No, Jim. I have to try the other clothing—from the second victim. Maybe I'll learn more. Please. I have to try."

Before he could say anything, she had opened the second box and removed the torn dress Wanda Simpson had been wearing on the night of her death. Quickly, she held it to her, running her hands along the jagged rips.

Jim knew he should try to stop her, but something held him back. Logically, he realized the odds were heavily against these murders having anything whatsoever to do with the disappearance of Jessica, but emotionally, he knew he had to let Gwyn try. For one thing, she would never forgive him if he didn't.

Gwyn suddenly spoke.

"—Yes. I have the victim."

"—She is being stabbed from behind."

"—She is falling."

"—Her head—her head hits something hard."

"—The assailant thinks she is dead."

"—She's still alive! I can hear her breathing!"

"—The man—he carries her to a fountain and dumps her in.

"—Water is filling her lungs."

"—She is drowning!"

It was too late to stop now. Everything she was describing was accurate, and his need to know more overrode his concerns.

"What else, Gwyn?" He spoke softly. "Can you see the attacker? Can you describe him?"

Again it was a few seconds before she answered him.

"Yes," she finally said. "I have the assailant."

Anderson decided to take a different approach. "Remember his face, Gwyn. Picture it in your mind. Try and remember every detail for the police artist. Are his eyes wide-set? What shape is his nose? Memorize his features."

She was quiet for a few minutes.

"Yes. I have it. I know what he looks like."

"Now look at his body. What is he wearing?"

She answered him slowly. "The same as before. A blue short-sleeved shirt and jeans."

Anderson watched as once again Gwyn's hands began shaking, then waving in the air as though to ward off an attack of some sort.

"The water—it's choking me. I can't breathe," she began. "Evil—so evil."

Anderson watched, horrified, as Gwyn began gasping for breath. "Come out of it, Gwyn!" he barked.

"The hands," she panted. "The hands are holding me. Let go! Let go of me!" Gwyn's hands went to her head and she began pushing at some unseen force.

Anderson had no idea what to do to help her, but some gut instinct made him reach out to her, grab her arm, and pull her from the spot where she was standing. Almost immediately, Gwyn began breathing normally. He helped her into a chair, only then noticing her color. Her face, neck, and arms had turned a bright red. She began running her hands back and forth over the splotchy skin on her arms as though it itched or was painful.

"Gwyn? Are you all right?"

She looked at him, as if only becoming aware of his presence for the first time.

"Yes," she answered him. "I think so."

"What—" he began. "What happened just now? And why is your skin discolored?"

Gwyn looked down at her reddened arms, then back up at Jim, perplexed. "I don't have the slightest idea."

As she spoke, her skin began turning gradually back to its normal color. The two of them watched in fascinated silence as the red drained away. In a matter of minutes, her skin was back to normal.

Jim was the first to speak. "That was the damnedest thing I've ever seen. Has that ever happened to you before?"

"No. I can't imagine what caused it." Gwyn hesitated, not sure if she wanted to continue, knowing Jim would probably not believe what she was going to say.

She decided to chance it.

"Jim. I want you to listen carefully to me. I know it sounds crazy, but I am dead certain there is a connection between these murders and Jessica's disappearance. I don't know what it is, but I have never been more sure of anything in my life. The water is somehow the key— both to the murders and Jessica. It isn't just the water the bodies were found in—I'm positive of that. I received this same image of water when Jessie disappeared, and that was months before the first murder happened." She stopped, waiting for his reaction.

"I don't know, Gwyn," he said to her. "Couldn't you be mixing everything up because of your concern for Jessie?"

"Damn it, Jim—no! Why are you doubting me all of a sudden? I'm telling you this killer has some knowledge about Jessie. And by God I'm going to find him—with you or without you!"

* * *

As Gwyn walked out of police headquarters, she was surprised to see a storm brewing. The sun had vanished behind swirling dark clouds that looked as though they could open up at any minute. The temperature had dropped dramatically, leaving no doubt that a spring storm was on the way. The gloomy weather seemed to match her mood as she ducked her head against the wind and headed for the police parking lot.

From inside the station, Sergeant Atkins peered through the dust-covered blind to get one last look at the blond lady who made him feel like Tom Selleck. He watched as she dashed for her car, making it just before the first raindrops started pelting down. He noticed another vehicle pull out seconds behind her. From his vantage point, he could see the lone occupant of the second car clearly, but gave it no thought as he turned from the window.

CHAPTER
FIVE

CHICAGO, 1962

"Hush, hush, little one. Mommie is sorry." The child sat huddled on her mother's lap as the woman rocked her back and forth—a hard, fast rock. "Be quiet, my sweet. Mommie loves you," she said as she rocked, the pats becoming harder and harder.

OMAHA, 1992

The woman's voice was cultured, melodic—and strained. Her hands played self-consciously with a white silk handkerchief as she spoke. "I know you must think we are overreacting. Betty has been missing for only two days. But we know her. She would never just take off without telling us. Certainly not with a serial killer on the loose and the murder of that college girl last month. She always calls us each evening—right before bedtime." The woman hesitated, uncertain. "You see, even though we live right here in town, Betty didn't want to stay at home and attend college. She wanted to be on her own. But she was young—only nineteen—and so she promised to keep in close touch. Then with the murders and all, we insisted she call us each evening."

The couple had been waiting for her when she arrived at the radio station. They were seated now in her office—tense, nervous. The woman's face seemed taut with fear, dark circles under her eyes. The man's eyes were bloodshot and he had a slight tremor in his hands. All the classic signs. Gwyn knew them well.

"And was she upset by these restrictions?" Gwyn spoke softly. "Did you get the feeling she thought you were being overprotective or trying to run her life?"

The woman's husband answered the question. "No. Never. Betty knew we were worried because of that other girl getting raped and murdered, and then those other women. She said it made her feel safe to check in with us each night."

"Did she have a boyfriend? Anyone special in her life that she might have taken off with for a few days?"

Mr. Crawford looked at his wife and shook his head. "Not that we know of anyway. Betty is an exceptionally beautiful young lady and dates a lot, but I don't think she has met any one special boy."

Mrs. Crawford interrupted her husband, "No. I'm sure she would have told me. Betty is our only child, and we've always been close. It wasn't uncommon at all for her to call me up and chat after she got home from a date." Her voice broke as tears welled up in her eyes. "I'm certain she would have mentioned someone new in her life."

Gwyn watched as Mr. Crawford walked over and put his arm around his wife's shoulder, pulling her slightly to him. He turned to Gwyn. "Can you help us?"

Gwyn thought back to those first few days after Jessica disappeared. Her anxiety, sleeplessness, and total, stark terror. It had to be the same for these parents. Their only child. Gone. She looked at them and prayed their daughter was just off on a small holiday from school—a harmless act of defiance or willfulness. She shuddered involuntarily. Something told her such was not the case.

"Mr. and Mrs. Crawford," she said kindly, "I will help you all I can. Believe me, I know what you are going through—the frustration and fear you feel. I can't, of course, guarantee I will be able to pick up anything, but I'm certainly willing to try." She glanced at her watch. "I have about an hour before broadcast time. Do you have an article that belonged to your daughter? Anything at all?"

Mrs. Crawford opened her purse and removed a round locket attached to a gold chain. "Yes. I thought you might need something. We stopped by her apartment and picked this up. She wore it almost every day." She opened the locket and held it toward Gwyn. "That is a picture of us on one side, and the other is Betty. We gave it to her on her eighteenth birthday."

Gwyn took the locket and sat looking at the lovely, dark-haired girl. Her father had been correct. Betty Crawford was indeed an exceptionally beautiful young lady.

She looked back up at Betty's parents, standing now—poised, bracing themselves for whatever was to come.

"I'm sorry," Gwyn said, "but I think it would be best if I did this alone. I don't want to upset you, and often what I see doesn't make any sense. It would be better if I did a reading and relayed my information to the police if I come up with anything."

Mrs. Crawford moved quickly around the desk to where Gwyn was sitting. She grabbed both of her hands in a frantic gesture. "No. Please. We can help more than the police. Something you see might make sense to us, but not to them." Her eyes searched Gwyn's face, pleading. "We won't fall apart. I promise you. Please! You must let us stay!"

Gwyn made her mind up quickly. "All right," she said. "I don't usually do it this way, but if you're certain—"

"Yes!" Mr. Crawford said. "We both agreed to come to you in the hopes you might give us even a small bit of information. We need to hear it all."

Gwyn nodded her head. "I'll need you to be quiet at the beginning. If I start receiving any images, I'll tell you what I see, and then it will be perfectly fine for you to talk to me and ask me questions. I won't lose the image once I have it."

Mr. and Mrs. Crawford sat back down in their chairs and watched in silence as Gwyn began rubbing her fingers over the gold locket. Almost at once she began to get an image. She forced her breathing to a slow pace, immersing herself deep into the vision.

"I see a room. Paintings, stuffed animals, large plants. A girl—your daughter I think—moving toward a door. She opens it. She is smiling—not afraid."

Gwyn's face contorted violently and her next words were guttural. "Evil! She is letting in evil! A black cloud. A cold black cloud." She began shivering. "A man. There is a man in the cloud, but I can't see him.

"Fear. I feel your daughter's fear now. She is backing away. Away from the cloud. Fists. She is knocked down. The man is hitting her. Over and over. Tearing at her clothes—raping her."

"Oh, my God!" Mrs. Crawford slumped against her husband. "Oh, no. Oh, God, no!"

Gwyn knew she should stop, but a compelling force urged her on.

"A cord. A telephone cord is wrapped around her neck. She can't breathe!"

"That's enough!" Mr. Crawford yelled. "For God's sake, that's enough!"

"No," Gwyn said, not willing to let go. "She is hurt. Bad. But I can still hear her breathing! Shallow. Very shallow. Muscles. Something about muscles. She is trying to tighten the muscles in her neck to keep the cord from sinking in!"

Mrs. Crawford's hands flew to her mouth. "We talked about that once! How if you can keep the neck muscles bulging, it it harder for someone to strangle you!"

"The man. He removes the cord. He thinks he has killed her! He picks her up. I still can't see him. Only a black cloud. A cold black cloud."

"Is she alive?" Mr. Crawford asked.

"I don't know. I think so." Gwyn forced herself deeper into the vision.

"Stairs. Short flight of stairs. Darkness. Outside. He has taken her outside. A tree. Bushes. No. She is in a room now. A small room. Low ceiling. On the floor. He dumped her on the floor. It's dark. I can't see. Wait. Boxes. Lots of boxes. The door closes. It locks.

"The cloud is going back to the apartment. Laughing! He is laughing as he cleans up the mess! A sick, hysterical laugh." The picture began fading and Gwyn slumped against her desk.

"I'm sorry," she said. "It's gone."

Mrs. Crawford spoke rapidly. "Harold, could the room she saw be those storage units out in back of Betty's apartment? Remember, each of the students were allotted a space for their overflow?"

"And to get there, you have to go down a short flight of stairs!" he answered her, already starting for the door.

"Mrs. Martin, would you call for an ambulance to meet us?"

Gwyn hardly had time to answer before they were gone.

Adam pushed away from the drafting board, rubbed his eyes, swore softly, and stood up. The design he had been working on looked much the same as it had when he had started, three hours ago. It was an important project—by far the largest one of his career. And Neb-Co had insisted he be the one to design their new agricultural building. It was to be the largest complex in Nebraska, and they wanted only the best. So far Adam had given them his worst.

He had three months to finish the design he had been working on for seven weeks. In three months, the corporation wanted to see what brilliant designs the young genius had come up with, and what he had now wouldn't do justice to a grade-school gymnasium.

He looked around at his newly refinished office and wondered if everything in his life was going to go down the toilet. Not that he really cared. Without Jessie and Gwyn he didn't give a shit, anyway. He would probably end up back on the streets from whence he came. Funny how he had managed to keep his background a secret—even from his wife. He hadn't really planned it that way, but the time had just never seemed right to tell her of his misspent youth.

At the age of five he was alone on the streets of New York—stealing to eat, and running errands for hookers who gradually turned him on to other things. When the law finally caught up with him, he was promptly enrolled in school and shuffled back and forth between foster homes, where most of the time he was told he would have to earn his own eating money. He was beaten, molested, and, when times were good, ignored. He learned to look out for himself, because it was a damn cinch no one else would. He learned the ways of the street and he learned one important truth: He was smart. Not just street smart, but book smart. He saw it as his only way out of the squalor.

When he left for Princeton, he did so with a full scholarship, a new wardrobe stolen from some of the best stores in the city, two thousand dollars he had saved running numbers, and a new background. He never looked back.

He wondered now what had happened to that street-fighter. Why had he let Gwyn slip away from him so easily? That wasn't his way. All his life he had fought for what he got, so why wasn't he fighting now? He had felt so helpless when Jessie disappeared—spent weeks combing the city, hoping to pick up something, but to no avail. Every day that passed wrenched a little more out of him, until now, he felt empty. No substance. No meat.

He heard a light tap at the door, and Brent entered. "How are you coming, partner? Got anything to show me yet?"

"Hell, no," Adam answered him. "I'm not any closer than I was seven weeks ago, if you want the truth."

"I don't think I can handle the truth, Adam—better lie to me. I'll sleep better nights."

Adam looked at his partner and knew he was only half joking. Brent Carlson had always been a nervous man— a worrier. At college he would spend every waking minute studying for a big exam—positive he would flunk it, positive he would never graduate.

Perhaps it was the drastic difference between the two men that accounted for their being drawn to each other. Brent knew nothing of Adam's background. What he saw was a capable, outgoing, extremely smart young man, who always seemed to be on top of things. He dated the prettiest girls, got the best grades, and had the most fun. And he always managed to draw Brent into the merriment.

Brent had felt honored that Adam wanted to spend his vacations with him in Omaha at his uncle's house. It never once dawned on him that Adam had nowhere else to go. It never once occurred to him that Adam was clinging to this family life the way a drowning man clings to a raft.

He still continued to look at Adam as being somehow bigger than life, although the last months had seen the beginning of an erosion process taking place. For the first time Brent was beginning to see Adam as simply a man—a vulnerable man, same as everyone else.

It was three minutes to airtime, and Gwyn sat listening to the last of the news broadcast, organizing her notes. The station's lead news story had been the discovery of a college student, raped, beaten, and strangled, but still clinging to life. She was listed in serious condition, but her prognosis was good. Gwyn was glad for the Crawfords.

Outside, she could see the rain lashing against the big glass windows. She couldn't seem to concentrate on the material in front of her. Something was nagging at her. Something important. It had to do with those images she had received at the police station—just a vague feeling she had missed something. What? She rubbed at the small ache beginning in the back of her neck.

Karen smiled up at the middle-aged woman standing timidly in front of her desk. Mrs. Henderson was terrified, of that she was positive. Her voice shook as she explained the array of clothing scattered on Karen's desk. "It was just an idea—I'm sorry to be taking up your time like this—I shouldn't have come—" she stammered. "My kids—they like these things—they thought I should show someone."

Karen looked down at the assortment of clothing. Each item looked as though the seamstress had been sewing several different outfits and mixed the patterns. The back of the denim vest was the rear end of a pair of jeans. The long pockets on the jumper were made from the legs of a pair of patched jeans. Out of a zipper, Mrs.

Henderson had created a unique headband. Multicolored strips of cloth were sewn into the seams of blouses and sweatshirts, so they could be worn inside out. They were, in fact, perfect.

She looked back up at the dumpy-looking woman in amazement. Who would have thought it!

"Mrs. Henderson," she said, "they are marvelous. Children's World will buy all you can get us. Or if you prefer, we will pay you a flat fee for each idea you come up with. As you know, we have many stores across the country—there is no way you could meet our demands. If you sell us the rights to mass produce, you would be making a lot more money for a great deal less work."

Mrs. Henderson appeared delighted and confused. "You'll pay me just for the idea? You really like them?"

Karen laughed. "*Like* them? I guarantee they will be all the rage by this time next year. You'll need to go talk with our legal department about all the details—I don't handle that end of it. And, Mrs. Henderson—"

"Yes, Miss Jackson?"

"You tell them if they offer you any less than five thousand for *each* idea, they will have to tangle with me."

By the time Mrs. Henderson left Karen's office, she had promised the petite whirlwind all future ideas, settled on her first name, Olivia, to be used in her line of clothing, been assured of a small percentage of all sales, and thought Miss Jackson walked on water.

Olivia Henderson was widowed, raising seven children all alone. She made ends meet by taking in ironing, cleaning house for other people, and sewing all her children's clothing. But she had remembered what it was like when she was young to always be wearing home-made clothes, so every outfit she made her children had a unique feature of one sort or another. Karen Jackson was no dummy. She saw immediately that Mrs. Henderson was a gold mine for Children's World. Better yet, she had her own market research in the form of seven children who let her know what would work and what would not.

It was a good bargain all the way around and Karen was pleased with her afternoon's work. Her company would gross several million from these designs, and Mrs. Henderson would not have to take in ironing to support her family.

She felt like celebrating. Maybe Gwyn would meet her at The Ark for drinks after her broadcast.

CHAPTER
SIX

Gwyn read the name from the large computer screen to her left. "Our next caller is Shirley all the way from Louisville, Kentucky. What's on your mind this evening, Shirley?"

"Good evening, Gwyn. First I want to tell you how much I like your show. I wouldn't miss it for the world."

"Thank you, Shirley, that's always nice to hear," Gwyn answered smoothly. "Is this your first call?"

"Yes. I've tried to get in before, but this is the first time I've made it."

"Well, good for you. Remember if our phones are busy, just keeping trying. We have seven lines to accommodate you. What's on your mind today, Shirley?"

"Well, I have a niece who was born with a caul, and I've been doing some reading that says this sometimes signifies the person will have psychic ability. Have you ever heard anything like that?"

"Yes. A little." Gwyn spoke into the mike. "In some cultures a baby born with a caul is believed to have second sight. And for you listeners who do not know what a caul is, it's just a fetal membrane that covers the newborn's face. I tend to believe that enough babies born with a caul *did* have extra psychic ability, or the belief would not have arisen in totally unrelated cultures."

"So you are saying my niece will probably be gifted like you?"

"No, no," Gwyn answered the woman. "I'm just saying the *percentage* must have been higher in these babies to give rise to the notion in the first place. Your niece may or may not have any more psychic ability than the next person."

"My husband thinks such an idea is crazy—says it smacks of witchcraft or something, and the whole idea is stupid."

"If there wasn't a reason for this rise, I'm afraid I would have to agree with your husband. But I believe that what happened was the baby's airflow was somehow constricted by the caul, which then triggered an area of the brain that would not have been activated had it not been for the caul. We've talked on this show before about many psychics who only began having second sight after a blow to the head or a high fever. Perhaps the caul acts in the same way. Of course this is pure speculation, but it would answer a lot of questions."

"Well, yes, it would," Shirley responded. "And it makes more sense to me when you explain it like that.

"Thanks for talking to me, Gwyn."

"Anytime, Shirley. Keep listening."

Gwyn looked at the computer screen and then into the next room where Mike Koerns, the engineer and backbone of her talk show, flashed her a thumbs-down sign. She took a deep breath, smiled, and nodded her head. All calls coming through to her were first screened by

Mike. They had worked a system out between them, and thumbs-down meant "idiot on line—proceed carefully."

"Our next caller is Martha from Cedar Rapids, Iowa. Good evening. You're on the air with Gwyn Martin. How can I help you today?"

The voice coming through her earphones was loud and fairly dripped with self-righteous indignation. Gwyn watched as Mike reached quickly for the control board, potting down to lower the tone.

"You can't help me at all, young lady," the woman said. "What you are doing is sinful and the work of the devil. I agree with the husband of that last caller. Everything you talk about on this show sounds like witchcraft to me. You should be ashamed of yourself."

Gwyn looked out the glass enclosure and rolled her eyes upward at Mike. He winked at her and laughed.

"Tell me, Martha," Gwyn spoke pleasantly. "Do you go to church?"

"Yes, I do," Martha fired back. "And I'll tell you right now I know how the devil works—he takes people like you and uses you to promote his filthy, sinful ways!"

Gwyn ignored the comment. "Do you sing in the choir, Martha?"

Martha sputtered, caught off guard by the question. "Yes. Yes, I do as a matter of fact. What difference does that make to anything?"

"Well, you know, Martha, I can't carry a tune at all. I don't have a talent for that. But I *do* have a talent for finding lost children, or sometimes knowing when people are in trouble. Are you going to tell me God could give you a talent for singing, but he couldn't give me a different talent?"

"Well—no—I mean—yes—but that's different. Singing is normal. What you do is strange and terrible. Not normal at all!"

Gwyn laughed gently. "I have a lot of friends who would tell you my *singing* is what is strange and terrible. So what is normal for *you* may not be normal for everyone. And what is normal for *me* may seem quite strange for others. Do you see what I am saying, Martha? You can't condemn an entire segment of the population because you don't understand a talent they have."

Martha's voice began to lose a little of its accusing tone, but she was not yet ready to concede. "Why do most of us not have even a small talent along this line, then? Why only a handful of people?"

Gwyn knew she had her now. "Martha," she said. "Do you have children?"

"Yes. Three. Two girls and a boy—all grown now."

"Tell me, when they were young, did you ever have a feeling something was wrong with one of them—a mother's instinct—and when you checked, sure enough, you were right?"

"Well, yes—sure—but I don't see—"

"It's the same thing, Martha. Only in a psychic these instincts are just much stronger. But the principle is the same. Everyone has *some* psychic ability, it's just that society has given them different names, like instinct, hunch, premonition, or—my personal favorite—*I just had a feeling!*"

Gwyn glanced at the clock and then back at the computer screen. Mike had printed four one-minute commercials. "Thanks for calling, Martha," she brought the discussion to a close. "I hope I was able to relieve your mind a little."

Martha's voice was pleasant now. "Well, actually you have. Thanks for the information. Good-bye now."

Outside the booth, Fred Wyatt, the station manager, gave Gwyn a thumbs-up as she moved to a commercial.

Damn, she's good! he thought. She never treated any of the callers with anything but courtesy, no matter what was said or how stupid the comment. It was this easy, considerate, pleasant manner that had catapulted Gwyn's show to the top of the ratings. He lived in daily fear that one of the national talk shows, like Talk Net, would steal her away from them.

Inside the booth, Gwyn rose and walked around, stretching her legs. Something was still nagging at her. Something important.

It had nothing to do with the broadcast. The program was going well. There had been a lively discussion on Uri Geller and whether or not he was for real. One of the callers reminded Gwyn that James Randi, a professional magician, has always claimed Geller was a fake. Gwyn knew absolutely that he was not.

She had met the handsome Uri years before when she was only twelve. Her father had taken her to one of his performances and then backstage to meet him. When she was introduced, he held her hand for a long time, then said to her, "Ah, pretty one. So we are in the same business, you and I?"

She knew immediately what he was referring to, and felt an instant bond with the man who was thrilling audiences throughout the world. He insisted on taking them to dinner that evening, and she astonished him by giving the waiter his order just as he was about to place it. He astonished them by bending a spoon and presenting it to Gwyn with a flourish. Throughout the evening they entertained themselves sending mental pictures back and forth, using napkins to sketch the images. Neither of them ever missed. These items still remained among Gwyn's most treasured possessions, and no one would ever convince her that Uri Geller was anything but the genuine article.

Gwyn saw Mike waving at her and sat back down at the large, kidney-shaped table. He always gave her a fifteen-second warning—time enough to replace her earphones and get back into the swing of things.

She waited until he pointed at her, then spoke into the mike. "Good evening again. You're listening to Talk Radio 620, KMOH, Omaha. This is the Gwyn Martin Show, and our next call is a local one. Hello, John. I haven't heard from you in a while," she said to the frequent caller. "What's on your mind today?"

"Hi, Gwyn. I was listening to your conversation with Shirley, and it got me wondering if you were born with a caul, or had a head injury or a high fever."

"No, John. Not that I know of anyway. Most psychics are just born with the gift, and there is no explanation for it. I fall into that category."

"How old were you when you knew you had these special powers, Gwyn?"

Gwyn thought. "Oh, gee. I'm not sure, John. Very young. That much I know. My dad told me stories about things I did when I was about two that just completely baffled them. My first actual memories came a few years later, though. By that time my dad had done a lot of research on the paranormal and thanks to him, I never went through much of the personal anguish that haunts many psychics."

John was an interesting, well-informed caller, and Gwyn could always count on him to liven up the broadcast.

"I was reading about a lady the other day—Josephine Hartley. She said when she was young, it got so she was afraid to go to sleep at night—afraid she might dream something bad about her family and it would come true. This never happened to you, then?"

Gwyn laughed. "Well, I wouldn't go so far as to say that. I did go through a few bad times along the way, that's only natural. But Josephine Hartley, who is probably the best-known psychic in the United States, had a horrible childhood because no one in her family understood what was going on with her. Also, her psychic revelations always came to her when she was in a dream state, which is why she reached a point where she was terrified to go to sleep at night. My visions always come to me when I'm fully awake, then I force myself into sort of a dream state, as I go deeper and deeper into the vision. My regular dreams have nothing whatsoever to do with any psychic ability."

John was on a roll now. "How does that work, then? Are you just walking along and you suddenly start seeing things in your mind, or what?"

"Yes. Sort of—but usually I work from an item and have to go into a deep concentration. Then I begin picking up images relating to the item. It sort of unfolds in my mind like a mini television scene—" She stopped.

That was it! That's what has been bothering me all afternoon. Of course. Why hadn't I seen it before?

CHAPTER
SEVEN

Jim Anderson sat in his office staring down at the police artist's sketch of the man Gwyn Martin had "seen." She had been pleased with the results, but Anderson was still not convinced. He didn't know a lot about the world of psychic powers, but he did know even the best psychics often misread the images they received. And Gwyn had been under enormous strain these last few months. How much credibility should he give this drawing? Did he dare not give it his full attention? He leaned back in his chair and lit another cigarette, oblivious to the two already burning in the ashtray. She had, he reasoned, been absolutely accurate in describing the murder scene. Was it such a stretch to imagine these killings being somehow connected to Gwyn's daughter? But how? What possible connection could there be between a serial killer and a missing child? At last he stubbed out his cigarette and hit the intercom switch. "Gordon, get me the files on the Martin case, and then I want you, Petterson, and Bozyk in here"——he hesitated, realizing Tucker, like himself, was operating on two hours sleep——"first thing in the morning."

* * *

He turned off the radio and sat silently listening to the raging storm going on outside the comfort of his office. Nothing. She had not mentioned the murders on her program. Perhaps she really didn't know anything that would place him in jeopardy. He didn't want to harm her, but his instincts told him she was somehow closing in on him. She had been to the police. Had she been able to give them anything concrete?

Never mind. He would wait a few days. He knew one person who could get that information for him.

Gwyn stuck her head in the door to Mike's room. He waved her in, made a few adjustments on the board, then turned to her.

"Dynamite program! After listening to the way you handled Martha, I know why I'm in here and you're out there. I would have just told the broad to stick it!"

"I considered it, Mike!" She laughed. "That kind of mentality just boggles my mind."

There had been three engineers working her program over the past seven years, but Mike was her favorite. At five feet eight inches, Mike was only slightly taller than she was, although no one ever noticed his height— certainly not the women he dated. His sandy-blond hair, quick smile, and friendly manner had hooked half the female population of Omaha—and the other half hadn't met him yet. He was, in the old-fashioned, good sense of the word, a charmer—and Gwyn adored him. They had hit it off right from the start, becoming fast friends as well as coworkers.

He had been with KMOH for almost three years, after

an apprenticeship of seven years at a small Kansas station, and his knowledge of every facet of broadcasting made him invaluable to their large AM station. Most importantly, he knew how to get along with people—an aspect that couldn't be overlooked in a business where everyone depended on the expertise of others. Gwyn knew that at least fifty percent of the credit for the success of her show went to Mike. It was his decision alone what calls went through to her, and he always managed to give her a good mix. Serious questions— lighthearted banter—and once in a while a "Martha."

"You're going to get wet out there," he said to her. "It's still coming down in buckets."

"I know, but I'm meeting Karen for drinks so I've got to run. How about you? Big date tonight, or do I even need to ask?"

"Nah. Think I'll stay home and read a good book. This night life is wearing me out."

Gwyn laughed. "Yeah, right, Mike! See you tomorrow—I'll ask for a book report!"

She stopped by her office, gathered up her things, and headed for the back door, anxious now to have some time to analyze this new knowledge that had come to her during the show. She heard a man's voice call to her as she was almost out the door.

"Mrs. Martin! Hold up a minute."

She closed the door against the heavy rain and turned to see Harold Crawford hurrying toward her. "I just had to come by and speak to you—thank you—for finding Betty for us," he said in a rush. "We got to her in time. She's hurt, but the doctors think she will be all right."

"Yes." Gwyn smiled at him. "I heard the news earlier and knew she had made it. How is she doing?"

"She was badly beaten, and has a broken leg. Her neck is lacerated and swollen from the cord, but we were told there is no permanent damage to her throat. I just came from the hospital. My wife stayed with her, and I'm returning there now, but we just wanted to let you know how deeply we appreciate what you did for us. The doctors said if we had been thirty minutes later, she wouldn't have made it."

"Well, thank God you were able to figure out where she was so fast. That is often the most frustrating part when I do a reading—trying to decipher it! I'm just thankful you both were insistent about staying. If we had waited to go through the police, we might not have reached her in time."

Mr. Crawford nodded his head in agreement. "But we did, and that's the only important thing. My wife and I want you to know that if there is ever anything we can do for you, don't hesitate to call us. There is no way we can ever repay you for giving us back our daughter."

"Just seeing your face is payment enough for me," Gwyn answered honestly. "And I want you to know I have already spoken with Captain Anderson about your daughter's attack. There wasn't a great deal I could tell him about this man, and I'm sorry for that. Sometimes my visions are clear on certain levels, and on other levels terribly mixed up. The only concrete information I could give him was the cloud of black—and that could mean anything. His clothes—his personality—anything!"

"You gave us the most important thing, Mrs. Martin," Harold said straightforwardly. "Betty!"

* * *

The streets were glassy from the increasingly heavy rainfall. As Karen turned left on Dodge she questioned the wisdom of meeting Gwyn tonight.

The Old Market was such a favorite of theirs, and it was their normal pattern to relax over drinks, then window-shop. Though their tastes in clothes were dramatically different, each enjoyed pointing out just the right boldly outlandish outfit for the other. The words "It's perfect for you" had become a long-standing joke.

Karen parked as close as possible, grabbed her umbrella, and dashed into The Ark. As always she was efficiently ushered to her favorite table by the bay window in the Olive Room. She ordered a glass of chablis and sat watching the rain pound everything in its path. Her choice of establishments suddenly seemed appropriate as she watched the gutters filling with water.

It was a horrid night to be out, but Gwyn had sounded glad she called. Excited, really—something new about the murders and Jessica that she wanted to talk with her about. Fleetingly Karen wondered why Gwyn had lumped the two together in her statement.

She was worried about her friend. First Jessica—then Adam. How much more would Gwyn be able to take before she cracked? It was astonishing that she had held herself together this long. Most women would have been in a mental ward by now with the strain. But Gwyn had always seemed to have a hidden reservoir of strength— an unfailing steadiness that pulled her through the worst of times.

Not like me, Karen thought. *If it hadn't been for Dr. Beckman I would be a basket case by now.*

She had not handled the disappearance of her godchild well. It was all she could think about. It invaded her dreams and consumed her every waking minute. Irrationally, she kept dwelling on that day, wondering if there was something she could have done—if there was something she saw that had not registered. She had stayed home from work that day with a headache, and had watched briefly from her kitchen window as Gwyn and Jessica played in the backyard. It had seemed only minutes later that she heard Gwyn yelling for the child and went to see what was wrong. *If I had only stayed by the window*. That thought kept playing in her mind. *If only*. Two powerful words that would drive her crazy.

She had finally gone to the yellow pages and looked under Psychiatrists. Captain Anderson had suggested they all get counseling to help them through their grief, but neither Gwyn nor Adam would go with her. *They should have*, she thought. *They are both in need of it every bit as much as I am. Probably more*.

Today had been good, though. For the first time in a long while she felt like she was back in control of her life. Olivia Henderson was the biggest "find" she had made in the last few months. It always gave her a euphoric feeling when she discovered a line that was sure to be a big seller. And the look on Mrs. Henderson's face when the legal department placed a contract in her hand calling for a fifty thousand dollar advance was something Karen would not soon forget.

"You look a million miles away," Gwyn's voice interrupted. "Sorry I'm late, but the streets are starting to flood a little, and I had to just creep along."

"You aren't late," Karen answered, waving her to a

seat. "I've only been here a few minutes myself. It's getting dreadful out—if either one of us had any sense, we'd be heading home."

"I know." Gwyn laughed. "I'm glad we're both devoid of brains, though, because the last thing I want to do tonight is be alone."

"What's up? You sounded pretty excited on the phone."

"Well, it's the damnedest thing," Gwyn said as she shed her coat and signaled for the waiter. "We had a caller today who asked me what happened when I did a reading. I was explaining that it was sort of like a television in my mind when all at once it hit me. The woman I keep seeing by the swing, she is never actively doing anything. I don't see her move toward Jessie, walk away, or anything. I just see her. Period. Like a large picture or one of those cutouts of movie stars."

"What do you think it means?" Karen sounded puzzled. "I don't see how that's going to help us at all."

"Wait. There's more. I went to see Anderson today, and when I did a reading on the victims' clothing I saw that same image of water that I always see when I do a reading by the swing. There is some connection between these murders and Jessie. I'm sure of it."

"Oh, Gwyn," Karen protested. "I'm equally sure you must be mistaken. It doesn't even make any sense. This killer only goes after women. There hasn't been any indication he has killed anyone else—certainly not children."

Gwyn shook her head. "No. I'm not saying he has harmed Jessica—or even that he has her. I only know this man has some information about her disappearance.

If I can find him, I'll be that much closer to finding my daughter." She stopped, then continued, dauntless, "The clincher is that the man I see in my vision is also one-dimensional—like a photograph. There has to be a reason I'm picking up this strange image in these two cases only."

Karen sighed deeply. "Couldn't it just be that you are tired and worried? Couldn't your mind be playing tricks on you because of the strain you've been under?"

Gwyn took a sip of the rum and Coke the waiter placed in front of her, waiting until he had departed before answering. "Karen, my 'mind' is the one thing in this life that I could always count on. I know a lot of psychics go through real troubles because of their special abilities, but that is not happening with me. I know what I saw today was real. Something strange is going on with these murders and it somehow involves Jessica."

"All right then," Karen answered her. "What is the next step and how can I help?"

Gwyn felt a weight lift from her shoulders. "Thank you, Karen. For believing me. And I *am* going to need your help. The first thing we have to do is figure out why the images I'm picking up of the woman and the killer are more like a photograph than the actual thing. I have probably the largest collection of books on the paranormal this side of the Library of Congress, and somewhere in one of those books we will surely find an answer. Also, I want us to start calling every major psychic we can reach. We will explain what I saw, and see if any of them have ever experienced anything like it, and if so what had caused it."

Gwyn's optimism was infectious, and for the first time

in months, Karen began to feel an excitement about the chance of getting Jessie back. Maybe there was still hope after all.

"All right then. I have a date with Brent tomorrow that I will cancel, and after work we can meet at your house and get busy. Actually, I could do some calling from the office tomorrow on the Watts line, if you have a list."

Gwyn's hazel eyes opened wide in astonishment. "You have a date with Brent? Brent Carlson?"

Karen played with her napkin self-consciously. "Now don't act so surprised. You know perfectly well you've been trying to get us together for years. He called this evening, just as I was leaving to come here. He was so insistent I finally said I would go." She stopped and looked at Gwyn squarely. "Of course you know the man is still in love with you."

Gwyn seemed taken aback. "With me? There was never anything between us, Karen. We were just good friends. Why—he stood up for Adam at our wedding, or have you forgotten?"

Karen spoke softly. "No, I haven't forgotten. I will always remember the look on his face when you said 'I do.' He looked like someone had just kicked him in the balls."

Gwyn shook her head back and forth, stunned. "I can't believe that. Brent and I are total opposites. We would never have made it together. Opposites may attract, but for the long haul personalities need to be at least somewhat alike. That was why I always wanted you two to get together. You are much more like Brent—and I mean that in the nicest way, because you are both my two favorite people."

Karen threw up her hands in mock surrender. "Okay—okay! Maybe he doesn't still have a thing for you. I haven't seen him in months, anyway. How about if I keep the date, but only for dinner? Then we'll still have most of the evening to work."

"Sounds good. And I'll bring over that list of psychics in the morning, in case you have time to call during the day." Gwyn sighed as she looked around. "Doesn't it feel good to be here in these wonderful surroundings? We must do this more often."

Gwyn's words filled Karen with joy. Many weekends had been spent shopping down here, Jessica in tow. So many shopping bags carried from the toy store, Jessica chortling gleefully. Gwyn frequently used to worry that they needed a separate toy room for all of Jessica's stuffed animals and dolls, many of them gifts from Karen. "It's a godmother's prerogative," she would laugh. It felt good to remember the laughter. *Please let this horror be over soon!*

CHAPTER EIGHT

It was a gorgeous September day. August's oppressive heat had been stilled by a light rain that had continued falling for three days, washing away the worst of summer.

The fifth day of September, was the sort of day adults remembered from their childhood and secretly wished they could turn back the clock to—returning once again to that carefree feeling of smelling crisp, fresh air after a rain, and knowing that the day is going to be absolutely perfect.

Gwyn had no hint of the horror this beautiful day would unleash in her life.

"It's a wonderful day for a picnic, Adam," she told her husband at breakfast. "Can you take a long lunch, and Jessica and I will set everything up on the patio?"

Jessica teetered over to her father, grabbing his legs and hugging him to her. "Please, Daddy, please! Picnic! Picnic!"

He reached down and gathered his daughter up in his arms. "Now how could I say no to the two best-looking women in Omaha? A picnic it shall be!"

Throughout the morning, Gwyn and Jessica made

preparations for the big event: Adam's favorite potato salad, baked beans, tiny ham sandwiches with the crust cut off, and Jessica's personal favorite—chocolate-chip cookies.

Jessica chattered away, as she had been doing for several months now. Her vocabulary was remarkably large for a child just past two years of age. Her parents were both positive they had a budding genius on their hands—or at the least an extremely bright, above-average child. She was their world, that much they knew.

Jessica disappeared into another room, and Gwyn walked over to the door to keep an eye on her. She watched her closely, always—aware of the many household dangers prevalent even in the best childproofed homes.

Crossing to the large dining-room hutch, Jessica sat down on the floor and began pulling at the bottom drawer. When she finally succeeded in opening it, she reached in and grabbed hold of Gwyn's best white damask tablecloth.

"Help, Mommie," she said, wrestling with the large cloth. "Special meal—use this!"

Gwyn groaned inwardly, knowing she should tell her daughter no, not for a picnic, but instead she laughed and went to help her. "What a good idea, Jessica. You're right. This is a special meal!" And they spread her expensive tablecloth over the redwood table on the patio.

It was a grand picnic. They started it off with a toast, using their best crystal, in keeping with the fine tablecloth. Wine for Adam and Gwyn, 7-Up for Jessica. They ate and laughed and told funny stories, both parents reveling in this perfect child they had created together.

It was over too soon, and Jessica begged her daddy to stay longer. He swooped her up and tickled her tummy. "No, darling. I have a lot of work to do this afternoon— but I'll be home again before long."

It was the last time he saw his daughter.

After Adam left, Gwyn placed Jessica in the infant swing, fastened the wooden bar securely, and began pushing her gently.

"Higher, Mommie, higher!" Jessica yelled, as she always did. And as always, Gwyn answered, "Not too high! You might sail away to the moon!"

It was a lazy, carefree day, and Gwyn let Jessica talk her into postponing her naptime, although she could see her child's eyes drooping as the swing rocked her back and forth. It wouldn't be long.

"I'm going in the house for a Coke," she told Jessica. "I'll be right back." And in the space of less than two minutes, her world was turned upside down.

When she saw the empty swing, she was stunned. "Jessica!" she yelled. "Where are you?" The silence was deafening, sending cold chills down her spine.

Frantically, she raced around the yard, screaming out her child's name. "Jessica! Don't hide from Mommie! Where are you?"

Karen heard her yelling and came running over. Together they checked every bush, every crevice, both of them becoming increasingly frantic.

Only minutes passed before Gwyn ran in the house and dialed 911. "My baby's missing!" she screamed at the dispatcher. "Send someone! Oh, God! Hurry!"

She returned to the backyard and stood by the swing, trying to force her mind into the other realm—to see if she could find her daughter in the same manner she had found countless other children. But the images she received were vague, meaningless. The white-haired woman. The overpowering water. Nothing made sense.

She could hear sirens in the distance, and realized she had to call Adam and let him know. She was sobbing when he came on the line. "Adam—oh, Adam! Something's happened to Jessica! She's gone! I can't find her!"

She would always remember his first words to her, and even though he never again repeated them in the weeks and months to follow, they were burned into her mind forever. "What the hell do you mean, you can't find her?" he screamed. "Weren't you with her?"

She tried to explain, but he cut her off. "I'm on the way. Call the police." And the phone went dead.

The two policemen had arrived and badgered her with their stream of questions—positive the whole thing was a publicity stunt to promote her radio show. It wasn't until Karen thought to call Captain Anderson that Gwyn was given a respite from the incessant questioning.

It wasn't long before Adam and Brent both came running into the house. Adam rushed over to Gwyn. "What happened? Have they found her yet?"

Gwyn shook her head, her eyes glazed with grief. "No. We've looked everywhere. Captain Anderson is on his way with more men, but she's just disappeared, Adam! She was in her swing—she couldn't have gotten out—someone had to have taken her!" Gwyn's voice began rising hysterically. "Oh, God! Where is she? What happened to her?"

Adam pulled Gwyn to him, folding her in his arms. "We'll find her. Don't worry. It wasn't your fault."

Somehow his words didn't comfort her. She had not even thought about blame, or where it might lie, until Adam mentioned it.

Brent walked over and put his arms around them both. "Gwyn," he said, "have you tried to do a reading?"

She nodded her head. "Yes, but nothing makes any sense. I keep seeing water—evil water—and a woman with white hair. That's all I see!"

Brent turned to the policeman. "Start checking every body of water around here—pools, saunas, anything a child might fall into."

The two officers looked at each other, uncertain.

"Do it now!" Brent ordered. "You start across the street, Adam and I will take this side."

The search continued for days. Posters of Jessica were plastered in every place of business in Omaha. Gwyn pleaded on television and radio for the return of her child. Money for a substantial reward was raised by many of Gwyn's listening audience. It remained unclaimed. Through it all, Gwyn tried over and over to reach her child with her special powers, to no avail. It was as though a brick wall had been erected in her mind between her daughter and herself.

Gwyn took a leave of absence from the radio station for two months, and spent all her time searching. At last she returned, knowing she had to get her life back on an even keel. At first, her audience besieged her with questions concerning Jessica, until finally she had to ban the subject to keep from losing her mind.

Adam became distant, remote, his dark, brooding eyes speaking volumes. He began to stay out later and later at night, until the time came that he did not even bother returning home. Gwyn hardly missed him, so wrapped up as she was in finding her child. Finally, they had separated, without ever really discussing why. And life went on.

CHAPTER NINE

Captain Anderson drummed his short stubby fingers absentmindedly on the Martin report. He had read through it again last night but could not see anything that would help them in any way. He was probably being a damn fool for even considering it, but out of respect for Gwyn, he would brief his men on the possibility of a connection. He looked up, annoyed.

"Where the hell is Petterson? This meeting was scheduled for eight o'clock."

"He had to go by the coroner's office to pick up his final report," Bozyk volunteered. "He'll be here shortly."

As if on cue, the door opened and Paul Petterson rushed in. "Sorry I'm late," he apologized. "You know Jerry. Doesn't think any of us know how to read so he always insists on going over the whole damn report so we won't miss anything."

Anderson laughed. Jerry Markham did indeed have an exalted opinion of himself, and considered policemen just a notch or two above Neanderthal man. But he was a first-rate medical examiner, and Anderson knew if there was any small detail that might help in their investigation, Markham would not miss it. For that, he would put up with the man's boorishness.

"All right, then," he began, "let's get started. As I'm sure you are all aware, the police commissioner has scheduled a press conference at three, and before you all start swearing, let me just say I think he is right in this case. We do need to warn the women of this town to be extra careful. Like it or not, we have a serial killer out there. If we don't catch him, he will very probably keep right on killing. The city needs to be made aware of this. Now. What exactly do we have on him? Tucker?"

Gordon Tucker rose. He was a large man, with steely blue eyes that seemed as though they could look into a person's soul. He was one of the best interrogators on the force, and a thoroughly dedicated investigator. When Anderson retired next year, he hoped the higher-ups had the good sense to offer his job to Gordon. They would have to skip over a couple of others with more seniority, but there was no question in Anderson's mind that Gordon was the man for the job.

"We found no footprints at the scene, Captain. That rock area around the duck pond is a favorite playground for children. The only prints we found were small ones—which means the killer used the rocks as stepping stones as he carried the body to the fence. The lab boys did find traces of dried blood on several of the rocks, and the blood type was that of the victim."

"Damn!" Anderson swore. "And what about prints where he entered the park?"

"Nothing, sir. He entered by the east gate. We could tell he dropped the body just inside the grounds for some reason, but again there were no footprints. He stayed pretty much on asphalt or concrete as near as we can tell."

"How did he get in the gate? Isn't it always kept locked?"

"Yes. The groundskeeper swears he checked all the locks on his last round. Of course that gate is hardly ever used, so he might have skipped over it, although he insists he checked it. At any rate, the lock was not jimmied. Either the killer had a key or is handy with a pick. The lock still works perfectly."

"Have we checked the houses on the east side to see if anyone saw anything that night?"

"Yes, sir. Nothing."

"Did we come up with any kind of physical evidence when we swept the area?"

Tucker grinned. "Lots, sir. Most of it bird shit, though."

"All right. All right." Anderson chuckled. "At least they got the point. Anything we can use?"

"We bagged about three hundred cigarette butts, lots of candy wrappers, trash, a pair of dime-store reading glasses, three pairs of sunglasses, a Saint Christopher medal"—he stopped and opened his notebook—"a pair of women's underpants, one lacy bra, three books, five caps, empty pop cans—do you want me to continue?"

"No. I think we get the picture. Hang on to everything, though. You never know. The saliva from one of those cigarettes could place our killer at the scene."

"Hold on. There is one thing we got that *is* important. The lab boys found a small hunk of brown corduroy at the top of the fence where the body was thrown over. It did not come from the victim, so we are assuming the killer snared his clothing as he was going over the fence. It isn't much, but it's more than we have had up to now."

"Good. Start seeing if you can trace it."

"Petterson, what do we have on this victim? Have you got a background yet?"

Paul Petterson was the newest member of Anderson's special task force. Only twenty-four, he had already distinguished himself by coolheadedness under fire and a bulldog determination to get at the truth in any situation. Blond-haired and freckled, he looked like a young college student instead of a homicide detective—a fact that usually worked to his advantage. Anderson knew he would turn out to be one of the best with a little more experience under his belt.

"Sir, the third victim, Lucy Higgins, was a prostitute with a list of priors a mile long. Up to now, she always managed to talk her way out of real trouble. She somehow got the court system to go easy on her, usually claiming she had a family to support. She did, indeed, have a family—three children, who she abused horribly. We have the kids at County General now, and according to the oldest boy, it was his mother who inflicted all the damage to them." Petterson stopped talking and flipped open a small notebook.

"The boy, Anthony, five years old, has numerous contusions and cigarette burns over his body. The three-year-old girl, Jenny, has a badly broken arm, abrasions, and burn marks. Gangrene had set in on the arm, and there is some question about whether or not it can be saved. The baby, seven months old, is suffering from malnutrition and cigarette burns."

"Damn it all to hell!" Bozyk exploded. "When are the

courts going to wake up and quit putting garbage like that back on the streets?"

Anderson nodded his head in agreement. "The first victim, Maria Gilbert, also had been turned in for child abuse. Maybe we're getting a pattern here. Bozyk, what have you been able to find out about Wanda Simpson? Is there even a hint of child abuse with her?"

"None, sir. As near as I've been able to determine, she is squeaky clean. I talked with her two children after the murder, and they gave no indication of having been abused. Her neighbors all have nothing but good things to say about her. Her husband is a popular high school teacher, and had students over at their house a lot. I can't help but think if she was abusing her kids, someone would have noticed."

Anderson lit a cigarette and inhaled deeply. "Still—when you were interviewing these people, we were not considering child abuse as a possible motive. Now it is a distinct possibility. If we can find any evidence that Wanda Simpson abused her children, we know what direction to head. Here's what I want you to do. Go to Children's Services and ask for Dr. Jacobs. She's a psychiatrist who has had a lot of luck getting abused children to open up. Get her to go with you when you interview the Simpson children again. She also will be working with us on this case and is due here tomorrow to give us a psychological profile of the killer. I want her briefed on all aspects of the case, and what you discover with the Simpson children could be important in her profile."

Bozyk nodded his head.

"And, gentlemen, I don't think I need to warn any of

you that the abuse angle is to be kept quiet. If Wanda Simpson did *not* harm her children, it would heap a lot of grief on her family unnecessarily."

"Now then, Paul, let's have Jerry's report," he continued. "Summarize—just hit the high spots."

Petterson opened a manila folder and scanned quickly down the two pages fastened inside. "The knife wounds were basically the same as on the other two victims. The thrust was upward, suggesting the killer was male. Normally a woman uses both hands on a knife, in a downward swing. Jerry said there was great force behind the upward thrust, and he feels confident it could have only been accomplished by a large, strong man." He paused briefly, then continued, "However, he did point out that the angle of the knife was such that there was an outside chance the killer could have been somewhat shorter."

"Covering his ass every way, is he?" Bozyk snorted.

Petterson answered smoothly. "The way he explained it, a large man swinging with his arm bent and a shorter man swinging with his arm locked straight out would cause the blade to go in at about the same angle. In any case, we are looking for a very strong man—short or tall. One of the thrusts broke two bones and went an inch farther into the body after that."

"How long had the victim been dead when she was placed in the water?" Anderson asked.

"About seven hours. Jerry estimated she had been dead about ten hours, and the tests he ran indicated she had been in the water close to three hours. Also her watch stopped at four thirty-five, probably from the water—the lab boys are running tests to see if they can ascertain that."

Tucker calculated rapidly. "That would put her death about six-thirty in the evening—still light out and a little early for her to be hitting the streets. Rather a strange hour for a hooker to buy the farm."

Petterson nodded and continued, "There was something else different about this victim. There were shards of green glass in her buttocks. Jerry guessed that someone, most likely the killer, had knocked her down and she landed on glass fragments of some sort. Some of the pieces were fairly large, and the lab is working to see if they can identify the glass."

Anderson got to his feet. "Anything else we should know about?"

"Yes, sir," Petterson answered. "She was stabbed twenty-three times. The killer kept stabbing her long after she was dead. Jerry estimated she had lost about three pints of blood before being dumped in the pond, although it was a little hard for him to be accurate on that figure because of the body being in water for that length of time."

"At least that tells us one thing," Tucker said. "Our killer is getting more vicious in his attacks."

Bozyk couldn't resist. "Yeah—or maybe he just didn't like what that bitch was doing to her kids."

Leon Bozyk was fifty-three, had twenty-nine years on the force, and a mouth that kept him in constant jeopardy with the top brass. He didn't give a damn about promotions or rank, and had once told Commissioner Rasnik if he would get his head out of his ass, he would be better off. He would have been fired on the spot had Captain

Anderson not intervened on his behalf. Anderson liked the man, vulgarities or no, and always included him in any special task force he headed. Bozyk was remarkably good at seeing through the bullshit suspects and witnesses often offered up. They might be able to do a snow job on everyone else, but not Leon Bozyk.

Anderson picked up the Martin report. "Okay. That about does it except for Gwyn Martin. Mrs. Martin did a reading from the victims' clothing and gave an accurate accounting of the murder scenes as near as I could tell. She gave us a description of the killer and worked with our artist, coming up with a detailed picture. There is only one problem. I'm not satisfied she is on target in this case."

Petterson was the first to speak. "But her information has usually been right on the money, hasn't it, Captain?"

"Yes," Anderson answered him. "But as you know, her child has been missing for nine months. Now she is convinced these murders have some connection to her little girl. I'm having a hard time buying that. I'm just afraid her judgment is not up to par right now, and we can't afford to send out fliers of this drawing when it could be some totally innocent person who has crept into her subconscious."

Bozyk said the obvious. "Well, we sure as hell can't afford to ignore what she says—she's been right too often. If that *is* a picture of the killer and we don't act on it, this city will have our butts—and rightfully so!"

"Why couldn't we just say this man was wanted for questioning?" Tucker interjected. "As someone who might have information about the murders."

Anderson nodded his head. "All right. We'll handle it

that way. But the men will have to be told there is a possibility he could be dangerous." He opened the file on the Martin case.

"If Gwyn Martin is right and there *is* a connection somehow, then we had better review what we have on her daughter's disappearance—which is precious little." He scanned down the report and the notes he had made the previous evening.

"Jessica Martin, age two, vanished from her parents' backyard on September fifth of last year. She has been gone now a little over nine months. We have no leads and no suspects. She was in a baby swing that she could not have climbed out of, meaning someone came into the yard and took her. Mrs. Martin was only in the house for less than two minutes, and saw no car in the alley or the front of the house when she returned. A neighbor, Karen Jackson, confirmed she saw the mother and child only moments before the child was discovered missing." Anderson stopped and lit a cigarette, seemingly lost in thought.

"Whoever took the child must have been watching the yard for the right moment," he continued. "Perhaps he—or she—parked a block or two away and that's why no car was noticed. Now, last night I gave this a lot of thought. If Gwyn is right about there being a connection, then the next logical step is that the killer is someone known to the Martins."

Tucker interrupted, "I don't follow you, Captain. Why would it have to be someone known to the Martins and not a total stranger?"

"I'm going by what Mrs. Martin herself told me. When she did a reading, she could not understand why she didn't pick up any hint of danger toward Jessica. Also, her child did not yell or kick up any fuss when she was taken. Gwyn had left the outside door open when she went in the kitchen for a Coke. She swears she could have heard her daughter if she began crying or let out a yell. At the time, I didn't think much about this, assuming the kidnapper covered the child's mouth or something. But in light of these latest developments, we have to entertain the possibility that it was someone known to Jessica. At any rate we've come up dry the other way, so maybe we need to take a look at people close to the Martins."

Anderson sighed deeply and shook his head as if trying to rid it of cobwebs. "And of course you all realize this is just a shot in the dark, anyway. If it were anyone except Gwyn Martin, I wouldn't even be exploring this possibility."

Gordon Tucker spoke up. "I think you are absolutely right, Captain. We can't ignore what Mrs. Martin tells us. She's worked with this department for seven years, and I have been amazed at her track record. All of us here have seen with our own eyes what she is capable of doing. Now, she might be mistaken in this case because of the involvement of her daughter, but that's something we will have to verify. I don't see any other course but to act on what she tells us."

"Right," Anderson replied. "Thanks for the vote of confidence. That's exactly how I feel. So here is what I want you to do. I have a short list of people who I know are close to the Martins. Tucker, you see both Mr. and Mrs. Martin for a more complete list, then divide up and start getting case histories on all of them. Find out where they were the day Jessica disappeared, see if any of them have a background of mental problems, or if anyone in their family has mental problems. I want a complete run-down of their personal lives and histories. I'll assign more officers to help, but I want all of you, personally, to go over every piece of information."

"Does that include Mr. and Mrs. Martin?" Petterson asked.

"Yes. Definitely," Anderson answered. "There might be someone in their background who has a grudge against them."

CHAPTER
TEN

Gwyn slid open the glass patio doors and stood surveying the damage wrought by the previous night's storm. All of her spring flowers had been pounded flat by the rain, small branches were littered over the lawn, and large puddles of water stood everywhere. As soon as it dried up a little she would have to get busy.

She was too tired to even think about it now. Last night had been bad again. Jessica consumed her every waking minute, and lately all of her dreams. She would awaken worn out from the dream-world struggles to recover her child.

Wearily, she headed next door. She forced herself to smile and entered Karen's kitchen with a cheery good morning yell. Not that she needed to pretend with Karen. Karen always understood. From the first day they met, each had accepted the other unconditionally. There had never been even a serious spat during those first months of feeling each other out. They became inseparable, and their friendship had only deepened over the years.

Gwyn helped herself to a cup of coffee and went to the den. She knew that's where Karen would be. She always had her morning coffee in this cozy room.

Karen's home had been decorated by a local design firm, but there were lots of personal touches that gave the den, especially, its own personality. A collection of European wood figurines, Danish porcelain, groups of candles, huge bowls of potpourri, the brass candlesticks on the mantel, all gave the room a lived-in touch. The walls were lined with signed prints, many that Gwyn had helped to pick out. They shared a mutual love of art.

Gwyn slipped easily into the overstuffed rocker near the fireplace, wrapping her hands around the porcelain coffee mug. Karen noticed the telltale creases around her friend's eyes. "Not much sleep last night?"

"No. More dreams—nightmares, really. Jessica will be almost within my grasp, then slip away. Somehow the dreams are more terrifying than anything I have gone through. I wake over and over in a cold sweat, shaking with fear."

Karen's eyes misted. It hurt to watch her friend's pain and she felt so damn helpless.

"I just don't understand why I haven't been able to reach Jessica," Gwyn continued, shaking her head miserably. "My own child! You would think the psychic impulses would be stronger between us!"

"Well, maybe we'll come up with something today," Karen said, trying to pull Gwyn out of her despair. "Did you bring me that list of psychics so we can begin calling?"

Gwyn reached in the pocket of her robe and handed Karen a sheet of paper. "Yes. I made this up for you last night. I called several from my list, but no one was able to help much. I couldn't get through to several of the top psychics. I'm hoping at least a few return my call today."

Gwyn glanced at the grandfather clock as it started chiming the hour. "We'd better get going. I still need to dress, and I want to see if I can pick up any images before I go in to work."

"Okay," Karen said. "I'm ready to take off now. I'll give you a call if I come up with anything."

Gwyn went out the kitchen door and crossed to her own backyard. She gazed at Jessie's swing moving slightly back and forth in the morning breeze. It looked forlorn. Empty. Would she ever see her child laughing gaily, yelling "Swing, Mommie, Swing"?

She focused her thoughts on her daughter. "Where are you, Jessie? Call to me, sweetheart." She put her hands to her head and tried to send her mind exploring. "Jessie! Where are you? Answer Momma, darling. Can you hear me? Are you safe?"

She went through this same ritual every day hoping against hope she would be able to get a fix on her daughter. She had driven to every section of the city, always searching with her mind, hoping for a miracle. It was going to make her crazy.

Then she saw it. A silver rainbow glinting in the morning sun—and at the end of the rainbow sat her child. Gwyn's knees buckled and she slid noiselessly to the ground.

Rosella Garcia hauled her gargantuan figure up off the overstuffed chair and walked once again into her son's room, as if expecting to see him appear there magically, safe at home in his own bed.

Manuel had been gone for three days, and she had no idea where he was. The only thing she was sure of was that he would be sick when he returned. Sick, hung over, spaced out, high—any of the clichéd terms that applied to a "user."

Rosella stared at the empty bed of her only child and crossed herself. *Dear God, what am I going to do? How can I help him?*

He had been to the clinic twice already, but nothing seemed to help. Only eighteen years old—still a baby— and his body wasting away with the poison of the streets.

He would be home. That much she knew. When he ran out of money and became so sick he couldn't stand up. Then he would return, begging her to help him. And she would. She always did.

She looked around as a tiny blond head peered around the corner of the door. "Jessica, honey! You're up!" She went over and lifted the little girl, hugging her close. "And how's the prettiest little girl in the whole wide world this morning?"

Jessica giggled and gave Rosella a kiss. "The prettiest little girl in the whole wide world is *great!*" She laughed. It was their own special greeting, and Jessica never tired of it.

"You were a sleepyhead this morning." Rosella smiled at her. "I had to eat my pancakes alone—but I saved some for you."

"I wasn't sleeping," Jessica answered her. "I was looking out the window at the city. It's so pretty in the morning."

Rosella put the tiny girl down. She looked cute in her pajamas, with her mop of curly blond hair in total disarray.

She had grown to love this child who had been placed in her care. She had to keep reminding herself it was only temporary. And maybe with the money she received she could send Manuel to a really good place. Like maybe that Betty Ford clinic she heard about all the time on television.

As she turned from Manuel's bedroom she winced as a pain shot down her left arm. It felt slightly different from the arthritis pain she was used to, but she put it out of her mind as she began preparing Jessica's breakfast.

"Yes, Adam." Gwyn spoke passionately. "I'm sure of it. Jessie is alive. Somehow I got through to her this morning. Maybe she picked up on my psychic impulses and responded in some way. I don't know. I won't even begin to try and explain it, all I know is that Jessie is alive."

Adam looked at his wife. "How can you put us through all of this again? My God, Gwyn, there is only so much a person can stand. How do you know you got through to Jessie? After nine long months you are telling me you finally located her?"

Gwyn's eyes burned and her throat ached from the tears she was trying to hold back. "No, Adam. I haven't found her. But I think she reached out to me this morning. Somehow we made a connection. I saw her. I saw her as clearly as I am seeing you now. There was a rainbow—a silver rainbow—and she was sitting at the end of it."

Adam crossed his office and took his wife in his arms. "Gwyn—honey—you have to stop this. Jessica is gone. We've done everything we can to find her but now we have to face reality. You are"—his voice broke as he continued—"you are just not making sense anymore. Maybe you should go see a counselor or something."

Gwyn stayed quiet, her face turning to stone. Slowly she extracted herself from his arms and stepped back. "A counselor? You mean like a shrink, don't you? You think I'm crazy? Is that it, Adam?"

"Listen, I'm sorry. I didn't mean it that way. It's just that these last months have been hard on you."

"Of course they've been hard," Gwyn shouted. "My—our—daughter is out there somewhere. Can't you understand that? I've found dozens of lost children and I can't even find my own child. How do you think that makes me feel, Adam? And how do you think it makes me feel when my own husband won't believe me when I finally get something?"

Adam shook his head back and forth wearily. "And what have you got, Gwyn? A silver goddamn rainbow? Is that supposed to mean something? It means just about as much as these serial murders having some connection to Jessie."

Gwyn's face paled. "How did you know about that? I was going to tell you as soon as—"

"The police were here, Gwyn. Not thirty minutes ago. They tell me they want a list of all our friends—that you told them this maniac killer also has Jessie. Now they think someone we know might be the killer! My God, Gwyn! Don't you see what is happening? Your subconscious mind is rebelling because you can't find Jessie.

Now you are beginning to see her in everything. You need to get some help, honey. Believe me. For once just believe me."

Gwyn tried to gather her thoughts. *Could he be right? Is my mind playing some awful game with me?* No. She refused to believe it.

She spoke slowly to her husband. "Listen to me, Adam. Please. Just hear me out. I wanted to be the one to tell you about the images I picked up at the police station. I'm sorry I didn't get here sooner—I had no idea they would come to you with this. But what the police don't know yet is that something queer is going on with these images. Now maybe you are right. Maybe my mind is playing tricks on me, but I don't think so. The images of the woman I kept seeing by the swing, and the image I picked up of the killer, were sort of like a picture. That has never happened before in any psychic vision I have ever had."

Adam interrupted, "There. You see? That's what I'm talking about? Your mind isn't functioning right anymore. You need to take a break from all this."

Gwyn felt like screaming but managed to hold on to a semblance of control. "Adam! Listen to me! There is some reason these two images are not moving and seem more like a photograph. Remember the white-haired lady I kept seeing by the swing? I saw her more like a picture than the real thing. Then when I held the victim's clothing, I saw the killer this same way."

"And what is all this supposed to mean, Gwyn?"

"I don't know yet, Adam. But you can bet your life I'm going to find out. Maybe someone is projecting an image into my mind somehow—I just don't know." She hesitated, wondering if she should tell him the rest.

"What?" he anticipated her. "What else aren't you telling me?"

"It's Jessie, Adam. She is in danger. Terrible danger. I didn't want to have to tell you this, but I'm sure that is why I reached her this morning. Something is going to happen to her if we don't find her fast."

CHAPTER ELEVEN

CHICAGO, 1970

He hid behind the kitchen door watching his mother as she moved about the house. He was going to have to make his move soon. It had been three days since she burned the girls, and three days was all she ever went without having one of her "fits." It was up to him. The girls couldn't take much more. At least he was strong enough now to get away from her.

He watched as she flopped in a chair and turned on the television with the remote control. Watching television! While the girls were in the bedroom wrapped in sheets, crying from the pain of the boiling water she had dumped on them!

"Germs," she had said. *"I have to get the germs off you."*

She was crazy. She did strange horrible things to them all the time. How he ever lived through it he would never know. But the girls were different. They couldn't take much more. He had to save them. He had to. There was no one else.

His eyes fell on the butcher knife lying on the counter where his mother had been cleaning a chicken—until her mind had wandered and she left, leaving the mess behind. Silently he eased out from behind the door, sliding his feet carefully so the floor would not creak. He inched his way over and picked up the knife, running his small fingers across the blade to check the sharpness of the instrument.

From the living room, he could hear her deep breathing and knew she had gone to sleep.

This is it. I might never have a chance again.

He stood over her with the knife clutched tightly in both hands. Her eyes opened briefly and a look of anger crossed her face. He brought the knife down with all the force his slight body could manage. He brought it down again and again and again.

OMAHA, 1992

Gwyn held the silk dress to her, letting her fingers move slowly over the many slashes. Jim watched her, fearing a replay of the previous day's events. He had advised against Gwyn putting herself through this ordeal again, but she had insisted.

"Children—pain—" she finally said, clutching her arm.

"A little girl—about Jessica's age. She is screaming. Her arm—the woman is twisting her arm. Oh, God! She broke it! She broke the child's arm!" Gwyn covered her face with her hands, shaking her head back and forth in disbelief.

Jim interrupted, "It's all right, Gwyn. The little girl is okay. She's in the hospital. Do you want to continue?"

Gwyn nodded her head slowly. "I can't seem to get by

the children. She burned them, Jim. With cigarettes! Even the baby!"

"I know, Gwyn. But they are going to be fine. Try again. Try to see what happened the evening Lucy Higgins died."

Gwyn picked the dress up from the table where she had dropped it and again closed her eyes. Her fingers played over the dress, in and out of the slashes left by the knife. There were many. Much more than on the clothing of the first two victims.

When she at last spoke, her voice was shaky, her breathing short.

"—Yes. I have the victim now. She is by a fence. Laughing.

"—She sees the knife. Starts to scream, but the knife goes into her.

"—Oh, God! Blood. Blood everywhere! The knife keeps slashing her. Over and over.

"—She falls. Isn't dead. She watches as the knife goes in again and again.

"—Her hand. Her hand is reaching for something. She tries to grab hold.

"—The knife goes deep. Deep inside her. Bones. I can hear her bones breaking as the knife plunges deeper."

"What about the man, Gwyn? Can you see the man with the knife?"

Gwyn didn't speak for a few minutes. Her head cocked to one side and she looked puzzled.

"—Yes. I have the assailant. It is the same man. Big. Handsome."

"What is he wearing?"

"—Jeans—blue shirt—same as before."

As she spoke the image of water began once again to blot everything from her vision. Her breathing became labored, shallow.

"A child. A child in the water. She is going under. Oh, God. Someone is holding her underneath the water! She is scared. She can't breathe!"

Gwyn's nostrils flared and she began gasping for air. "Let her go! Let—her—go!"

Once again Jim took hold of Gwyn's hand and pulled her toward him, away from where she was standing. She collapsed in his arms, sobbing.

"A little girl—in trouble—drowning!" she babbled. "Oh, God, Jim. What does all this mean?"

He held her to him, shaking his head. "I don't know, Gwyn. I just don't know. Let's get some coffee and go back to my office to talk about it. I think we both had about all we can stand of this room."

Gwyn sipped the coffee slowly, her mind going over the bizarre vision again and again.

Jim opened a notebook, anxious to get her thoughts down while they were fresh.

"You said the victim reached for something when she was down. What? Do you have any idea?"

Gwyn tried to think. "The edge of something. A flat edge—like a big box—only it was off the ground a few inches. I'm sorry. I know that isn't much help, but I didn't see that part plainly."

Jim smiled at her. "You did wonderful, Gwyn. Anything you can tell me puts us that much closer. You mentioned a fence. What kind of fence? Chain-link? Picket?"

"No." She shook her head slowly. "It was a high wooden fence—like around a backyard. She was in the corner—a fence in back of her and to the left side."

"And are you certain about the clothing? Jeans and a blue shirt? Each time the same?" Jim asked, keeping his voice pleasant. "We had reason to believe the killer wore brown when he killed Lucy Higgins."

Gwyn picked up fragments of Jim's thoughts. *No way. Killer wouldn't be dressed identical each time. She is mistaken.*

"No," she said softly. "I'm not mistaken, Jim. But there is something I have to tell you about these visions."

When she finished talking, Jim shook his head wearily. "I don't know, Gwyn. I just don't know what to think. There seems to be something going on here that isn't consistent with your past dealings with us. You are able to describe what happened to the victim down to the last detail, but the killer seems to be eluding you. And I don't know what to think about these cardboard images." He walked over to a filing cabinet and removed a folder. He flipped through a few pages, running his finger down the typed notes.

"She is being stabbed from behind—" He scanned down. "The man—he carries her to a fountain and dumps her in." He stopped reading. "And yet you just told me you never see this man actually doing anything?"

Gwyn thought back. "That's right, Jim. I saw the knife going in her. I saw her body going toward the fountain and then felt her drowning. *But I never saw the man actually do it!* Yet I know the man I see is the killer.

I know it just as surely as I know this man has information about Jessica!"

After she left, Jim absentmindedly ran the fingers of his left hand through his mop of unruly gray hair that refused any and all attempts of either comb or brush. The case was shaping up to be a real bitch. Where to go next?

Suddenly decisive, he grabbed his hat and walked toward the door. A change of scenery was needed, for his sanity, to clear his head. Whenever his mind was sluggish Jim went to the Ak-Sar-Ben Aquarium. The graceful, fluid motions of the fish calmed him and often his best ideas surfaced after an hour observing the movement of these creatures of the sea. Damned if he wasn't desperate for a good idea!

Gwyn drove down Herrington Boulevard with the car windows down. Wind whipped wisps of blond hair from the bun she had fashioned carelessly that morning. She paid no attention. It felt good to feel the fresh air rushing against her skin.

Why was everyone so determined to convince her she was wrong? She knew what she had seen. It might not be logical—or probable—but somewhere in this city there was a serial killer who was somehow connected with her daughter's disappearance. Where was he? What was he doing at this very minute?

Up ahead she saw the tall steeples of Saint Michael's, and eased over into the right lane to exit. She didn't notice the car following her at a distance do the same.

* * *

Gwyn walked to the front of the church, her high heels sounding loud in the empty sanctuary. For some reason she felt uneasy—edgy. She looked around, half expecting to see someone else, but no one was there. She knelt, made the sign of the cross, and lit one of the many candles on the altar. "Please, God," she prayed as she had done every day for nine months, "please help me find Jessica and keep her safe wherever she is."

At the back of the church, partially hidden by the confessional, solemn eyes watched her every move. He had been following her for days now. Watching. Waiting. Biding his time, waiting for the perfect moment. It was almost time.

CHAPTER TWELVE

Leon Bozyk stood in the outer office of Children's Services, waiting impatiently for Dr. Jacobs to join him. He didn't like working with women. Never had. Actually he didn't much like working with men either. He got more done on his own.

He was a loner. Always had been, except for the six months he had been married back when he was thirty. She had been a whiny, bitchy little thing who tried to take over his life. When he failed to return home for two weeks, she finally got the hint and packed her bags, cleaned out their savings, sold the furniture, and left. Some men might have been annoyed by her crassness. Not Leon. He went on a three-day drunk to celebrate.

Since then, he made it a point not to go out with a woman more than three times. It seemed to him after the fourth date they began to think they had a "relationship," with all the bullshit *that* entailed.

He was, although he didn't know it, an attractive man. The skinny, pockmarked youth he had been was gone. His dark brown hair was cut short, framing a large, ruddy-complexioned face—the sort of face one might expect to see on a New England fisherman. It was weathered and lined, but instead of detracting from his looks, it enhanced them.

He was a good detective. He had learned to read people well from all the years he had spent on the streets. He had been bounced back to pounding a beat by almost every superior he had ever worked under, so he had lots of experience. He was liked by the old-timers on the force, and tolerated by the younger ones. At least everyone knew where they stood with Leon Bozyk. If he thought you were acting like an ass, he did not hesitate to tell you.

At last the door to Marlo Jacobs's office opened and she exited, holding the hand of a small boy. "Sue," she said to the receptionist, "would you take Timmy back to his mother? She's in the waiting room. Tell her I'll be back here at five if she could meet me then, or if not, find out when would be convenient for her and make an appointment." She knelt beside the boy. "Will you come back to see me, Timmy?" The boy nodded his head solemnly.

She waited until the child was out of the room before turning to Leon. "I'm Dr. Jacobs," she said as she extended her hand. "I'm sorry you had to wait, but Timmy had a lot of fears to work through before he opened up to me. I didn't want to stop once he did."

"That's all right," Leon mumbled. "Are you ready to go now?"

"Yes, Detective—?"

"Bozyk. Leon Bozyk."

"That's quite a mouthful, Detective Bozyk. Mind if I call you Leon?"

"Whatever," Leon answered ungraciously.

Marlo Jacobs smiled pleasantly. "Captain Anderson described you as a grouchy curmudgeon whose bark was worse than his bite. Can I assume he was right in that statement?"

Leon took her arm and headed out of the office. "Obviously the captain doesn't know me very well," he said. "Actually my bite is far worse than my bark."

Marlo laughed easily. "I don't doubt it for a minute, Detective. Not for a minute."

It was a thirty-minute drive to the Simpson home, and Leon found himself talking easily to the doctor about the case. She asked intelligent, well-informed questions and seemed genuinely interested in any thoughts he had regarding the investigation. She wasn't too hard to look at, either, he had decided. She appeared to be in her late forties or early fifties, medium height, nice figure, and outstanding legs. She wore her brown hair short in one of those styles that suggested maybe she was active in sports. The kind of a hairdo, Leon thought, all women should wear. No fuss. No bother. And a man could touch it without getting in trouble. He found himself wondering about her personal life.

He glanced over at her. "Do you have a private practice as well as work for Children's Services?"

"Not anymore," she answered him. "I gave that up about a year ago. I guess I just got tired of talking to bored housewives about their sex life. Of course, I had always done a lot of work with children, but there were so many more who really needed me—abused, damaged children who were falling through the cracks in the system. There are two and a half million reported cases of child abuse every year in the United States, and that's only the tip of the iceberg—most we never hear about. Anyway, after my husband died, and my two children were grown and gone, I realized there was no reason I couldn't just devote at least a few years to these kids. So I closed up shop, and here I am."

"How do you stand it? Doesn't it get to you seeing what some of these kids go through?"

She nodded her head. "Oh, yes. Sometimes the only way I can cope is just to go home, mix a stiff drink, and have a good cry. Not very professional, but effective. And how about you?"

"What do you mean?"

"You see the sordid side of life every day, also. How do you handle it?"

"I don't know," Leon answered truthfully. "I've never given it much thought."

"My husband used to say people were like pressure cookers. If they don't let off steam once in a while, they end up blowing their top. He said policemen, especially, have to beware of the 'pressure cooker' syndrome."

Leon was instantly on guard. "Are you trying to do a number on me, Doc? Find out what makes me tick? Pigeon-hole me in some mumbo-jumbo psychological niche? I suppose your husband was a shrink, too."

Leon was not certain what he expected Marlo Jacobs's reaction to his words to be, but it was certainly not the reaction he got.

"Mr. Bozyk," she said coldly, "kiss my ass."

They finished the drive in chilly silence, but once at the Simpson home, Marlo Jacobs seemed to put her feelings aside as she interviewed the two children. She was friendly, open, and caring. She soon had them talking to her as though they had known her all their lives. When she felt she had their confidence she asked Leon to leave the room. He joined their father in the kitchen.

"What's this all about, Detective?" he asked. "I can't see what possible good talking to my children will do. They certainly know nothing about their mother's murder."

Leon cleared his throat uncomfortably. "Uh—Mr. Simpson, this is just standard procedure in a murder investigation. We have to cover all bases. Your children might have seen or heard something along the way— something they forgot that might be important."

Jack Simpson seemed to dissolve before Leon's eyes. He put his coffee cup down on the counter and sank heavily into a kitchen chair, his eyes filling with tears.

"I just can't believe this has happened. I don't know how I'll ever manage without Wanda. She was such a terrific wife—such a good mother. Everyone liked her. Who would do such a thing?" he rambled.

Leon recognized true grief when he saw it. The man was going through hell. If Wanda Simpson had ever abused her children, he was quite certain her husband knew nothing about it. He had obviously adored his wife.

Marlo Jacobs entered the kitchen. "All done," she said to the two men. She crossed to Jack Simpson, extending her hand. "Mr. Simpson, you have two lovely children. Thank you for letting me talk with them."

"You were right, Detective Bozyk," she said as soon as the car door closed. "I did not pick up even a hint of child abuse with those children. They seemed like happy, well-adjusted, normal kids. Of course I could be wrong. It's impossible to tell with only one visit, but my instincts tell me there was no abuse involved here."

Leon felt relieved. At least Jack Simpson would not have that to deal with.

"I did notice one strange thing, though," Marlo continued. "The house is a modest one, but the contents are extremely valuable. There are original paintings on the walls that must have cost a small fortune, not to mention the antiques. The children showed me through the house, and every room is decorated top-of-the-line. I know a little about home furnishings, and either the Simpsons have money in their background, or they are paying teachers a hell of a lot more than they did in my day."

CHAPTER THIRTEEN

Two hours later in the conference room at police headquarters Tucker, Petterson, Bozyk, Captain Anderson, and Police Commissioner Rasnik sat behind a table littered with microphones. Rasnik, considered a pompous ass by most of the men seated with him, raised his arm for silence, waiting for the room to quiet before speaking.

"Yesterday morning the body of a woman, Lucy Higgins, age thirty-two, was discovered in the duck pond at the zoo. Our investigation has determined she was killed by the same person or persons as the two previous victims, Maria Gilbert and Wanda Simpson. The deaths of these three women, who have no connection to each other, lead us to believe we are dealing with a serial killer. We want to warn the citizens of Omaha to take extra precautions. Women should travel in groups, or at least pairs. Don't go out alone, especially at night. These deaths have occurred in three different sections of the city, so there is no telling where the killer may strike next. This latest victim was slain at six-thirty in the evening, so don't assume you are all right during daylight hours."

Commissioner Rasnik stopped and looked out at the sea of reporters, reveling in his moment in the sun. He continued dramatically, "A serial killer is a city's worst nightmare. They strike at random, with usually no rhyme nor reason as to their choice of victims. Because of this, it is one of the toughest crimes to solve."

Bozyk held his hand over the microphone in front of him. "No, shit," he mumbled to Anderson.

"So now if there are any questions, we will try and answer them."

"Are there any suspects yet, Captain Anderson?" a reporter yelled, effectively bypassing the commissioner.

"No. Not yet," Anderson answered.

"Do you have any leads in the case?"

"Yes. We have some physical evidence that might pan out. Nothing I can give you, though."

"Were all three victims stabbed with the same knife, Captain?"

"Yes. We believe the same knife was used on all three women."

From the back of the room a reporter called out, "Captain Anderson—Captain Anderson."

Anderson pointed at the man.

"The commissioner stated there was no connection between the victims, but that's not quite true, is it?"

Anderson swallowed hard. "The only connection we have come up with is that they were all women in their early thirties, and they all had children. Other than that, no. Next question?" He pointed to another reporter.

But the man in the back was not to be put off.

"What about child abuse, Captain?"

The room fell instantly quiet, and Anderson knew he could not sidestep the question.

"There was suspected child abuse in two of the cases, not in the third. There is no reason at this time to think that has any bearing on the murders."

The reporter would not drop the issue.

"*Suspected* child abuse, Captain? Lucy Higgins's three children are in the hospital right now. And I just finished interviewing Maria Gilbert's neighbors and they say she abused her children daily. That sounds to me a little more than 'suspected.'"

Anderson was irritated and it showed.

"There was no child abuse in the Simpson case, though. You can't establish a pattern if only two of the victims share a common denominator."

"You did check, then, to be certain Mrs. Simpson did not abuse her children?"

"Well, yes, of course, just as a matter of policy." Anderson tried to sound casual. "But there is absolutely no indication of anything like that in her case. We heard nothing but good reports on Wanda Simpson from beginning to end, and I think it is unfair to her family to suggest anything to the contrary."

Another reporter took the ball.

"Do you think it is possible the killer just goofed in the Simpson case, and is really after abusive mothers?"

Anderson forced a smile. "Gentlemen, I know you are all after an angle to liven up the evening papers, but I'm afraid you will have to come up with something else. As of now, our department has no leads in the motive for these killings—if there even is one. Next question, please."

"What about Gwyn Martin? Has she been in to see you yet?"

"Yes. As always, Mrs. Martin has given us all the help she can. I can't discuss anything she had to say, though. That is her policy as well as ours."

"Captain Anderson, isn't it true that a serial killer usually keeps right on killing until he is caught? And sometimes it takes months and years before that happens?"

Anderson cursed the commissioner's remarks. "Only if he stays on the move. Then it is harder to trace him. If this killer stays in our city, we will get him. You have my word on that."

He picked up the remote control from the table by his chair and flipped the television into darkness. Damn fools. All this ruckus over three women who weren't worth spitting on. They should be giving him a medal for ridding the city of vermin, instead of trying to hunt him down like a rabid dog.

So Wanda Simpson was a model citizen and mother? Shit. She was the worst of the lot as far as he was concerned. He walked over to a drawer and removed a small packet of photographs, handling them carefully by the edges. He could hardly stand to look at them. They made him sick to his stomach. He knew Wanda Simpson's fingerprints were all over the photos. He had watched her casually flip through them as she quoted him the price.

He had discovered the lovely Mrs. Simpson quite by accident. He had been at a hotel bar in Kansas City when he overheard the men in the next booth talking. They had just returned from Omaha with their "buy." The more he listened, the more outraged he became. Finally, he heard what he had been waiting for. The fat man referred to a Simpson woman. The rest had been mere legwork.

It had taken him only three days to track down the bitch and arrange his own "buy." And he had taken extreme pleasure in the look of surprise on Wanda Simpson's face when she realized she had made her last sale.

He sat looking at the disgusting photographs, trying to come to a decision. Finally he went to the closet, pulled on a pair of gloves, then removed an envelope from a box in his desk. They were ordinary envelopes, the kind sold at discount stores and supermarkets. There was no way the police could trace them back to him. He turned one of the photos over and printed his message in block letters, then slid them all into the envelope. At the last minute he remembered not to lick the flap or the stamp, moistening them instead with a dampened towel. Then, using the same block letters, he slowly printed the address.

The evening broadcast was all about the murders and the commissioner's warning. Gwyn tried to steer the discussion on to other topics, but her audience would not be denied. Even her out-of-state callers kept returning again and again to the subject of Omaha's serial killer.

"Good evening, Gwyn," an elderly woman with a high-pitched, twangy voice said. "After listening to the press conference this afternoon, does it make you nervous that maybe the killer might think you can identify him, and come after you?"

Gwyn tried to make her voice steady. "No. Not really. I wasn't able to give the police much concerning this serial killer. He would just be putting himself in more jeopardy by coming after me, because I don't know anything more than the police know anyway."

"And of course you wouldn't tell us if you *did* know more, right?" the woman said, pressing the issue and making Gwyn uncomfortable. "I heard Captain Anderson say today that you made it a policy not to discuss anything you do with the police, so we don't really know *what* went on, do we?"

Gwyn bypassed the question. "The main thing we know right now is that the city should be alerted to the danger. Let me repeat what the police told us today. Women should travel in groups and absolutely not go out alone at night, and even in daylight hours it would be best to at least travel in pairs. Don't stop for anyone on the highways, or open your home to any stranger—no matter who he says he is. A few years ago a serial killer gained access to his victims by posing as a telephone repairman, so trust no one until the police have apprehended this man."

Gwyn was relieved to see "John from Omaha" flash on the computer screen. "Good evening, John. Nice to hear from you," she said truthfully. "What's on your mind today?"

John's warm voice filled the air waves. "Hello, Gwyn. Sounds to me like your audience is putting you through the old wringer tonight."

Gwyn laughed. "Oh, not really. I know everyone is concerned about what is going on. That's only natural. It's just that I can't discuss specifics about the case. I don't know any more than the police, and they will keep us informed on a 'need to know' basis, I'm sure."

"Well, Gwyn, my question is about police forces in general. How do they react, normally, to working with a psychic on a case? From everything I've ever read, it seems the police never take a psychic seriously—even make fun of them to some extent. What are your thoughts about that?"

Gwyn was glad for the chance to talk about something else. "John, about the only time police make fun of psychics anymore is in fiction. In real life, only the most backward of police forces won't take help from a psychic. A few years back that wasn't the case, but during this last decade there has been an explosion in the field of parapsychology. Almost everyone you talk to believes there is a *sixth sense* that flourishes in certain people. It would be lunacy for the police not to take advantage of someone who can give them even a small bit of information about a crime."

"What happened when you first went to the police and told them you could help them solve a crime? Did they take you seriously?"

"That was seven years ago, John. And I think at first they might have been a little skeptical, but they acted on my information, nevertheless."

John chuckled. "You know, if I were a criminal, I'd be a little hesitant to commit a crime these days. I was reading about this psychic who was just sitting at home and saw a murder, saw where the body was thrown, and even described the vehicle the killer was driving. The police were able to find the body and track the killer just from this man's information."

"Yes," Gwyn answered him. "That would be Nelson Palmer. Without his help, the murder would probably not have been solved."

"Gwyn," John said earnestly, "I want you to do me a big favor."

"Certainly, John—if I can."

"I want you to take good care of yourself and be extra careful until this maniac is caught."

"That's a promise, John," she answered him.

In the room across from Gwyn, Mike printed in the name and city of the next caller on the computer, then answered another flashing line. "Hello, this is the Gwyn Martin Show. May I have your name and city and a brief description of what you want to discuss with Gwyn?"

The voice coming through the phone was raspy, almost unintelligible.

"Please. You must stop him."

"I'm sorry," Mike said into the phone, "this is the Gwyn Martin Show. Did you wish to speak with her? If so, I'll need your name and—"

"Stop him!" The voice on the line sounded frantic. "Tell her—tell her to watch out!"

Mike reached over and punched a button, activating the tape recorder attached to the phone. It was probably just a crank call, but he wasn't taking any chances.

"I can't understand you," he said. "Would you mind repeating that?"

There was silence, then he heard the phone click and the start of the familiar dial tone.

"Damn!" he swore softly. "Every loony in a five-state area must be calling in tonight."

In the control room, Gwyn suddenly felt an icy chill run through her body. Her hands began to shake uncontrollably and she rapidly brought the discussion to a close. Her eyes flew to the computer. Thank God. There were three minutes of commercials. Quickly she took off her earphones and ran into Mike's room.

"What happened just now, Mike?" she asked him as soon as she saw he had the commercial running. "Did you get a phone call you didn't put through to me?"

He looked at her in surprise. "How the hell did you know that?"

"Who was it, did he say?" she asked, ignoring his question.

"No. It was just a nuisance call. Something about your being careful—and, oh, yeah, he asked me to 'stop him'—or something like that."

"Mike," Gwyn pleaded, "this is important. I think that call was from the killer. I can't explain it, but I'm certain it was. Did you get it on tape?"

"No, I'm sorry," he said, shaking his head. "There

wasn't time. I put the recorder on, but he hung up. Damn it! I should have thought about this possibility and been taping all the pre-calls."

"Are you sure it was a man's voice?"

Mike tried to think. "No. I guess I'm really not sure. Whoever it was, he was trying to disguise his voice— you know, sort of a ragged whisper."

"And what did he say—exactly?" Gwyn asked. "Try to remember."

Mike played the conversation back in his mind. "First he said, 'Please—you've got to stop him,' or something like that. Then he repeated, 'Stop him—tell her to watch out.' "

Gwyn knotted her forehead in concentration. "Well, that doesn't even make any sense! Why would the killer say for you to stop *him*? Are you sure he didn't say, 'stop *me*'?"

"No." Mike shook his head. "He said stop *him*—I remember that for certain."

Gwyn looked puzzled. "Maybe I was wrong then. Perhaps it wasn't our serial killer. I was just so sure—"

Mike looked at the clock. "You have thirty seconds. Are you going to be able to finish the show?"

"Yes. Go easy on me, though. Just nice, normal callers, okay?"

"You've got it. No Marthas the rest of the evening. And I'll tape all incoming calls, in case our friend gives us another shot at him."

Gwyn left the station, driving slow, trying to sort out the incredible events that seemed to keep bombarding her from all sides. At the last minute, she decided not to take the interstate to her home. Instead she pulled off onto the access road, then wound around to the area near the university. She had about an hour before Karen arrived at her home, and driving had always been a release for her—especially here, in this lovely section of the city.

The sun was just setting, bouncing off the trees and houses in a dazzling display of light. The streets were virtually empty, and as Gwyn drove she became more and more aware of the strange lack of any activity. She knew the reason, and reached over, snapping the locks down on the doors of her car. No use taking any chances.

Both the murder of the college girl and the attack on Betty Crawford had occurred around here in this high-class, established part of the city. Gentle hills and narrow streets discouraged outside traffic. Ivy-covered two-story brick homes were the norm. The whole area had a timeless quality that kept real estate prices at a premium. There was a waiting list of families wanting to purchase even the smallest of homes in this neighborhood, and college students considered themselves extremely lucky to land an apartment in this prime location. With the abundance of maple trees lining the quiet streets, it was an unlikely area for violence. Residents always joked that the area only became noisy in autumn when fallen leaves crunched beneath feet or automobile tires.

Something told Gwyn they were not joking now. She shuddered as she remembered the attack on Betty Crawford she had witnessed. So many things happening. How much more could she take?

Whenever she did a reading where violence was involved, it left her drained—physically and emotionally. It was hard to feel the pain and terror a victim was going through. Hard not to let it affect her.

What was it about the serial killings that so unnerved her? She could feel the fear of the victims, certainly, but there was another element at work. She had been able on the last victim to pick up an essence of evil—only it was the evil of the victim as she harmed her children, not the killer. There was also an overwhelming feeling of horror and evil emanating from the strange visions of water—but was this a separate thing altogether? At home by the swing, months ago, she was seeing this same image of water. She had to admit it, she hadn't really tuned in on any feeling of evil directly connected to the serial killer. Why?

She had also received an overpowering impression of evil coming from the man who attacked the Crawford girl. That was normal in cases involving violence. Why then wasn't she getting this same feeling about the serial killer? Or was she just kidding herself because of the possible connection to Jessica?

It was almost dark now, the only sunlight coming from a faint glow in the western sky. Automatic yard lights began popping on all along the quiet streets. Gwyn passed a van with the words "Black Jack's Pizza" written on the side. She imagined fast food delivery places were doing a booming business right now, when people were afraid to venture out after dark.

She suddenly realized she was famished. It had been hours since she had eaten. If she hurried, she would have time to grab a Big Mac on the way home. She ignored the ache beginning at the base of her neck that often accompanied a psychic experience. No. She could not stand any more trauma tonight. She reached over and turned the volume up on her car radio, forcing her mind away from the other realm. Enough was enough.

CHAPTER FOURTEEN

"Before we get started, I have to tell you. One of the shops in Regency Court has a blouse that would be striking with your blue suit. Shall we take a look at it this weekend?" encouraged Karen.

It used to be a normal pattern. Adam would good-naturedly entertain Jessica so Karen and Gwyn could shop and try the latest fashions. How they loved it! They would go to all the boutiques in this elegant mall and try on clothes for hours, then shyly sneak into the Godiva chocolate store and sinfully purchase a sampling of the beautifully decorated candies. While resting on the wrought-iron benches strategically placed in the center of the mall, they would take off their shoes and munch chocolates, congratulating each other often on their wise and absolutely necessary purchases. And what atmosphere! There was lush greenery, a waterfall at the end of a long hall, and skylights overhead. It always refreshed their spirits. How long ago it seemed since they had spent a day in carefree amusement.

"Yes." Gwyn nodded in agreement. "I'll look forward to it. And is that a new outfit you're wearing? Trying to impress Brent?" Gwyn grinned.

"Well, everything else was dirty," excused Karen. "And don't get any ideas. It was just a quiet, friendly dinner. We went to Trini's, which, by the way, still serves the best Mexican food in town. Now, let's get to work or we'll be up all night," she said as she stared at the heaping piles of books covering Gwyn's living room.

"Do you really expect us to wade through all this or are you going to sleep on them like Edgar Cayce so they will magically implant themselves in your mind?"

Gwyn laughed. "No. I'm afraid I don't have his talent. We'll have to do this the old-fashioned way. Would be nice though, wouldn't it?"

"Where did you get all these books, Gwyn? These aren't the kind of books you can walk in a bookstore and pick up," Karen asked as she thumbed through a pile. "Many of these were out of print before you were even born."

"Oh, from everywhere, I guess. I studied at the Psycho-physical Research Laboratory in Princeton. The director there took a liking to me and whenever new books arrived, she gave me the old ones. Also my father began collecting books for me as soon as he realized my 'special' talents."

"Isn't it odd that you were in Princeton at the same time as Adam, yet you never met until you were both here in Omaha?"

"Well, not really. By the time I was around, he was already in an architectural firm, so there was no reason our paths should have crossed."

"How is he?" Karen asked. "Have you seen him lately?"

Unexpectedly, a wave of sorrow washed over Gwyn.

She tried, without success, to keep her voice from betraying her emotions. "Oh, yes. I saw him this morning. I told him everything that was going on, and he suggested I see a psychiatrist. Can you beat that? The first real hope we've had that Jessica is alive, and he wants me to drop the whole thing."

Karen saw Gwyn's pain and tried to ease it. "Give him time, Gwyn. I never saw a father as crazy over a child as Adam was about Jessica. I can't even imagine what he must have gone through—and is still going through. At dinner tonight, Brent told me Adam still cannot do his work, and spends hours on the phone every day calling agencies and missing children hot lines. He has even been trying to get a line on illegal underground adoption markets—thinking maybe someone took Jessica to sell."

Gwyn was clearly surprised. "Then why did he brush off my efforts so casually? He would hardly listen to anything I had to say."

Karen avoided her friend's eyes. "Perhaps," she said quietly, "it's because what you're saying is so hard to believe. And maybe also because if he believes there is a connection to this serial killer, then he has to entertain the possibility that his little girl is in the hands of a psychotic madman. Maybe he just can't deal with that prospect."

"Yes, I see what you mean," Gwyn said softly. "I'm not crazy about that idea myself. And on top of everything else, someone called the station tonight and spoke with Mike—warned him, really. Said to 'stop him,' whatever that means. Also that I should 'watch out.'"

Karen looked shocked. "Was it just a crank call do you think? Or was it the killer?"

"I don't know. At first I got really bad vibes—just *knew* it was our man. But when Mike described what was said, I wasn't so sure. If it was the serial killer, why wouldn't he have said, 'stop *me*'? I imagine Mike was right. It was probably nothing more than some pervert making a nuisance call."

"Please don't go taking any chances, Gwyn." Karen spoke earnestly. "It makes me nervous that you are on the radio every day, reminding this killer there is a damn good psychic around who might be able to finger him."

"I know just what you mean. My audience wouldn't drop the issue tonight, either. Did you catch any of the show?"

"Yes. Brent and I listened to the first part on the way to the restaurant. He remarked that he didn't like the way it was going—said it could be dangerous for you."

Gwyn shrugged. "There isn't much I can do. I'm not about to quit a job I love because of this maniac. I won't give him the privilege of running me off my own show! Besides, the more I learn about this killer, the closer I'll be to figuring out these visions and finding Jessica." She stopped talking and looked around. "Speaking of which, we had better get cracking."

They had been working for three hours when Karen broke the silence. "Here's something. It says that when conducting experiments in telepathy, a negative observer can adversely influence the outcome. Is it possible a negative mind is somehow interfering with your powers?"

Gwyn put the book she was reading aside, arched her

aching back, and shook her head. "No. I don't think that could be it. What it means is that a negative mind might keep the psychic from being able to complete an effective reading. That still wouldn't explain the photograph-like appearance of the two people I saw."

"Have you found anything at all?"

"No. Not really. Nothing I didn't already know. It is possible for a psychic with a great deal of power to force her thoughts into another person's mind. But that can't be it. First of all, I was tested at every major parapsychological institute in the United States—including Rhine—and I don't want to sound like I'm bragging, but my test scores were always among the highest. There were only a handful of psychics ever tested at Rhine who outdid me in clairvoyance, telepathy, or precognition. So the chances of another psychic being here with enough power to influence my mind is just astronomical."

"Were there any areas you were weak in or had no abilities?"

"Only two. Retrocognition, which is seeing past events, and psychokinesis, which is the ability of the mind to move objects. And neither of those would have any bearing on what I am seeing."

Karen was fascinated with the conversation. "Did you actually do tests to see if you could move an object with your mind?"

"Only a few times. I was able once to make a chair move slightly, but the experience left me weak and sick to my stomach. I decided to stick with the areas I was naturally good at."

"Unbelievable," Karen said, shaking her head. "Just unbelievable. And what's this about testing high in telepathy? We've been friends for lo these many years, and you're just getting around to telling me you can read my mind?"

Gwyn laughed rakishly. "That's right! Your deepest, darkest secrets are known to me. I'm just waiting until you're extremely rich to begin the blackmail!"

Karen made a face at her and burst out laughing. "I only *wish* my life was exciting enough to elicit a little blackmail! But seriously, how good are you at thought transmission?"

"Not good at all anymore," Gwyn answered. "When I was younger I was better at it—but even then, it was more in the line of controlled experiments. However, I did go on a few dates where I picked up snatches of thought that sent me running home to Daddy!"

"How about Adam? I would think the possibility of being able to read your husband's mind would put a real damper on a marriage! I mean—even the best of men must have less than noble thoughts *part* of the time."

Gwyn looked away at the mention of her husband, and Karen was instantly sorry she had brought his name up again.

"No. I've never picked up anything from Adam. Not a word. I think that was one of the things that attracted me to him—gave him a mysterious quality I liked. Anyway, I rarely try to consciously pick up on other people's thoughts. It's sort of an invasion of privacy."

Gwyn looked at her watch. "It's after eleven. What say I make us a plate of cheese and crackers to counteract all the coffee we've consumed, and then let's call it a night?"

Karen nodded her head wearily. "That sounds good. How about a small glass of wine to go with it?"

"Good idea, but I'm fresh out. Would you settle for rum?"

"No, wine sounds better for cheese and crackers. It's a little late to hit the hard stuff, anyway. I'll just run over to the house and get a bottle of white zinfindel." She hauled herself up off the floor and slipped on her shoes. "Anyway I've been on that floor so long, the exercise will feel good."

They were both so used to running back and forth between their two houses that neither one gave any thought to the commissioner's warning.

Karen closed the front door behind her and started across the yard separating the two houses. "Shit," she swore softly as her high heels sank into the rain-soaked earth. Quickly she stepped back onto the cement, realizing she would have to follow the sidewalk—a little longer distance, but preferable to ruining her shoes.

The clipping noise of her heels sounded loud in the quiet night, and she suddenly began to feel apprehensive. *Don't be such a baby!* she said to herself. *There's more light near the street than between the houses, anyway.* Almost as soon as that thought struck her she had another one. *More light for someone to see me, too.*

She reached her driveway, and crossed to the large railed veranda that ran almost the length of the house. She stood for a few seconds looking out into the moonless night from the safety of her porch. There was no one around. She was just letting her nerves get the better of her.

* * *

Gwyn moved about the kitchen uneasily. She glanced at the large double windows over the sink, then without really thinking about it crossed over and drew the curtains. She opened the refrigerator, took out a round ball of cheese, and began stripping the wax casing. *Something's wrong,* she thought as she rummaged in a drawer for a knife to cut the cheese. Only when her hand closed around the knife did it hit her.

Karen! She dropped the knife and ran.

Gwyn cut across the yard, her running shoes able to handle the soft ground better than Karen's heels. Just as she reached the corner of her house, a man burst from between the two homes, nearly colliding with her. She screamed as she felt his arms go around her.

"Gwyn. It's okay. It's me."

"Brent? Is that you?"

"Yes. I was in back. I heard Karen yell. Where is she?"

"At her house," Gwyn answered him as she sprinted away. "Come on." She would deal later with what Brent was doing in their backyard. At the moment she was only glad for his presence.

When they reached the porch, he stopped her. "No, Gwyn. Stay out here. Let me go in first." His voice had a commanding tone to it, and she hung back, letting him take the lead.

Karen's front door was standing open, and they could hear her voice from inside. Brent went through the door quickly, then stopped. Karen was standing in the middle of the living room, both hands covering her mouth as she shook her head from side to side, moaning.

"What is it, Brent?" Gwyn asked from the doorway.

He stepped to the side, allowing her to view the wreckage in Karen's home. Gwyn rushed to her friend. "Are you all right? What happened?"

Karen seemed to be in shock. "I don't know. My house—my beautiful house. It's ruined."

Gwyn held her as they both looked around at the damage. The furniture had been shredded, pictures slashed, mirrors broken, and the drapes hung in ribbons.

Brent recovered first. "Where's the telephone, Karen?" he asked gently. "I'll call the police."

She pointed toward the den, and then seemed almost to choke as she spoke. "My clock—oh, God. Not my clock." She ran for the den.

Brent flipped on the lights and the three of them stood transfixed, staring at the remains of Karen's grandfather clock. It was hacked totally beyond repair, and on the wall in black spray paint was printed the words:

KEEP YOUR MOUTH SHUT BITCH
OR YOU ARE NEXT

CHAPTER FIFTEEN

Detective Bozyk opened his notebook. "When was the last time you were home, Miss Jackson?"

She looked at him through tear-filled eyes. "About three o'clock this afternoon. I came home to clean up for a dinner date, then returned to my office. I had an appointment at five and knew there wouldn't be time to change if I waited until then."

"And when you returned you found things as they are now?"

"No. I was at Gwyn's house all evening—after my dinner date." She turned to Brent. "You brought me to Gwyn's about eight, wasn't it?"

He nodded his head. "Yes. It was just a few minutes after, as I recall."

"And then what?" Bozyk continued. "When did you leave Mrs. Martin's home?"

"Just a few minutes ago," Karen answered. "Just shortly before Brent called the police."

"Did you notice anything out of the ordinary before you went in the house?"

"I was a little jumpy because I felt like someone was

watching me. I didn't see anyone though and decided it was just my nerves."

"Think carefully, Miss Jackson. Was there any specific reason you were feeling nervous?"

"No. Really there wasn't. Usually I cut across the yard to go home from Gwyn's. But the rain had softened the ground, and my heels sunk in when I started across. So I took the sidewalk, instead. I was under the streetlights, and for some reason that made me more edgy than the darkness. I remember thinking anyone could see me plainly. When I reached my porch, I looked around, but didn't see anyone."

"And then you entered the house?"

"Yes. I always keep a key in a pot of flowers on the porch. I took it out, unlocked the door, and went in. I think I screamed when I saw . . . saw the wreckage." She closed her eyes tightly, trying to halt the flood of tears that was once again starting.

"Miss Jackson," Bozyk continued, "listen to me. This is important. When you went in the den and saw what was written on the wall, what was your initial reaction? What did you think those words meant?"

"Well, I . . . I don't know. I suppose I thought the murders." She hesitated a few seconds. "No. Wait. I remember now thinking about Jessica. For some reason she popped into my mind when I read the words. But just fleetingly. I don't know anything about her disappearance that I haven't already told the police."

"Can you think of any detail at all concerning Jessica or the serial murders that might make you a threat to the kidnapper or killer?"

Karen shook her head from side to side slowly. "No. I'm sorry. I don't know anything—except . . ."

"Yes? Except what, Miss Jackson?"

"Well, I have always had a feeling I saw something without really seeing it, if you know what I mean. Something about Jessica. About that day. Just a nagging itch that won't go away. Dr. Beckman, the psychiatrist I have been seeing for about a month, tells me that is just a normal reaction to a bad situation. Everyone wants so badly to help, they convince themselves they might know more than they really do."

"In this case, Miss Jackson, you might actually know more." He looked at the petite, attractive woman. "If you don't mind my asking, why are you seeing a psychiatrist?"

Karen managed a slight smile through her tears. "It's okay, Detective Bozyk. I'm not embarrassed about it. I just was having some hard times trying to cope with Jessica's disappearance. I'm her godmother, and she was such a special little girl." She glanced at Gwyn. "We all loved her so much. And Captain Anderson suggested we should get counseling to help us through the ordeal. I finally decided to take his suggestion, that's all."

Bozyk nodded his head and changed the subject. "When you approached your house this evening, did you notice anything unusual? Lights that you hadn't left on—that sort of thing?"

Karen thought a minute. "No. I didn't really pay any attention. I always leave three lights and a radio on—sort of my own personal alarm system." She seemed to be concentrating. "I believe the lights I had left burning were still on and no others," she said. "I remember we turned the den lights on when we entered that room."

"We?" Bozyk said. "I was under the impression you entered the house alone."

"I did," Karen answered him. "But in just a few minutes Brent and Gwyn came in. They were with me when we checked the den."

Bozyk turned to Gwyn. "And how did you happen to come over at that time?"

"Karen had run over to her house for a bottle of wine. After she left I started getting uneasy. It was sort of like what Karen described. I felt like someone was watching me. Then all at once I just knew something was wrong. I dropped what I was doing and dashed over here." She hesitated. "I ran into Brent at the corner of my house. He said he had heard Karen yell and then we both came to check."

"Do you live around here, Mr. Carlson?" Bozyk asked.

Brent shook his head. "No, sir. I live across town."

"May I ask what you were doing here then? You dropped Miss Jackson off and yet you were still hanging around over three hours later?"

Brent looked indignantly at the detective. "I wasn't just *hanging* around. I was worried about the girls being alone. Especially since Gwyn's radio show, where it was readily apparent she might be able to identify the killer. I just wanted to keep an eye on the house to make certain no one bothered them, so I parked in the alley."

"Have you ever done this before?"

Brent looked down at the floor. "Yes, sir. A few times."

Bozyk looked at Karen and Gwyn. "Did either of you know Mr. Carlson was watching the house?"

They both shook their heads, and then Gwyn spoke. "Detective Bozyk, Brent is a friend of ours—both Karen and myself. He is Adam's partner, and was best man at our wedding. He is also godfather to Jessica. I'm certain he was only trying to help."

Bozyk was not convinced, but decided to drop it. "When you were watching the house, did you see or hear anything out of the ordinary?" he said to Brent.

"No. Nothing. I saw Karen walk home, and then heard her yell. That's all."

"All right, then, I guess that about does it," Leon said. "We have no way of knowing if this was done by the serial killer or someone with a sick sense of humor." He turned to Karen. "My men will be done here in a few minutes, then I suggest you lock up and spend the night with Mrs. Martin. You can contact your insurance carrier in the morning and they will help you get started on repairing this damage.

"And, Mr. Carlson," Bozyk added, "I'll station a man outside so you don't need to stand vigil."

Brent nodded, closemouthed.

CHAPTER
SIXTEEN

Anderson picked up the pile of memos on his desk and started sorting through them. The string of convenience store robberies had been solved during the night. An off-duty police officer had made a midnight run for diapers and saw the robbery in progress. He had apprehended the thief as he left the store.

His men now had a suspect in custody for the rape and murder of the college girl last month, and the near murder of Betty Crawford—a pizza delivery boy who had been apprehended near the university during the night, and had since confessed. Good. One less homicide to worry about.

He scanned down the report, then smiled. The delivery truck was black, as was the uniform the man was wearing. Gwyn's "black cloud." There was no doubt about it. She was good. Damn good.

In the heart of the city, there had been two knifings and one shooting during the night, but no deaths.

Ak-Sar-Ben, Omaha's prestigious racetrack, had had a moment of excitement when a woman had removed her clothing, scaled the fence, and run nude partway around the track behind the horses in the eighth race. Anderson chuckled, picturing a jockey glancing around and seeing who was gaining on him.

He picked up the last report and sobered quickly. Karen Jackson's home had been vandalized the previous evening, and a message left that indicated it could be the work of his serial killer. What the hell was going on? Why Karen Jackson?

The events of the last few days kept running through Anderson's mind as he carefully studied Leon's report. First there was the murder of Lucy Higgins. Then the incredible story Gwyn Martin gave him in the evidence room. Now her neighbor gets her house trashed with a threat to keep her mouth shut. About what? What could Karen Jackson know? And even if she did know something, did it have any bearing on the murders?

There was no forced entry to the house. The back door was bolted from the inside, so the only access to the home was the front door or through the garage. The automatic garage door did not appear to have been tampered with, and the inside door leading from the garage to the house was still locked.

Miss Jackson's car had been left at her office, so conceivably someone could have removed the opener from her car, entered through the garage, picked the lock, and, when finished, locked the garage door again as he exited.

Then he would have had to return the opener to the car.

No. He wouldn't have gone to that much trouble.

More likely, he entered through the front door, using the key or picking the lock. But again there was no evidence the lock had been tampered with.

Anderson lit a cigarette and leaned back in his chair. Someone she knew? Someone who knew she kept a key in the flowerpot? That seemed the only logical answer. He hit the intercom.

Sometime during the short night Gwyn had flung back the covers, and she lay there now, her body glistening with a thin layer of sweat. She was awakened by the sunlight that streamed in, forcing her eyes open, and forcing the dream into conscious thought.

"Jessica!" she said aloud as she emerged from the nightmare, her body jerking involuntarily. Slowly her mind began to adjust. She was home. In bed.

It had been so real! Jessica crying—calling to her. They had all been in the dream: Adam, Brent, Karen, Jim. All searching. Jessica had been lost in a forest—animals all around—clawing at her. No one could reach her.

Gwyn swung her long legs over the side of the bed and sat up, remembering. A dog. Someone had brought a Labrador retriever and it worked its way through the dense trees to her child. Jessica began laughing—petting the big friendly animal. But then it began snarling viciously and turned on her.

A tremor ran through Gwyn's body as she focused on the dream. Jessica had begun running—trying to escape the dog. She was screaming, calling for her. That was all she could remember. At that point she had awakened.

Gwyn reached for her robe. Thank God it had only been a nightmare. It meant nothing. Still, it made her uneasy as she entered her kitchen and began making coffee.

She jumped when Karen spoke to her. "Good morning. Kind of a short night, wasn't it?"

"Oh, damn, Karen!" Gwyn laughed, covering her chest with one hand. "I forgot all about your being here. You about gave me a heart attack!"

"I'm sorry I startled you," Karen said. "I heard you yell out Jessica's name a few minutes ago. Another nightmare?"

"Yes, and I don't think I've quite got my bearings yet. Even though I know the dreams don't mean anything, they still unnerve me."

Gwyn plugged in the coffee maker and crossed over to Karen, putting her arms around her. "And how about you? Did you get any sleep last night?"

"Not much. I just lay there thinking of all the hours, and days, and weeks I spent hunting for just the right little vase, or the perfect shade of mauve for my drapes. And now everything is destroyed!"

Gwyn's eyes misted over. She alone knew what Karen's home meant to her friend. With no family, and no special man in her life, she had devoted much of her time to furnishing her home. It was her pride and joy.

"Well," Gwyn said. "Let's look on the bright side. At least you weren't home to encounter the intruder. And your insurance will pay for the damage. It's been a long time since we went shopping. We'll just start over and fix everything up even better than before!"

Karen smiled for the first time, aware that Gwyn was trying desperately to cheer her up. "All right, friend. You have a deal—but I'm not starting until this maniac is caught. I couldn't handle working on my house while he is still running loose!"

"Have you thought of any reason why that message was left?" Gwyn asked, sobering again.

"No. I can't imagine. I spent half the night trying to make some sense out of it—but I haven't a clue. Not a damn clue!"

"Well, I'll tell you one thing—I don't want you staying there until the police have this nut safely behind bars. It will do us both good not to be alone just now."

"I agree, Gwyn. And just between you and me, I wouldn't object to having Brent parked outside. That detective Bozyk—he thought it was strange for Brent to be watching the house, but I'm sure he was only trying to help. And right now, we can use all the help we can get!"

"Yes," Gwyn said thoughtfully. "But it *was* curious, his being there, don't you think?"

Bozyk, Petterson, and Tucker filed into Anderson's office.

"I know you haven't had much time to compile backgrounds on people close to the Martins," Anderson said. "But in light of what happened at the Jackson house, I think it is imperative we give this our full attention."

Anderson glanced at his watch. "We have a few minutes before Dr. Jacobs gets here to give us a psychological profile of the killer, so let's go over what we have so far. Tucker?"

"Captain, we have received a good deal of information already, especially about Mr. Martin," Tucker said. "He has a police record, so we were able to get quite a lot on him."

"Adam Martin has a police record?" Anderson asked incredulously. "I can't believe it!"

Tucker continued, "He not only has a police record, but we have juvenal reports on him from about the age of eight." He opened a file and handed it to Anderson.

Jim scanned quickly through the report.

Age eight—found roaming the streets of New York, running errands for prostitutes. Enrolled in school, placed in foster care.

Age ten—arrested for theft, placed in different foster home.

Age eleven—attacked another child, would have been sent to correctional institute but a teacher intervened on his behalf.

Age fourteen—charged with raping the daughter of his foster parents. Charges dropped. Placed in different foster home.

Age seventeen—arrested for running numbers—charges dropped for lack of evidence.

In all, the boy had been placed in thirty-seven different foster homes—inner-city foster homes, which Anderson knew were a far cry from the high standard of foster care found elsewhere.

He looked up from the report. "Nothing since the age of seventeen?"

Tucker nodded. "There was a note attached to his records saying that a child psychologist who had evaluated him considered him dangerous. However there were also dozens of letters from teachers praising him and talking about how bright he was. In fact, with everything stacked against him, he still managed to graduate second in his class from high school. He was given a full scholarship to Princeton."

Anderson shook his head. "Incredible. Just incredible."

Tucker took another sheet from the file. "His record at Princeton was exemplary. He graduated with honors, held class offices, and was well liked by the students and teachers. Not a hint of going back to his old ways. He worked for an architectural firm in Princeton after graduation, and they had nothing but good things to say about him."

"Well, it looks to me like he left his past behind him," Anderson said. "Keep digging, though. We can't afford to overlook anything here.

"What about Mrs. Martin? Anything on her background we can use?"

"We couldn't find anything that would help us in any way. Her mother died in a car wreck when Gwyn was four years old, and she was raised by her father. She has never been in any trouble—not even a parking ticket. Her parents moved around a few times when she was small, but finally ended back where they had started in Oregon. Her father was a lumberjack, and was killed about five years ago by a falling tree. There are no other family members that we could find. No aunts or uncles or grandparents. All in all, we couldn't find anyone who had a bad word to say about her, let alone have a grudge big enough to want to harm her daughter."

"And her friend? Karen Jackson?"

Tucker removed another file. "So far we don't have much on her. She was raised in Missouri by a great-grandmother. School records show she was a bright student but somewhat of a loner. She has no police record, and has worked for Children's World for eight years."

Bozyk spoke up. "Why was she raised by a great-grandmother? What happened to her mother or grandmother?"

Tucker closed the file. "I don't know. We received no information about that. Her school records in Missouri start at the age of eleven, and they have no records prior to that."

"Isn't that a little odd? I mean, even when a kid transfers to another state his records have to go along with him. Why wouldn't they have a completed file?"

Anderson interrupted, "Why don't you find out, Leon. It's probably nothing, but see if you can track them down."

He turned to Petterson. "What have you learned about our man in the alley, Brent Carlson?"

"He was easy to trace. Mr. Carlson has lived all his life here in Omaha. He graduated close to the top of his class from high school—was liked by those who remembered him, but wasn't heavily involved in school activities, and many people I talked with could not even remember him being in their class. His entire family—mother, father, two sisters, and a brother—were killed when their family home burned. Brent was ten years old at the time, and had been spending the night at a friend's house. He had to be hospitalized for a short time when he learned his family had been killed."

"Was there any question about his possible involvement in the fire?" Bozyk asked.

"No," Petterson answered. "It was a faulty gas line

that led to the explosion. The company settled out of court and Brent came into a great deal of money on his twenty-first birthday. He was raised by an uncle here in Omaha, who took him in and treated him as though he was one of his own. I talked with the uncle and his children, and they had nothing but good things to say about Mr. Carlson."

Bozyk interrupted again, "I just think it was odd as hell for him to park in that alley for three hours and watch the Martin house. Why didn't he tell his partner, Gwyn Martin's husband, if he felt she might be in danger? And he admitted he had done that sort of thing before. I don't know—if we're looking for someone with a screw loose, he just might be our man."

Petterson closed his file and looked at Bozyk. "I wondered about that, too. I thought it was a little strange since the two men were good friends at college and now partners in a firm. Why wasn't it Adam Martin in that alley, or even the two of them? If they were concerned about the safety of Mrs. Martin, why was Carlson there alone?"

Bozyk nodded his head. "Exactly."

Gwyn checked the traffic to her left, then eased her car off the ramp into the flow of commuters. It was a thirty-minute drive to her station when the traffic was heavy, as it was now. She stayed in the right-hand lane, having no desire to compete with drivers hell-bent on knocking a couple of minutes off their commute time.

She reached over and tuned in KMOH for the morning news. The lead story was the apprehension of the

University Strangler, as he had been dubbed by the press. Gwyn turned the radio up.

"—the man, twenty-two-year-old Jason Shelby, was arrested near the university at three A.M. this morning. Officers were suspicious when they discovered a pizza delivery truck in the area at such an odd time. A three-mile chase finally ended when the suspect turned down a dead-end street and was cornered by police."

Gwyn could hear her heart beating in her ears and she felt suddenly nauseous. *The truck she had passed! Oh, no. Please don't say he harmed another girl!*

"—Jason Shelby has confessed to the two previous attacks, and police say he was apprehended before anyone was injured during the night."

Thank God. She would never have forgiven herself if another person had been killed because she had refused to respond. She had sensed something was wrong, but had ignored it—forcing her mind away. When was she going to learn that she could not deny her gift—or curse, as the case may be?

Manuel Garcia jabbed at the keyhole several times without success. He lifted the ring of keys up to eye level and studied them intently. Red. The key with that little edge of red plastic was the right one. He tried again. After three attempts, he finally managed to unlock the door.

"Mama! I'm home!" he called out, and collapsed on the couch. He waited, his head buzzing, for her to come and minister to his needs. He needed food. It had been four days since he had put anything into his system except the drugs. His arms and legs were heavy, leaden. It had taken all his energy to drag his wasted body home. "Mama. Please. I need you."

The door to the bathroom opened, and Rosella walked over to her son. Her face was pale, and still wet from the water she had splashed over it. She had been sick at her stomach again. No doubt she had picked a bug up from somewhere. She looked at the emaciated form of her only child. *Please, God,* she prayed, *don't let Manuel catch it. His poor body couldn't stand a bout with the flu.*

"It's all right, baby," she said kindly. "I'll fix you some soup."

He looked up at his mother. "I'm sorry, Mama! This is the last time. I swear to God it is!"

She had heard the same thing a hundred times before. The promises. The lying. The cover-ups. It was a sickness, deep within him. His father had been the same. Drank himself to death when Manuel was but five years old. "It's in the genes"—that's what the experts were saying now, and she believed them. There was just an ache in some people that all the love in the world couldn't ease.

And then there was Jessica. With enough love and life in her for twenty people! She didn't know how she would have managed these last months without that delightful child. It reminded her of the old days, when she cared for other children. Each child left in her care had been special to her. Parents stood in line to have her keep their young ones. She would always be proud of that, even if she hadn't had much luck with her own.

It was strange, though, that Jessica's mother was still unable to come for her. The little girl talked about her constantly, and Rosella encouraged it. She didn't want her to forget—that had been one of the stipulations.

She reached over to shut the flame off under the soup, and another pain shot down her left arm. This time the pain didn't stop.

The image Gwyn received was fleeting and came out of nowhere. A large woman. Pain. Quickly she pulled her Dodge Dart out of traffic and over onto the shoulder. The images were coming rapidly now. Jessica. A woman—clutching her chest and falling. *Where? Where are you?*

Gwyn put her hands on her head and tried to force her mind deeper, but the image was gone as rapidly as it had appeared.

"Damn!" she swore as she smashed her hand against the steering wheel in frustration. "Damn, damn, damn!"

CHAPTER
SEVENTEEN

When Gwyn arrived at the radio station, most of the staff had already heard the news about Karen's house. The general manager offered to hire a bodyguard for Gwyn until the killer was apprehended, and several of the office girls asked if she would like to move in with them until everything was over. Gwyn was touched by their concern, but insisted she would be all right.

"Now don't be so pigheaded, Gwyn," Mike chided her. "There has been enough said on your show lately that this asshole *might* decide to come after you. And the fact that all this happened right next door to you is a little too close for comfort in my book."

"I'll be fine," Gwyn insisted. "Karen is going to stay at my house for a few days, so there will be two of us. And don't worry, Fred," she said to the manager, "if I get uneasy about anything, I'll take you up on your offer of a bodyguard."

The open friendliness of the people in Omaha never failed to impress Gwyn. Of all the places she had ever lived, Omaha alone had this quality. Almost a small-town atmosphere. People always seemed to have time to say a kind word or offer help. Throughout the horror of the last nine months, the concern and caring actions of the community had sustained her. But now she needed to be alone—to make some sense out of the vision she had received.

She finally was able to close the door to her office and leave the endless stream of questions and comments.

Her hands were shaking. The strain was beginning to show. She automatically went over and began making coffee, thinking to herself all the while that she should lay off the caffeine. When the ringing of the phone split the air in the quiet office, she jumped, spilling coffee grounds onto the counter.

She reached for the telephone. "What is it?" Her voice sounded ragged and sharp to her ears.

"I have a collect call for Gwyn Martin from Josephine Hartley," she heard the operator say. "Will you accept the charges?"

Gwyn's tone changed markedly. "Yes, Operator. Yes, put her on."

Gwyn recognized the husky, deep-throated voice of Josephine Hartley the moment she spoke. She had listened to the famous psychic on talk shows a number of times.

"Miss Hartley—I'm so glad you returned my call. I was afraid I wouldn't be able to track you down."

"You were lucky, my dear," she answered. "I've been in London for the last several weeks. I returned early this morning and when my secretary told me about your problem, I could hardly wait to get you on the phone."

"Does that mean you can help me?" Gwyn asked expectantly.

"I'm not sure. But I do have one or two ideas to

discuss with you. Have you ever read about Wolf Messing?"

"Yes. Of course," Gwyn answered, her hopes dropping. "But I don't think—"

"Hear me out, dear," Miss Hartley interrupted. "As you know, Joseph Stalin did not believe in psychics and challenged Wolf Messing to prove he had the ability to cloud men's minds. Whereupon Mr. Messing went into a Moscow bank, presented the teller with a blank sheet of paper, and she let him withdraw a hundred thousand rubles. He accomplished this feat by projecting his thoughts into the teller's mind. She was absolutely convinced he had handed her a legitimate withdrawal form."

Gwyn spoke quickly. "Yes, Miss Hartley, I know that story well. He also was able to reach Stalin's house in the country by convincing the guards he was the head of the Soviet secret police. But I don't see how his experiences could have any bearing on what I'm seeing."

"What I am getting at," Josephine continued, "is that someone is clouding your mind—much the way Wolf Messing was able to convince a bank teller and a guard they saw something that they in fact did not see."

Gwyn shook her head. "No. I just can't accept that explanation. *I* am the psychic here. In Messing's case, *he* was the psychic. I can't believe that another psychic would just happen to be in Omaha, just happen to be involved with my daughter, just happen to have committed three murders, and just happen to have so much more psychic ability than me. You see what I am saying? It isn't a *reasonable* solution."

Josephine Hartley's deep voice came back on the line.

"Yes. I see what you mean. But it wouldn't *have* to be another psychic. I agree that the odds aren't great that another Wolf Messing is operating in Omaha, but, my dear, *someone* is responsible for the cardboard images you are picking up. Let's explore some other possibilities."

"Like what?" Gwyn sounded confused. "Who else would be able to project images into my mind?"

"Someone close to you, perhaps? Someone you see, but your mind won't accept as a killer so it tricks you into seeing a different image?"

"I never thought of that," Gwyn answered truthfully.

"If a gifted psychic can project an image into another person's mind," Hartley continued, "then perhaps subconsciously she can project into her own mind."

"But that would mean my need to protect a killer is stronger than my need to find my little girl," Gwyn protested. "I just don't see how that would be possible."

"Perhaps not, and I do have one other idea to throw at you."

"Certainly. Fire away."

"A few years back I was conducting experiments on distance as a factor in thought transmission. I was connected by phone to a psychic in London named Lawrence Husselman. It was all a controlled experiment with observers on both sides. We had a wonderful time sending images back and forth, and he sounded like such a neat man that I got to wondering what he looked like. I asked him to concentrate on his features, and I would see if I could pick them up. I received an image of an extremely handsome man, and we agreed to meet later in the year."

Josephine's laughter came over the line. "Well, let me tell you, the man I met in London had no resemblance at all to the image I had received. He was short, bald, and an altogether ugly little man. But he thought of himself as attractive, and that is what I picked up."

"So you are saying I might be getting an image of how the killer *perceives* himself, instead of how he really is?"

"Well, it's only one of many ideas, but that could be it, certainly."

"Josephine, I can't thank you enough for the help you have given me," Gwyn said. "I have a feeling that somewhere in the ideas we've tossed around is the answer. I'll just have to sort it out."

"You are very welcome, my dear. If there is anything else I can help you with, don't hesitate to call."

"By the way," Gwyn said. "Whatever happened on your date with the ugly little man? Was it a disaster?"

"Not on your life." Josephine laughed. "I married him!"

CHAPTER
EIGHTEEN

Sergeant Atkins looked down at the envelope addressed to the captain in uniform block letters. He decided to chance Anderson's wrath and disrupt the meeting. It could be important. Carefully, he picked the envelope up by the edges and headed down the hall.

"What is it?" Anderson sounded annoyed by the interruption.

"Maybe nothing," Atkins answered. "But this letter just came for you, and it looks a little odd. I thought it might be important." He handed the envelope over. "At least there has been an effort made to disguise the handwriting."

Anderson picked up his letter opener and slit the top of the envelope. He removed the small pile of photographs and spread them out on his desk.

"Jesus Christ!" he swore as he looked at the nude pornographic pictures of children.

Anderson picked the envelope up and looked again for a letter. "What the hell do you suppose these mean?"

"Check the back of the pictures," Tucker suggested. "Maybe there'll be something there."

Carefully, Anderson turned the photos over. Across

one of them, printed in the same block letters, was written: WANDA SIMPSON'S SUNDAY SCHOOL CLASS.

Anderson put the photographs back in the envelope and handed them to Atkins. "Sergeant, take these to the lab and check for prints. We have Wanda Simpson's on file, and I want to know if her prints show up on any of these. Also, I want a saliva test on the flap and stamp. Tell lab I want the results immediately, and then you get them back to me here."

He turned to Bozyk. "Check your notes. What church did the Simpsons belong to?"

"First Presbyterian on Bellevue," Bozyk answered without looking. "She *was* active in church events. I had to get a schedule of her events and interview several church members after her death. And she did teach Sunday school—that much I know. Everyone spoke highly of her, though. I never got so much as a hint of any scandal."

"Do you think there is any chance those pictures could be on the level?"

"Hell, I have no idea!" Bozyk said, shaking his head. "I do know Dr. Jacobs mentioned the contents of the Simpson house were extremely valuable—way out of line for a teacher's salary. Maybe this was her answer to a second income!"

"And it fits the pattern," Tucker said. "When average-type citizens get involved in illegal activities such as this, they generally shop out of town and pay cash for expensive items with a high resale market. So much harder to trace than a bank account, and most people don't pay much attention to the contents of a house—and couldn't tell the difference between a masterpiece and a flea market special, anyway."

Anderson lit a cigarette and leaned back, suddenly feeling old. "You realize what it means if we can verify these photos were taken by Wanda Simpson—this city will explode with indignation. And before it's all over, the press will probably be nominating our serial killer for sainthood!" He looked at Bozyk. "I suppose there's no way her husband could not have known about it?"

Petterson interrupted, speaking for the first time since Atkins had brought in the photos, "This is just all unbelievable to me, Captain. I attended Jefferson High School, and Jack Simpson was the best teacher I ever had. That was about ten years ago, right after they first moved here. He helped me—and a lot of other kids— over some pretty rough times. He's a hell of a great guy! I can't believe any of this bullshit!"

Bozyk nodded in agreement. "That was my impression of the man, also." He pulled out his notebook and flipped quickly back several pages. "When I first interviewed him after his wife's death, he made the remark that Wanda was 'such a good organizer and money manager—always shopping for bargains.' I've got to tell you, I doubt like hell he knew what she was up to—if in fact she was up to anything."

At exactly that moment Atkins opened the door and hurried to Anderson's desk. "Sir, I'm still waiting for the full report, but I thought I should let you know—lab found about a dozen clear prints belonging to Wanda Simpson on the photos."

"Well, I'll be damned!" Petterson swore softly. "That little bitch!"

Bozyk spoke. "Captain, if we can determine Jack Simpson was not a party to this, could I break it to him? I'm certain he will want to get his children out of town before it hits the papers."

Anderson nodded his head. "Yes. Of course. You can just imagine what their lives would be like around here once this breaks."

He sat quietly at home, the only sound coming from the pencil he tapped unconsciously against the desktop. Was there anything he had overlooked? Anything at all to tie him to the killings?

He had lined his car trunk with plastic before dumping the Higgins woman in it, just as he had done before with the other women. Then yesterday he had scoured the car, inside and out, just to be on the safe side.

He was getting careless. He knew it. He had killed Lucy Higgins in broad daylight. Only sheer luck had prevented him from being seen. He had to be more careful. Too many people would suffer if he was caught.

The pictures. Was there any way they could trace the printing back to him? He remembered reading once that experts could distinguish a person's handwriting even from print. Damn. Had he been careful enough?

What if someone remembered him from the bar? He had spoken with the Higgins dame only briefly. Had anyone noticed?

Careful! I have to be more careful!

* * *

Gwyn sat closeted in her office, her fingers drumming nervously across the top of the large oak desk that comprised half of the room. There were two hours until airtime, and she had asked not to be disturbed.

Someone I know?

Someone who perceives himself different than he really is?

Another psychic?

The possibilities somersaulted through her mind like tumbleweeds caught in the wind.

She looked at the spread of framed photos on the wall of her office. Jessica's face laughed down at her as she took her first step, ate chocolate ice cream, and cuddled her favorite stuffed bear.

For some reason Gwyn found herself remembering the other Jessica. The little girl in the pipe. The whole world had held its breath, willing the plucky blond-haired child who sang "Winnie the Pooh" to make it. How that mother must have suffered, knowing her baby was only yards away, but not able to reach her. That was how Gwyn felt. So close, but helpless. Wanting so desperately to reach her child, but unable to.

She stared at the grouping of pictures. What was it about them? Was she missing something?

"Gentlemen," Dr. Jacobs began, looking out into the sea of police officers and detectives, "I don't think there is any question now but that your serial killer was an abused child. Most likely, the abuser was a mother, but it could have been any female in whose charge the child was left. At any rate, he is now killing this person over and over again in the form of other abusive mothers."

"Are we dealing with a true psychopath here?" Anderson asked. "And is this killer likely to start killing others, or will he stick to his pattern of abusive mothers?"

"I can't answer that question, Jim," Marlo answered. "Anyone who kills like this is deranged in some way. To what extent we have no way of knowing. Tomorrow he may decide that all brown-haired women remind him of his mother, and go after them. Or he may see a woman spank her child, and decides she needs to die. What I can tell you is that he will continue killing."

Leon Bozyk sat at the back of the crowded room studying Marlo Jacobs, barely listening to the questioning going on. He had heard all this psychological shit a thousand times before and could reel off the theories as easily as she. None of it made much difference anyway. Maybe later. In a courtroom. After police work had nailed the loony. But not now. Of course the killer was insane. So what else was new? He would keep on killing? No shit!

He had to admit the good doctor looked damn fine today, though. She was dressed in a yellow sweater number that showed off her figure. High heels, too. He always liked women in heels. Did something good for their legs and the way they walked.

She had been on his mind for two days. He kept remembering her soft, easy laughter—her warmth. *Probably learned it from one of her damn books. The Psychology of Charm—Psychoanalysis in the Working Place.* He snorted.

Gordon Tucker rose from his chair next to Leon. "Doctor, I just wanted to say a word about how much I admired your husband, and to extend my sympathies. I know it's been almost a year since his death, but his memory is still an inspiration to us all."

"Thank you, Gordon." Marlo smiled. "He was an inspiration to me, also."

Leon blanched. "Who the hell was her husband?" he asked as Tucker sat back down.

Tucker looked at him strangely. "Matthew Jacobs. Didn't you know?"

Leon sucked in his breath and for the first time in his life felt like a complete ass. No. He hadn't known.

Ten years ago a thirty-eight-year-old police lieutenant had walked in on an armed robbery at an Omaha bank. It was the young officer's day off, and he had simply gone in the bank to cash a check. He could have easily blended in with the other customers, but he chose to offer himself to the heavily armed junkies when it became evident they were going to take hostages in their escape from the bank. Later, they had left him for dead, shot in the back, when they made their final switch of vehicles. But the lieutenant had hung on, given a description to the police, and the men were apprehended.

The shots he took left him paralyzed from the waist down, but he continued to be as active as he could in police work. He gave speeches, wrote papers on police policy, and taught classes. He worked with the handicapped and always had time to listen when an officer needed encouragement.

That young officer had been Matthew Jacobs. No wonder Marlo Jacobs had told him to kiss her ass when he had wised off about her husband. He remembered now that Lieutenant Jacobs had been bedridden for the last couple of years, so it couldn't have been easy on her.

Leon suddenly became aware that Anderson was speaking to him. He rose awkwardly from his chair. "Yes, Captain?"

"I want you to go over our files with Dr. Jacobs. Bring her up-to-date on all the information we have."

Miserably, Leon nodded his head. "Yes, sir."

"I'm sorry," he said to her as soon as the others had filed from the room. "I didn't know. I . . ."

She cut him short. "No, Leon. You don't owe me an apology. It's I who should apologize to you." She laid her hand on his arm. "I overreacted. It was obvious you didn't know who my husband was, and I should have told you right then. I can't imagine why I didn't. It was childish of me, and I apologize." She smiled up at him. "Can we start all over again?"

Leon looked at her in amazement. What an astonishing woman. With those few words she had made everything right between them again and put him at ease.

"I think that's a great idea," he said to her, then added, "You're some kind of lady, Doc, you know that?"

Her eyes twinkled as she grinned, giving him a big wink. "Damned right!"

Gwyn still sat staring at the photos of Jessica on the wall. What was it that was bothering her? She had looked at those same pictures every day for nine months without having this feeling. She tried to retrace her thoughts.

She had been looking at the pictures, and then began thinking of the other Jessica. Why? What had brought the little girl from Midland, Texas, to her mind?

Winnie the Pooh!

Gwyn rose and walked over to the picture on the wall. Jessica smiled out at her, clutching her favorite stuffed animal. Her Pooh bear.

Jessica had the bear in her arms that day. In the swing. And yet Gwyn was positive she had seen that bear only recently.

Where?

At Karen's house!

She tried to think. That night in the den. Among the rubble. She had seen Jessica's Pooh bear. It hadn't registered because many of Jessie's toys were at Karen's house. But how did that bear get there if Jessica had it with her on that last day? Could Karen have picked it up from the yard? Or was the bear somehow connected to that funny feeling Karen had that she had seen something without really seeing it?

Quickly she picked up the phone and dialed Karen's number at Children's World. "Come on—come on," she said aloud as the phone rang. "Please be there." On the fifth ring, Karen's answering machine came on and Gwyn said simply, "Need to talk to you. I'll call back later."

She grabbed her purse and headed out the door, stopping only long enough to ask the station manager if he would mind running an old tape for the evening's broadcast.

"I have a lead on Jessica," she told him without explaining further.

"It's hard to say," Marlo said, shaking her head. "Without more to go on, we're only guessing about what kind of childhood these people had."

She spread the files out on the desk in front of them. "Take Adam Martin. He would seem to be the most logical one to have suffered abuse. But was it enough to have turned him into a psychotic killer? There is no indication he has been in any trouble since his teen years, yet so often feelings start erupting later that can directly be tied back to the abuse one suffered as a child. And according to at least one doctor who dealt with him, he was potentially dangerous."

"What about the others?" Leon asked.

"Again, we're just guessing," Marlo said. "Brent Carlson could have been deeply traumatized by the death of his family. And we have no way of knowing if he was an abused child either before or after their deaths. Even Gwyn Martin could have had a troubled childhood—many psychics do. She obviously adored her father, but we know nothing concerning her relationship with her mother. And we really don't have any information yet on Karen Jackson."

"I have a call in to the school officials in Missouri," Leon said. "That should give us a little more to go on with Miss Jackson. I can't imagine why it wasn't sent in the first place—just a note saying the files were not available."

"Leon," Marlo began. "Do you really think one of these people is the serial killer?"

"No," he answered her truthfully. "I don't. But I'm not so certain that one of them doesn't have information that could lead to the killer. Information he—or she—might not even realize they have. Mrs. Martin has been so reliable in the past that we can't take what she tells us lightly. If she thinks there is a connection between her daughter's disappearance and these killings, then I, for one, would be willing to bet she's right. And if she *is* correct, then logically we have to focus on people close to her."

Marlo laughed. "That doesn't sound much like the reaction of a hardened street cop. I thought you guys weren't supposed to believe in stuff like that."

He laughed with her. "I started believing the day Gwyn Martin found the Bateman woman. She gave the police all the credit, but I'm here to tell you, we didn't have a clue as to where Helen Bateman was." He briefly told her the story. "I was with Anderson when we got to that farmhouse, and I must admit we both thought we were on a wild goose chase. I don't know who was more surprised that we had found him, Hank Reynolds or the two of us. Anyway, we always took Gwyn seriously after that."

"I'd like to meet her sometime," Marlo said. "She sounds like a fascinating woman."

Gwyn removed the key from the flowerpot and unlocked Karen's front door. She had done the same thing a hundred times before when she took care of the house when her friend was on buying trips, but she felt strange about it now. *Don't be silly*, she told herself. *Karen won't care.* But the feeling persisted as she walked slowly through the damaged, quiet house.

She entered the den and crossed to the corner where many of Karen's lovely possessions lay smashed beyond recognition.

There it was. Jessica's Pooh bear. She knelt down and picked up the soft toy, cuddling it to her.

She didn't see the figure sitting in the large chair, or hear footsteps on the thick carpet as the person came up behind her, bringing a brass candlestick down hard on her head.

CHAPTER NINETEEN

The newspaper headlines blared the shocking news to the citizens of Omaha.

WANDA SIMPSON INVOLVED IN CHILD PORNOGRAPHY RING

————————Police today confirmed the existence of a child pornography ring operating in Omaha and surrounding cities. Parents at the First Presbyterian Church were shocked and outraged to discover their three- and four-year-old children had been drugged and photographed in pornographic acts. In a bizarre turn of events, it was learned that Wanda Simpson, the children's Sunday school teacher and the latest victim of the serial killer, had for years been using her class as unknowing subjects in child pornography.

Twice a month Mrs. Simpson took her class on all-day outings. It has now been learned that she drugged the children early in the morning, and spent the day taking lewd pictures of them, often with men. She then sold these photographs all over the state. Doctors have confirmed that the children involved had been molested.

Mrs. Simpson's husband, Jack Simpson, teaches history at Jefferson High School and from all indications had no idea his wife was involved in the pornography. Police confirmed their investigation cleared Mr. Simpson. They are certain his wife acted alone and her husband was not involved in any way.

School officials at Jefferson have reportedly accepted Jack Simpson's resignation in the wake of these latest developments, although they were quick to point out he was one of Omaha's finest teachers.

SERIAL KILLER STALKS CHILD ABUSERS
————With the confirmation yesterday that all three murder victims were in some way connected with child abuse, police are now concentrating their efforts in this area. There has been widespread interrogation of employees at crisis centers, social services, and abuse hot lines. Police believe the killer had to come by his knowledge of the abuse through some agency dealing with trauma to children. Anyone with information along this line should contact local authorities.

HAPPY ENDING FOR HIGGINS CHILDREN
————In the aftermath of their mother's death, three young children are going to have a chance at a better life. Five-year-old Anthony Higgins and his two younger sisters are going to be adopted by Mr. and Mrs. Charles J. O'Riley. Patrolman O'Riley was one of the two officers who found the battered children the day following their mother's death. All three children had extensive injuries resulting from abuse by their mother. It was initially believed that Jenny Higgins, age three, might lose her arm due to gangrene, but doctors have now confirmed they were able to save the little girl's arm. All three children are now on the road to recovery.

Patrolman O'Riley said he and his wife had been visiting Anthony, Jenny, and Nellie in the hospital, and the three

children literally "stole their hearts." Since no other relatives could be found, the social service office is granting a
petition that the children be placed in the O'Riley household
pending permanent adoption proceedings.

This reporter could not help but wonder what would have
been in store for those three children if their mother had not
met her death at the hands of Omaha's serial killer.
Sometimes good comes from the worst of circumstances.

Anderson closed his Sunday edition of the *Omaha
World Herald*, tossing it carelessly on the already clut-
tered couch. He was glad for the Higgins children.
Charlie O'Riley was a good man with a heart full of
love. At least something was going right.

They had broken the news of Mrs. Simpson's involvement in pornography yesterday, and his office had
become a zoo. Parents had to be notified and the children
in the photos identified. It had not been easy to watch the
crumpled faces as mothers and fathers realized what their
children had been subjected to. The families would never
be the same again. The only comfort any of them had
was the fact that the children were heavily drugged, and
perhaps would have no memory of the abuse.

He was glad Jack Simpson had been able to leave the
city before the worst of it broke. The mood of the
outraged parents would certainly have resulted in action
being taken against him and his children. Already, the
Simpson home had been the target of random shootings.

I'm too old for this shit, Anderson thought. *It's time
for the younger men to take over. I've seen enough.*

He walked into his kitchen and viewed the mass of
dirty dishes. *Not even a damn clean kettle to heat water
for coffee!* He sat down heavily in a chair by the table.

Those poor babies! That was what was really getting to him. It burned in his gut that anyone, especially a mother, would take advantage of those little ones. And for what? So some perverted asshole who couldn't make it with a woman could get his jollies. And so she could buy "pretties" for her house! *Damn bitch!*

He wished Molly were here to talk with him. She had always had a way of righting the world—of bringing everything into perspective. He looked around the kitchen. He could almost hear his wife saying, "It would help if you would get off your duff and put our home in order." He decided it was time.

He had been working for about two hours, and slowly the small house was beginning to look like a home again. The dishes were all washed and put away, his clothes were in the dryer, and the living room was at least picked up. The physical activity had been good for him, and gradually Jim's mood had lightened. It was the first time since Molly's death that he had spent any time on the house. It felt good to at last see some order returned. He still could not bring himself to remove Molly's things, but perhaps that day would come.

He was startled by the ringing of the doorbell.

"Adam!" he said, surprised to see the tall, handsome man on his doorstep.

"Captain Anderson, I need to talk with you, if you have a minute," Adam said without preamble. "It's about Gwyn."

Jim swung the door open wide. "Certainly, Adam. Come on in."

He motioned Adam to a chair, thankful he had cleared away the litter. "What's up?"

Adam shook his head, confused. "I'm not sure, Captain. Gwyn seems to have disappeared. I can't locate her anywhere. Did she say anything to you at all about going somewhere to check on Jessica?"

"To check on Jessica?" Jim repeated. "Why, no. Has she learned something?"

"That's just it, Captain. I don't know. The station manager said she left before broadcast time on Friday, saying she had a lead on Jessica. And that's the last anyone has seen her. I located her car at the airport, but none of the airlines had any record of her taking a flight out."

Jim felt a knot begin in his stomach. *Oh, God, no. Don't let anything have happened to Gwyn.* He tried to control his emotions when he spoke. "Have you checked with Karen Jackson? She would probably know if anyone would."

Adam nodded his head. "Karen is the one who contacted me. She was staying with Gwyn because of the damage to her house, but Gwyn never came home. She finally called the radio station, and found out Gwyn had left suddenly before airtime." He stopped, groping for words. "Don't you see? It must have been something important. Gwyn would never take off like that when she had a broadcast to do. She's much too conscientious. Not to mention leaving Karen alone at our house without even telling her where she was going."

"Does she have any relatives nearby? Or friends? Anyone she might have gone to if she needed help acting on whatever information she received concerning Jessica?"

"No. Not that I know of anyway. She has no family, and as far as I know, Karen was her only good woman friend. Of course Gwyn never met a stranger. She has a lot of casual friends, but no, not anyone she would go to in a crisis."

Anderson tried to sound reassuring. "Well, don't worry, Adam. I'm sure she is just running down a lead on Jessica. But I'll put a bulletin out on her nonetheless, and start searching myself."

Adam rose and extended his hand. "Thanks, Captain. If you hear anything at all, give me a call. I'm going to continue looking, but I left the answering machine on, so you can leave a message."

Jim closed the door behind Adam and grabbed for the phone. His instincts told him Gwyn Martin was in trouble. Big trouble. *I should have assigned someone to her,* he thought. *Damn it all to hell! If she is hurt, I'll never forgive myself!*

Gwyn lay on the bed taking in her surroundings for the second day. At least it was morning now, and the tiny window near the ceiling was letting in enough light for her to see again.

She had regained consciousness in total blackness. When? Two nights ago? It had been a terrifying experience to wake in darkness, unable to move. The only sound she could make was a muffled hum because of the wide tape stretched tightly over her mouth. She twisted again, trying to loosen the ropes that held her flat to the bed. It was no use. She looked at the silver duct tape wound around and around her wrists and ankles, then at the ropes securing her to the top and bottom of the iron bed. The only movement she could make was a slight rolling motion, which was beginning to cause pain where the tape pulled against her raw skin.

Her mouth was dry, and her throat felt swollen. It was becoming increasingly hard to swallow, and she wondered how long a person could live without water. She tried to think. How many hours had she been here? Since Friday evening. This was the second day of light so it must be Sunday. Sunday morning. That would mean she had been here about forty hours. Surely someone was missing her by now.

She looked around the room. But where *was* she? She couldn't be at Karen's home. She had been all through Karen's house a hundred times, and knew no such room existed. This was a child's playroom as near as she could determine. An attic playroom. There was no door, but Gwyn could see a set of stairs that obviously swung down from the floor to the lower section. If she could only work loose, she could lower the stairs and escape. She didn't think anyone was around. She had heard no sounds at all for two days.

She had occupied much of her time yesterday trying to guess what kind of a child used the playroom. She had finally decided that both a boy and a girl must use the room. There was an elaborate train set assembled on the floor, and the usual assortment of bats and balls. But there were also dainty dolls and tea sets, suggesting a little girl played there, also.

Everything was geared toward a child except for an array of weight-lifting equipment and a rack of clothing

that ran the entire length of one of the walls. The
clothing was divided into sections, and Gwyn had
decided the family who placed them there consisted of a
man, a wife, a teenage daughter, an older, more sophis-
ticated daughter, and a grandmother. And of course the
two little ones. *Where were they? Would they return
home and find a dead body in their attic? Had they
moved, and left all this behind?*

Was she in the country, or in the city? She had tried to
do a reading, but the combination of a splitting headache
and her terror had left her unable to concentrate. Maybe
today. She would sleep awhile, then try again.

*No! I mustn't sleep! I can't waste this daylight. I have
to figure a way out of here.* Tears burned at her eyes and
she forced them back. She could not afford the luxury of
crying. If her nose became plugged she would be unable
to breathe.

Dear God, she prayed for the hundredth time, *please
let someone find me!*

Karen stood surveying Gwyn's living room. In her
anxiety of the last two days, she had done what she
always did to relieve tension—she had cleaned. Gwyn's
house now shone from top to bottom. She had begun the
job casually Friday evening, waiting for her friend to
return. Then yesterday as she waited for word, she had
tackled the job in earnest.

Where the hell could she be?

She had done everything she could think to do. She
had called everyone who might have an idea of her
whereabouts, but had come up blank. She had checked

the hospitals, bus terminals, airport, and rental agencies. Nothing.

The piercing sound of the telephone caused Karen to jump nervously. She raced to the kitchen and grabbed the receiver up on the second ring.

"Gwyn?" she asked quickly.

Adam's voice came on the line. "No. I'm sorry, Karen. It's me. I take it you haven't heard anything, then?"

Karen's hopes fell, and she sank down on a kitchen chair, her trembling legs suddenly giving out on her. "No, Adam," she said, her voice sounding raspy to her ears, "have you?"

"Not much. I did locate her car at the airport, but I checked every flight out, including private ones, and she was not listed."

"Well, at least that's something!" Karen's spirits began to rise. "Maybe she didn't want anyone to know where she was going so she used another name. Did you check under Calvert?"

"No." Adam's voice also began to take on a note of encouragement. "No, I just didn't think of that possibility. I'll check right away. I just returned from seeing Anderson, and he is putting a missing person's report out on her. I got the feeling he was going to give this his full attention, Karen, so maybe we'll hear something before long."

"Call me as soon as you have checked again at the airport," Karen said quickly, knowing Adam was anxious now to get away. "I will probably be at my own house, at least for a little while. I can't begin straightening up until after the insurance adjusters have completed their reports, but I do need to get some clean clothes and water my plants."

"Fine," Adam answered. "Don't worry about it. I'll call both places as soon as I know anything."

Karen replaced the receiver and stood looking at the phone. The thought crossed her mind that she should call Brent and let him know what was happening.

No. Maybe later, after they had more information.

CHAPTER TWENTY

Anderson entered headquarters and headed for his office. He had put the wheels in motion concerning Gwyn's disappearance—there was nothing else he could do for now.

The precinct was strangely quiet, or maybe it just seemed that way in comparison with the madhouse it had been yesterday. He sat down wearily at his desk and lit a cigarette, at the same time silently saying a prayer for Gwyn's safety. He had not realized how much she had come to mean to him over the years.

Gwyn had been the one to visit Molly religiously all during his wife's illness. Gwyn had been there for him after Molly's death, helping him with funeral arrangements and seeing to it that he ate—even though she had her own personal problems at the time. It was Gwyn who nagged, cajoled, and encouraged him to start taking better care of himself. Much like a daughter. It suddenly dawned on him that he had indeed grown to love Gwyn as though she were the child he and Molly never had.

Damn it. He felt so helpless. First he had let her down by not finding Jessica, and now she had disappeared in much the same way. Would they still be looking for her

months from now? Not knowing if she was alive or
dead?

He jumped as the unfiltered Old Gold burned down
into his fingers. *The same as Jessica!* Maybe that was it.
And if so, then logically it had to tie in somehow with
those closest to Gwyn.

He picked up the phone and dialed Bozyk, but got no
answer.

Leon Bozyk woke slowly, trying to get his bearings.
He wasn't in his own bed, that was all his foggy mind
could comprehend. Gradually, his brain started clearing
and he remembered.

He rolled over and pulled the naked woman lying
beside him up close. She opened her eyes and smiled at
him.

"Good morning, Doctor," he said. "Did you sleep
well?"

"Like a top," she answered him, planting a kiss on his
shoulder. "And you?"

Leon turned his arm to where he could see his watch.
"Considering it's now ten-thirty and the latest I have
slept in fifteen years is six o'clock, I'd say yes, I slept
damn fine."

Marlo propped herself up on an elbow and looked
down at him. "How about some breakfast? Biscuits and
gravy and we can call it lunch as well?"

"All this, and you cook, too?"

Marlo laughed. "Well, actually I was thinking of
brunch at the Marriott. Didn't you say you needed to
check in at the precinct about noon?"

"Just to see if that file on the Jackson woman has

arrived," Leon answered. "I talked with a school secretary and she said she would overnight whatever material was available. I don't know why, but I'm beginning to get the feeling there is something mysterious about Miss Jackson's missing files. The secretary wouldn't give me any information over the phone—just said I'd have to wait until she cleared it with her boss."

"Why don't you call now and check?" Marlo suggested. "Maybe it's in now and we could stop by and pick it up before we go to eat."

Leon swung his long legs over the side of the bed and reached for the phone. "Good idea. Stay right where you are, though. If it isn't in, I have a much better plan for my only day off in weeks—and it doesn't include breakfast!"

Marlo chuckled softly as he punched in the number and waited while the duty officer went to check. She jumped at the next words out of his mouth.

"What the hell do you mean, her records are sealed? Son of a bitch! They can't do that! We're in the middle of a murder investigation here." He stopped, listening to the officer. "Illinois? A judge in Illinois ordered her records sealed and the courts won't release them? Well, we'll by God see about that!"

He slammed down the phone and turned to Marlo. "Why the hell would a judge seal the records of an eleven-year-old girl? And can he do that? Keep it from us?"

Marlo nodded. "I think a judge can do just about whatever he wants as far as minors are concerned."

Leon shook his head angrily. "We'll just have to get another court order, then. And that could take days."

* * *

Gwyn heard the noise of the stairs being lowered and jerked awake. Had someone found her or was the person who had placed her here returning? She could hear the thud as the stairs locked into place, then footsteps coming.

Her eyes opened wide with relief and she felt a lump in her parched throat.

Karen! Thank God!

Somewhere in the back of her brain a warning signal was going off. Why was Karen carrying a tray of food and a pitcher of water?

She closed her eyes, trying to think. Was she dreaming? Maybe no one was there at all.

She opened her eyes and saw Karen standing over her. But it wasn't Karen's voice that began speaking.

"I'm sorry I had to leave you here so long without food and water," the deep voice said. "But sometimes Karen gets stubborn. She wouldn't leave your house and this is the first chance I've had to come."

Gwyn shook her head from side to side, making guttural noises behind the tape covering her mouth.

"I'll remove the tape," the voice said, "but you'll have to promise not to yell."

Gwyn nodded her head vigorously, not understanding what was happening but thankful for the chance to speak.

Karen picked up a jar of Vaseline from the tray and began gently loosening the tape from Gwyn's mouth. When one side was freed, Gwyn immediately tried to speak, but could only whisper. "Karen—what are you doing? Why—?"

"Be quiet now," the husky voice said. "I'll have this tape off in a minute, then you need some water."

Gwyn lay quietly as the job was finished, her mind going in a thousand directions. *If only I could think!*

Once the tape was off, Karen quickly untied the ropes fastened to the top of the bed and helped Gwyn into a sitting position. She held a glass of water to her lips and Gwyn welcomed the cool liquid as it loosened her dry throat.

At last she could speak normally. "What are you doing, Karen? I don't understand?"

"I'm not Karen. I'm Jake. Karen is still trying to find you."

Gwyn looked closely at the person standing over her. The voice was different. The clothing was different. Even the mannerisms were different from her friend's, but there was no mistaking that it was Karen.

Gwyn tried again. "What do you mean, Karen is still looking for me? What's going on, Karen?"

"I'm not Karen!" the voice said impatiently. "I told you, I'm Jake."

"All right, then—Jake," Gwyn said. "Where am I? Why do you have me tied up like this? And where is Karen?"

All at once the ramrod stiffness that Gwyn had noticed before became bouncy—almost flirty—as Karen whirled away, smiling coquettishly.

"You might as well tell her, Jake. It looks like she's too dumb to figure it out on her own." The husky voice had changed into high-pitched singsong. "After all, she has a right to know why she must die."

Gwyn sat quietly, too stunned to comprehend what

was happening. *A twin? Did Karen have a twin?* She stared at the woman closely.

"What's the matter, honey?" the strange voice said sarcastically. "Cat got your tongue? Or do you only want to talk to Jake? Well, too bad! You've got me now!"

A multiple! It suddenly sunk through to Gwyn. *Karen is a multiple personality!* My God, how could she have been friends with her all these years and not known?

Gwyn's voice shook as she tried to think what to do. "Who are you?"

"I'm Lily. And I hate you almost as much as I hate Karen. You're both trying to ruin it all."

"What, Lily?" Gwyn asked. "What are we trying to ruin?"

"Everything. You and your snooping, and Karen going to that damn shrink. She'll find out about the rest of us. She'll try to make us go away." Her face hardened. "And don't think Karen will save you. She doesn't even know this room exists. I removed the handle from the kitchen ceiling years ago. No one has ever even noticed the attic entrance."

The switch was almost imperceptible. One second she was talking to Lily, and the next moment Jake was back.

"Enough of this," he said as he took long strides toward the bed. "You must eat now."

He fed her carefully, and Gwyn gladly took in all the food. As she ate she tried to think if there was a way to overpower Karen. She was larger, and certainly stronger. At least she would be when she regained her strength. One on one, there was no way Karen would be a match for her.

The voice that was Jake spoke. "Don't worry about

Lily. I won't let her harm you. Sometimes she tries to hurt Karen, but the rest of us can usually stop her."

A memory from her college days slowly surfaced in Gwyn's mind. The persecutor. Most multiples had a persecutor personality who was at war with the rest of the personalities. This was the personality that would harm the others. She had a thought.

"Did Lily do the damage to Karen's house?" she asked.

Jake nodded his head. "She was trying to warn Karen to stay away from Dr. Beckman. Also, she didn't like Karen helping you try to find Jessica. She felt threatened and lashed out."

Gwyn's heart pounded so loud in her ears she was afraid Jake could hear it. She tried to steady her voice as she spoke.

"Jessica? How would that be a threat to Lily? Does she know something about my daughter?"

"Not really. Only Aunt Sylvia knows about Jessica, and she doesn't come out much anymore."

"Jake, listen to me," Gwyn pleaded. "You have to help me. I have to get out of here and find my daughter. Could you please let me talk to"—she felt foolish saying the words—"to Aunt Sylvia?"

Jake shook his head. "I told you. She doesn't come out very often. She's old now, and getting forgetful. Anyway, I can't let you go. You'll go to the police, and then they will find out who killed those women."

"My God, Jake," Gwyn said quickly, "did Lily kill those three women, too? You have to stop her, don't you see that?"

Jake rose and looked down on Gwyn. "You know Lily

didn't kill those women," he said. "You saw the killer. You described him to the police and to Karen, remember?"

It hit Gwyn almost before Jake finished speaking. *I saw a man! A tall, strong man. It was the Jake personality. He killed those women.*

Before she could think how to respond to this development, Jake was pushing her back down on the bed. He once again fastened the ropes securely to the top of the bed.

"Please," Gwyn begged. "Couldn't you leave my mouth free? It's hard to breathe with the tape covering my mouth?"

He hesitated, uncertain. "I'm sorry," he finally said, "but I must." And he placed a new strip of tape over her mouth. But in his hesitation, Gwyn suddenly realized that Jake would not harm her. He may have viciously killed three women, but he had no quarrel with her. As long as the Jake personality was around, she would be safe.

Marlo Jacobs exhibited no embarrassment at the surprised look on the captain's face when she and Leon entered his office together.

Anderson rose, extending his hand. "Well, good morning, Marlo. How nice to see you again. I didn't know you were in the building."

"I just got here," she answered him. "With Leon. We wanted to pick up some material on the Jackson woman."

Anderson turned his attention to the detective. "I have been trying to reach you."

Leon averted his eyes. "I—uh—was out for a while, Captain. What's up?"

"Gwyn Martin is missing. No one has seen or heard from her since late Friday afternoon. Tucker and Petterson are both on duty but tied up on other matters. I was hoping you would lend me a hand."

"Sure, Captain. What would you like me to do?"

"We need to concentrate on the material we have gathered on Gwyn's family and friends. I can't help but think we are missing something there. First Jessica, and now Gwyn herself. Furthermore, Gwyn told her boss at the radio station she had received new information about Jessica. Now, if this information was that important, why didn't she contact my office? I can't believe Gwyn would have gone to check on something if she thought for a minute it might be dangerous. She is too level-headed to have gone off half-cocked."

"I agree," Bozyk said. "That doesn't sound like Gwyn at all. Especially knowing that if she ran into any trouble at all, it might put her daughter in jeopardy."

Anderson continued, "To be on the safe side, I assigned men to tail Adam Martin, Brent Carlson, and Karen Jackson. I know that Adam and Karen have been out seaching for Gwyn, but on the off chance they might be involved, I'm having them covered and I want you to interview them again as to their whereabouts on Friday." He shook his head, spent. "This is all I can think to do, which in the long run will probably mean nothing."

Bozyk remembered the Jackson report. "Captain, I don't know if it means anything, but I received information this morning about Karen Jackson. It seems all of her early records were sealed by a judge in Chicago some twenty years ago."

Anderson was clearly surprised. "Sealed? I thought about the only time records were sealed was in the witness protection program. Since when do minors qualify?"

Marlo interrupted, "Maybe I can help on that issue. Sometimes, when a minor has committed a criminal act or been subjected to a horrifying experience, a psychiatrist will suggest the sealing of records to protect the child from future embarrassment or harassment. That could be the case here."

"And our only way around it is to get a court order to have them opened?" Anderson asked.

"Usually yes, but because it has been so long ago, maybe the judge would open them if you only requested it of him personally. There is a big difference between a school system asking for those records, and a Homicide captain."

Bozyk nodded his assent. "I'd say it's worth a try, Captain. It would certainly save us a lot of time."

Exactly one hour later, Captain Anderson slammed the phone down in disgust. "The retired Honorable Judge J. McClure is on a three-week fishing trip in Canada. If he calls home, his wife will give him our message. That means our hands are tied until tomorrow. Even if I can get a court order today, it can't be served until the Cook County courthouse opens in the morning."

CHAPTER TWENTY-ONE

Gwyn's brain reeled under the weight of her new knowledge. *Her friend! Her best friend!* It didn't seem possible. It had been Karen who murdered those women. And it had been Karen who took Jessica. *Where? Where would she have taken her? And why?*

She remembered those feelings of dread that had been washing over her lately. They had always occurred when Karen was close by. Just a few days ago as she was getting in her car. That same feeling. And then Karen had crossed the yard to talk with her. She hadn't realized the relationship, but it was clear now. Crystal clear.

Poor Karen. I have to remember she knows nothing about all this.

She thought about the images she had picked up from the victim's clothing. *Incredible. The personality of Jake was so strong, I actually saw that person instead of Karen.*

Josephine Hartley's words came back to her. "Perhaps you are picking up how the killer *perceives* himself, not as he really is."

And the woman by Jessica's swing? The elderly, gray-haired woman with the friendly eyes? It had to be the personality of Aunt Sylvia! But why had she taken Jessica? And where?

Gwyn tried to sort it out in her mind. Karen had helped her look for Jessica that day. Where was her daughter during this time? Could one of the other personalities have harmed her?

No. She knew Jessie was alive. She had seen her by that rainbow only a few days ago.

I have to talk with Aunt Sylvia! There is no other way.

Downstairs, Karen was startled by the sound of the phone. Panic filled her. *How could I have gone to sleep? Now, of all times!* She dashed into the den and picked up the phone. "No, Adam, I haven't heard a word."

Manuel Garcia sat on the front row of chairs in the small chapel trying to remember the words to the "Hail Mary." His head was splitting and there was a hot fire burning in his gut.

He looked at the plain pine coffin gracing the altar. He was going to miss his mother. When things got really tough, she had always been there for him. Not that he had ever been much of a son. Rosella Garcia had worked hard all her life trying to provide for him, but he had never been able to kick getting high once he had a taste of it.

Even now, with his poor mother stretched out in front of him, his mind could only return to his aching need. His grief at losing his mother was tempered somewhat with the knowledge that her small estate would allow him to hit the streets again with cash in hand to purchase some magical painkiller.

And he was even going to make a profit on the kid. He looked down at the tiny blond-haired girl sitting primly next to him. She was a cute kid. Good-natured and bright. His mother had adored the child, but he sure as hell couldn't take care of her—and they hadn't heard a word from that Jackson lady in almost two months. Rosella had said not to worry, but the way he figured it, the broad had dumped the kid. Anyway, it didn't matter. If she ever *did* get around to checking, he would be to hell and gone from this city.

He was supposed to meet the buyers in the morning. He'd have to stay straight until then. After he had the kid out of his hair, he'd sell his mother's things and stay high for a month.

The priest began walking around the coffin and the smell of incense filled Manuel's nostrils. Outside, he could hear the slow tolling of the bells as they paid their last respects to Rosella Garcia. He wept.

Brent Carlson finished the morning paper and sat looking thoughtfully at the articles concerning Wanda Simpson and the serial killer.

Why didn't it make him feel any better to know the serial killer was only after abusive mothers? That should let Gwyn off the hook as a possible victim, right? Wrong. She might still be able to identify him. There was still a chance the killer might decide to eliminate that likelihood.

But if the killer was only going after abusive mothers, why had he trashed Karen Jackson's house? Why had he left that cryptic message on her wall? Of course, that might not have been the work of the serial killer, but somehow Brent felt that it was. He was a practical man—a logical man—and it was not consistent with rational thought to believe there was no connection. Just as he could see no connection between Karen and the murder victims.

Was there a chance Karen knew something about this killer? That didn't seem likely. Could the message have really been intended for Gwyn? It was common knowledge they were friends and neighbors. Had the killer decided to strike at Gwyn in this manner? Again, not likely.

Brent kept kicking the possibilities around in his mind. No. There was an element missing somewhere.

Bozyk pulled his car up in front of the impressive town house that belonged to Brent Carlson. He could see a man sitting in an old car across the street, seemingly reading a newspaper. Anderson's boy.

"Mr. Carlson," he said when Brent answered the door. "I wonder if I might have a word with you?"

"Certainly Detective—Bozyk, wasn't it? Come on in."

Leon looked around at the plush surroundings and decided he was in the wrong business. "Quite a place you have here. I take it the architectural field must be extremely profitable."

Brent looked uncomfortable. "Not enough for all this, no. I came into quite a lot of money on my twenty-first birthday. And I invested it well."

Leon used the statement. "That would be the money you received from the insurance company, right? From the fire?"

Brent didn't rattle but answered curtly, "Yes. That's right, Detective."

Leon decided to see how the young man reacted when pushed. "Almost half a million, wasn't it? Must have given you quite a jump on other men your age. Not everyone gets set up for life like that."

Brent's voice was icy cold. "Not everyone loses their entire family because a workman failed to notice a gas valve had never been hollowed out. The company had installed a new furnace only that morning, but couldn't waste their time waiting to see if the damn thing was functioning right. Half a million? At the time that meant nothing to me. I used to lay in bed plotting ways to torture and kill the man responsible." He looked squarely at Bozyk. "So how does that grab you, Detective? And what the hell is this really all about?"

"I want to know where you were between the hours of four and midnight last Friday, Mr. Carlson."

"Why, Detective?" Brent shot back in fury. "Am I a suspect in something, now?"

Bozyk kept his face impassive. "Just answer the question, Mr. Carlson."

"All right. Let's see—Friday? At exactly four o'clock I was at St. Joseph's church on Broadway. I was best man at my cousin's wedding. She was really more of a sister to me, since I had lived with their family most of my life. Have you ever been to a Catholic wedding, Detective? First there is the ceremony—that takes at least an hour. Then there is the photo session—another hour. After that everyone goes to a big hall for the reception—and of course there's the dinner and dance. If you want to verify my whereabouts, I can give you the names of about five hundred guests. Would that do?"

Bozyk shifted, uncomfortable. "I'm sorry, Mr. Carlson. We have to push a little with this. We're running out of time. Gwyn Martin has been missing since Friday, and we are talking to everyone who might know anything."

The effect on Brent Carlson was instant and devastating. His face crumpled before Leon's eyes, and the chilly demeanor vanished. If it was an act, Leon decided, then Dustin Hoffman better move over.

"My God. What happened? Hasn't anyone heard from her since Friday?" The words tumbled from Brent's mouth. "Why didn't someone let me know?"

All at once everything fell into place for Leon. The man's vigil in the alley, his nervousness when questioned. Brent Carlson was in love with Gwyn Martin! And he would bet his last dollar Gwyn was unaware of it. He wondered if Adam suspected his partner's feelings for his wife.

Leon quickly told him the details of Gwyn's disappearance. "Would you have any idea where she might have gone, Mr. Carlson?" he asked. "Any idea at all?"

Brent shook his head solemnly. "No. But I'll start looking right away. Do you know where Adam is? I need to talk with him. There's no sense in us covering the same ground twice."

"All I know is that he has checked at the airport. However, I think I can locate him for you," Bozyk answered, not mentioning the fact that both of the men had tails on them. "Let me see what I can do."

* * *

Gwyn heard the scraping noise as the stairs once again began descending. She watched as Karen this time pulled the steps back up into the attic after her, locking them in place.

She ignored Gwyn and went right to the train set, making adjustments and checking to see if all the cars were lined up right on the track.

Gwyn watched the strange spectacle in silence. *What was she doing now?*

Karen crawled over to a small metal box and flipped the switch located at the top. The electric train started chugging around the track, its piercing whistle sounding like the real thing to Gwyn's ears.

Karen sat on the floor, clapping her hands joyfully. "Go train," she said in a small childlike voice. "Go fast!"

The child personality! Gwyn remembered now that almost all multiples had at least one, sometimes many more. What was it she had read? "—frozen in time at the age some horrible trauma occurred."

What had happened to Karen in her childhood? Something awful. Some abuse that started when she was very young and continued for many years. Not normal abuse—if there was such a thing—but something worse—much worse.

Tears burned at Gwyn's eyes. *I'm so sorry, Karen. I'm sorry for what you must have gone through!*

She must have made a small noise, because Karen suddenly looked up and noticed her on the bed. She put both hands on the floor in front of her and pushed herself up, in exactly the same manner a child would rise from the floor.

She leaned over and shut off the train, then teetered toward the bed. "Bad mommie! Mommie tie you up?"

Gwyn nodded her head and tried to force the tape from over her mouth.

Karen reached up and pulled the tape away. It came off easily, because of the residue of Vaseline "Jake" had used.

"Hello, sweetheart," Gwyn said. "Can you untie me? The rope at the top?"

Karen shook her head back and forth. "Mommie will get mad. I mustn't make Mommie angry. She will hurt me."

"No she won't, honey," Gwyn said. "I won't let her. See how big I am? I won't let anyone hurt you."

"Mommie might burn me," Karen insisted. "Want to see?" She began undoing her blouse.

Gwyn gasped in horror as she saw the hideous scarring on Karen's body. It extended across her back, down her arms, over the chest, and even onto her breasts. *Oh, God, what insanities has my friend been subjected to?* All of their shopping trips—Karen's insistence on her own dressing room—the long-sleeved blouses. It all fell into place.

Karen began fastening her blouse, fumbling with the buttons as only a child would do.

Gwyn tried again. "I'm sorry your mother burned you. If you will help me, maybe we could get away from here."

Again the switch was so sudden Gwyn missed it. The

child's voice now became cold, calculating. "You aren't going anywhere, Mrs. Martin, so just relax."

"Who are you?" Gwyn asked.

"I'm Gloria," the voice said. "And I run things around here. You won't have any luck trying to con one of the others into letting you go. *I* decide who comes out. If I see one of the others is weakening, I will simply make them go away."

Gwyn realized instantly that this was the personality she needed on her side.

"Gloria, would you please let me talk to Aunt Sylvia? Even if you don't let me go, I would like to know where my daughter is."

Gloria seemed to be thinking it over, but when she spoke her words were not encouraging. "I don't have as much control over Aunt Sylvia as I do the others. She is old now, and set in her ways. Personally, I think she has gotten senile these last few months. She forgets things and doesn't make a lot of sense when she talks." Gloria's voice was aloof, dispassionate. "I've tried to find out what she did with the kid, but she refuses to tell me."

"She's all right then? Jessica?" Gwyn asked rapidly. "She wouldn't have harmed her, would she?"

"Aunt Sylvia? Harm anyone? Of course not. She is the original mother hen. She was even furious with Lily for tearing up the house—knew it would hurt Karen, and she can't stand to see any of us in pain."

"Does Karen know about any of you?" Gwyn asked. "Does she even suspect?"

"No. And that's because I'm very careful about when I let anyone out. All through the years, I've tried to make sure Karen doesn't have a lot of 'holes' in her memory.

Usually, she thinks she just dozed off, or was daydreaming." Gloria stopped, concentrating. "Except lately. I think she is beginning to suspect something is wrong. She doesn't know what, though. Thinks maybe she's getting Alzheimer's."

"Gloria," Gwyn began tentatively, "what happened when you were small? How did Karen get scarred so horribly?"

"Oh, from all sorts of things. Boiling water, hot knives, you name it, that bitch used it. Her favorite was holding Karen under water until she almost passed out. She would also make her sit in water for hours, until her skin was all wrinkled and soft. Then she would use a harsh lye soap, which she made herself, and scrub the child's body raw—inside and out. Lovely person, Karen's mother. Got just what she deserved. When Jake was eleven, he killed her."

Gwyn closed her eyes against the horror. "I'm so sorry," she said. "Karen is my best friend, and I had no idea she had been through such a nightmare."

"Karen doesn't remember," Gloria answered. "That's where we all came in. When the pain would get to be too much, we would hand it off to someone else. Sort of like that game of hot potato the kids play. If you hand off quickly enough, no one feels the heat."

"What does she think the scars are from?"

"When she went to live with her great-grandmother, the woman told her she had been in an accident when she was little. Karen accepted that explanation. She blocked everything from her mind about those early years. Her great-grandmother was kind to her, especially so since she knew her own daughter and granddaughter had been totally mad."

"Karen's grandmother, too? Had she treated Karen's mother the same way when she was little?"

"Oh, not near to the extent her bitch of a daughter abused Karen. But she was crazy, and died in a state hospital for the insane."

"And now Karen? Is the same thing happening to her?"

Gloria became indignant. "Of course not. There is nothing wrong with Karen. If she had not had all of us to help her, she might have ended up the same way, but we saved her from that."

Gwyn knew that what Gloria was saying was probably true. No one could have lived through those atrocities unscathed. "The others" had indeed saved Karen's life, and probably her sanity as well.

"What about the murders, Gloria? What if Karen gets blamed for those? Is it fair to make her suffer for what Jake did?"

"I'm sorry about that possibility, but Jake really had no choice. All of those women were harming either their own or other children. They were vile, evil women and deserved to die. I thought putting their bodies in water afterward was a nice touch on Jake's part. Sort of helped make up for all the times Karen was nearly drowned."

"There's one thing I don't understand," Gwyn continued. "Karen is so small. How was she able to lift those bodies? It doesn't seem possible."

Gloria seemed impatient with her. "My dear, you haven't been listening. Karen didn't kill those women. Jake did. And Jake is quite strong. You see all this weight-lifting equipment? Jake uses it religiously. He has always protected us. When Karen was fourteen, three teenage boys cornered her in an alley and attempted to rape her. Before it was over, Jake put two of the young men in the hospital, and the third had to have extensive dental work. The word spread, and no one bothered Karen after that."

Any hopes Gwyn had been harboring about overpowering Karen suddenly vanished. If she tried, Gloria would merely call Jake.

She changed the subject. "What are you planning on doing with me? Jake said he would not let Lily harm me, but you can't leave me here tied up forever. Someone has surely noticed my car in your driveway by now, anyway. Why don't you let me go? I won't tell anyone your secret. I promise."

A note of aloofness returned to Gloria's voice. "Jake left your car at the airport Friday evening. There's no reason for anyone to suspect where you are. And we haven't decided what to do with you yet. No one wants to hurt you, not even Lily, really. But we can't let you expose us, either. It's a shame Aunt Sylvia ever took your daughter. If it wasn't for that, we would not be in any danger now. And it's only a matter of time before Karen remembers about Jessica's Pooh bear. She saw the child with it, and then later it was here at her house. Just as you remembered it, so will Karen in time. Then I don't know what we will do. Karen could not handle the concept that she had anything to do with Jessica's disappearance. It would be too much for her I'm afraid."

"If you would find out where Aunt Sylvia took Jessica

and let me go get her, Karen would never have to know. Wouldn't that solve everything?" Gwyn pleaded.

"If we could trust you, yes. And if Aunt Sylvia would agree to tell us. As I told you, I know most everything that goes on around here, but I don't know what she did with the child. Jessica was asleep up here earlier on the day she disappeared, then during the night Aunt Sylvia left with her. She returned shortly before dawn that next day, alone. That's all I know."

My God. All the time they were searching frantically for her daughter, she had been safe—asleep in Karen's attic! It didn't seem possible. Why, then, hadn't she been able to reach Jessica?

"Do you think any of the other personalities know where she is?" Gwyn asked.

"I believe Tommy, the little boy you met earlier, has played with Jessica. But he is too small to tell us anything."

Gwyn's hopes rose. "Does he play with her here? At this house?"

Gloria shook her head. "No. Not anymore. He used to before she left, though. They played up here a lot. Sometimes Jessica played with Amy, too. She's five. Or one of the others. Your daughter enjoyed coming to Karen's house. There was always someone to play with."

Memories of Jessica talking about her "invisible" friends came flooding back.

Mommie! Mommie! Want to play with Amy!
Tommy play? Gwyn had heard her say to Karen.
Patty—Tracy—Robert—Tim—Angela.

She and Adam had laughed about their child's lively

imagination, and all the time she was talking about Karen's child personalities! She knew what none of the rest of us even suspected.

"But Tommy has played with Jessica since then? Isn't that what you said?" Gwyn asked.

"Yes. I heard him talking one day a month or so ago. I didn't know whether to believe him or not, since I control who comes out." She rubbed her forehead in concentration. "How odd that I wouldn't know. He said he had been to see 'Wessie,' but that was all I could get out of him."

Then she's safe! Thank God!

"I have to go now," Gloria said. "Karen will get suspicious if I'm out too long. Especially today, when she is trying so hard to find you."

"Gloria," Gwyn said as she looked down at her wrinkled, wet skirt. "I need to use the bathroom. I've soiled myself twice already."

This news seemed to upset Gloria and her hands flew to her face in a gesture of disbelief. "My Lord. Of course. How cruel of me. I'm sorry—so very sorry!"

Gwyn watched the transformation of the aloof, re-moved Gloria, into the caring, concerned . . . who? Was it still Gloria or had another personality emerged?

"Gloria?" she began tentatively.

"No. I'm Carrie. I can't believe no one thought about your—your personal needs." She began undoing the tape from around Gwyn's wrists and ankles. "And your skin is getting raw. Don't worry now. I'll fix you up." She helped Gwyn stand.

Needles of pain shot through Gwyn's legs as she tried

to support her weight. She would have fallen, but strong arms went around her, holding her into position.

"You better let me help you walk around a bit," a deep voice said, and Gwyn knew Jake was back.

CHAPTER
TWENTY-TWO

Leon located Adam at the home of Gwyn's station manager, Fred Wyatt. He relayed the information to Brent, who called the number and requested Adam wait for them there. Leon decided it was as good a time as any to talk with Gwyn's husband, and followed after Brent as he drove to the residence.

Adam was waiting in his car when the two men drove up. Leon pulled his green '79 Ford around in front of Adam's white '90 Lincoln, and thought again he must be in the wrong business. The brilliant white of Adam's car set off the man's dark good looks. Normally, Leon did not pay much attention to what other men looked like, but it was hard not to notice Adam Martin. He looked rather like a young Rock Hudson. In contrast, Mr. Carlson looked like a young Doris Day. Blond, blue-eyed, and freckled.

As Leon approached Adam's car, the man opened the door and got out, waiting for him. "Have you heard anything yet?" he asked anxiously.

"No, I'm sorry, Mr. Martin, we haven't," Leon said. "And I was wondering if you would mind answering a few questions for me?"

Brent walked up to the two men at that moment. "Better watch out, Adam," he said. "Detective Bozyk is going to give you the third degree. He just finished with me."

Adam turned to the detective. "What's this all about? Surely you don't think Brent or I had anything to do with Gwyn's disappearance?"

"I'm sorry, Mr. Martin," Leon said, "but we have to explore every possibility. Would you mind telling me where you were Friday between the hours of four and midnight?"

Brent Carlson's reaction to that same question was nothing compared to Adam's outrage. "What the hell is the matter with you people? I'm the one who reported Gwyn missing, remember? I've been out hunting for her since six this morning. And what are the police doing to find her?" he spat out. "Questioning me! Son of a bitch!"

Leon stared at the man without changing expression. "If you would just answer the question, Mr. Martin, we could all be on our way."

"Why the hell should I?" Adam shot back. "This is lunacy. Sheer lunacy!"

Brent interrupted. "Adam, we don't have time to waste here. Just tell the man so we can get going. Gwyn's life may depend on us, and we don't have time for this bullshit." He cast a dark look in Leon's direction.

Adam ran long fingers through his thick hair in a gesture of impatience. "Of all the damn, dumb things— Friday? I don't know. I think I worked late at the office, and then went home—alone." He turned to Brent. "Was Friday the wedding?"

Brent nodded.

"Yes, that's right then. I had planned on going to the wedding, but with everything that had been happening, I decided to skip it. I stayed at the office until about seven, then went home. Will that be all now, *Detective*?"

"Not quite. Can anyone verify this information?" Leon asked.

"No, damnit!" Adam shouted. "I worked at the office— alone. I drove home from the office—alone. And I stayed at my apartment—alone."

"All right, then, Mr. Martin," Leon said. "I'm sorry I had to question you, but you must understand that in an investigation we can't overlook anyone just because we don't *think* he could have been involved. We have to *know*. And for what it's worth, your wife means a great deal to several of us on the force. We are doing everything we can to find her."

Adam didn't answer as he got angrily into his car, his face set in cold fury.

Gordon Tucker drove down Tenth Street until he finally located the sign. Carl's Glass Works. He pulled up in front of the small factory, glad to see another vehicle parked in the vacant lot. He had talked with the owner, Carl Swenson, who had agreed to meet him. Damn nice on a Sunday morning.

The door swung open, and a short, pudgy man gestured.

Gordon got out of the car and walked toward him, extending his hand. "Mr. Swenson? Detective Tucker. And I sure appreciate your taking the time to help me."

"Yah. Glad to help," Swenson answered. "The grand-kids, they were driving me crazy, anyway."

"As I told you on the phone," Tucker said as they entered, "we traced this green glass to your factory. What I need to know is what it is used for, and if you have a list of who purchased the glass."

"Yah, yah. I understand. May I see the glass, please?"

Gordon removed several pieces from the plastic bag he was carrying and handed them to Mr. Swenson.

Carl walked over to a littered desk and flipped on a bright light. He held the glass under the light, then picked up one of the larger shards and studied it intently.

He nodded his head. "Yah. This is mine. One of the lesser grades. I think I remember who bought it, but let me check my files to be safe."

Tucker was surprised. "You mean you can remember everyone who purchased this particular glass?"

Carl nodded again. "Yah. Is not so hard. There is only one." He opened a filing cabinet and pulled out a folder. "Here it is," he said proudly. "I was right. This glass was used for light fixtures at Micky's Tavern on State Street. Micky Cahn. He wanted this special color, and I made him a good deal. I think his tavern must get a little rough at times. Always he is coming back for replace-ments."

Gordon couldn't believe his luck. Tracing that glass could have taken weeks. Instead he had the information handed to him on a silver platter!

"Mr. Swenson—Carl—I can't thank you enough for your help," he said.

"Yah, yah. Anytime," the little man answered him.

* * *

Gordon read the notice printed on the glass door to Micky's Tavern. Open Sunday—1:00 P.M.–12:00. He checked his watch. Two hours yet.

He knocked loudly on the door, hoping Mr. Cahn had come in early, but got no response, then walked around to the alley. It was littered with trash and broken bottles. Three cats scurried out of the large double sanitation dumpster as he approached.

He spotted the broken green glass immediately, and crossed to the west side of the dumpster. He knelt down and picked up one of the pieces. There was no question in his mind that it was the same. He looked at the dumpster again. Gwyn Martin's "box"? A tall wooden fence enclosed the section of alley directly in back of the tavern, and the area to the west of the dumpster formed a neat little square. Easy enough to corner someone, and just as Mrs. Martin had described it.

There were several large stains on the cement below the glass, but the rain had washed away whatever had caused them. They could have been made by anything, but Gordon had a hunch this was going to turn out to really be his lucky day. He returned to his car and called for the lab.

Grace Phelps neatly folded her copy of the Sunday morning paper and wondered if she should call the police. That new volunteer, Carrie Jackson, had taken some call last Wednesday involving cigarette burns. She had heard the sharp intake of breath as the young woman listened to the caller, but when she had asked her about it, Carrie had told her the matter had been settled.

Carrie was one of her best volunteers on the hot line.

She could almost always convince an out-of-control mother to seek help before she harmed her children. She certainly didn't want to get her into any trouble. Help like that was too hard to come by. What could she possibly know, anyway? The callers all remained anonymous.

Of course, once in a while the hot line was used by a neighbor or someone who suspected battering was going on. But in those cases, where the name of a potential abuser was left, it was always turned over to Social Services.

No. If that caller had left someone's name, Carrie would have reported it.

And besides, she wasn't too sure she would even want to tell the police if she *did* know something. After twenty years of watching the horrors children went through at the hands of violent adults, it did her heart good to know that at least three abusers had gotten a taste of their own medicine!

She decided to leave well enough alone.

Paul Petterson waited in the central offices of Children's World. He was glad the large retail clothing store stayed open on Sunday. Now he wouldn't have to wait another day to get the information he needed.

It had already been verified by their lab that the piece of corduroy taken from the top of the fence at the zoo had come from a Children's World factory. Now all he needed to do was see if the company kept any kind of records concerning what it was used for, or who the purchasers might be. He had little hope that any such records would exist.

A middle-aged woman opened the office door and introduced herself to Paul. "Hello. I'm Mrs. Appleton. How can I help you?"

Paul handed her the small scrap of material and explained what he needed.

Mrs. Appleton smiled and shook her head. "I'm sorry, but I don't think I can be of much help. This material *is* ours, all right, but we have a number of outfits made from this corduroy. Girl's jumpers. Boy's suits. And it has been real popular this year. Trying to trace an entire outfit would be like looking for a needle in a haystack— let alone determining where this small hunk came from."

"You don't keep records, then, of who buys different outfits?" Paul asked.

She smiled at him wryly. "Detective, that would be like asking Wal-Mart if they kept records on who purchased razor blades at their stores. No. We are far too large an operation to keep individual records."

"Can you tell me this, then," Paul continued, "what is the largest size clothing made from this particular corduroy?"

"Yes. I can help you there," she answered him, "but it will take a few minutes." Mrs. Appleton crossed to the desk and started punching in numbers on a large computer. In a few minutes she looked up at Paul.

"This corduroy was used exclusively in our Junior line. The largest waist size would be twenty-four, with a pant inseam of twenty-six inches."

Paul swore softly. *Just some kid. Just some damn kid climbing the fence!*

CHAPTER
TWENTY-THREE

At least she was more comfortable now. That was a blessing. "They" had helped her walk, use the tiny bathroom in back of the clothes rack, and change clothes. They had even replaced the tape binding her wrists and ankles with soft cloth.

She had begun to think of them not as Karen, but different, unique individuals. Jake had helped her walk until her circulation was restored. Carrie had helped her clean up in the bathroom. Gloria had gotten her clean clothing from home and changed her wet bedding. Carrie had rubbed Vaseline over her chapped wrists and ankles, and Jake had fashioned bindings, from soft strips of cloth, which were much more comfortable.

Karen moved between the behavioral states so rapidly, it was often hard for Gwyn to keep up. One second she would be talking to Carrie, then a subtle change of posture and tone of voice would indicate Gloria was back.

All of the personalities she had met in the last hour had been concerned for her comfort and apologized for the raw skin on her wrists and ankles. In spite of all that had happened, Gwyn felt an inherent kindness and gentleness in most of the personalities. She could even understand the killings, really. If what Gloria had told her about those women was accurate, then she could see why someone who had suffered the abuse Karen had suffered would react in a violent way.

Everything that had been happening over the last several months was now becoming clear to her. The visions of water that seemed to encompass such evil— the red, splotchy skin—all connected to Karen's childhood and the trauma she had endured. Somehow when Karen was in one of the personalities that remembered the abuse, Gwyn had been able to zero in on it.

The only thing that remained a mystery to her was why the Aunt Sylvia personality had taken Jessica. Had she noticed her alone in the yard and thought her abandoned? Of course if Gloria was right, and that personality was growing senile, there was no telling *why* she might have taken her. It was imperative that she talk with Aunt Sylvia.

As if in answer to a summons, Gwyn heard the now familiar scraping sound that accompanied the dropping of the stairs. Who would it be this time?

She watched in fascination as Karen emerged, walked over and picked up one of the dolls and began crooning to it.

"Poor baby. Poor baby. Mustn't cry. Mommie loves you. Mommie loves you."

Karen sat down on one of the small child-size chairs. She began a back-and-forth motion with her upper body that reminded Gwyn of a mother trying to rock a baby without the benefit of a rocker. It also reminded her of the motion she had seen patients at a mental hospital use. Back and forth. Back and forth. All day.

Gwyn didn't make a sound. Whoever this personality was had not noticed her, lost as she was in some childhood fantasy—or nightmare.

In a few minutes Karen got up from the chair and gently laid the doll down in its doll bed. She then walked over to a chest and took out a nightgown.

"Come, baby. We must take our naps now," Karen said as she began undressing the doll. When she finished with it, she began removing her own clothing.

The true horror of what Karen had experienced was burned into Gwyn when she saw her friend's naked body. Where pubic hair should have been, there was only mangled scar tissue.

Oh, God! What had that woman done to her?

Karen slipped on her nightgown and curled up in a fetal position on the floor with her doll. She continued the back-and-forth movement as she chanted in a childish voice.

"Hush, baby. Hush, baby. Don't cry. Mommie loves you."

The two men still sat talking, parked in front of Fred Wyatt's house. Adam was out of ideas. He looked at his partner expectantly.

"What about Mike Koerns?" Brent asked. "Gwyn's engineer at the station. She always seemed to have a good relationship with him. Could she have gone to Mike for help?"

"No. I've already checked. As a matter of fact he's out looking for her, also. When he heard she was missing, he immediately called in one of the other engineers and took off. We are keeping in touch through Karen." Adam's voice broke. "Last time I called in, he hadn't come up with anything."

The sky began to darken suddenly. Brent looked out Adam's car window up at the billowing clouds and knew their time was running short. The radio had promised another spring storm and it was approaching rapidly. Already he could see jagged strips of lightning to the south. Somewhere Gwyn was out there. In need of help. Every nerve ending in his body told him they had to find her—and fast.

"All right," he said to Adam. "Let's think. If Gwyn received some new information about Jessica, where did it come from? Do you have any idea who she might have been talking with or heard from?"

Adam shook his head. "The station manager said she received one long-distance call earlier in the day, but no calls went through to her in the final two hours before she left. If that call had anything to do with Jessica, I don't think she would have waited two hours before acting on it. At any rate, we can't find out anything about that call until tomorrow—unless Anderson decides to pull rank with the phone company."

"Did she make any calls that they know of?"

"She tried to reach Karen at work. Karen had a message waiting for her when she returned to her office, saying Gwyn had called and would try again later. That was shortly after four, and she left her office about that same time. We figured she tried to reach Karen, then left to follow up on whatever information she had."

Brent shook his head, puzzled. "It just doesn't make

any sense to me. I can't imagine Gwyn taking a flight out of the city or just disappearing without letting at least one person know where she was going. I assume you checked the answering machine at work?"

"Yes. She hadn't called."

"When was the last time you talked with her?"

Adam tried to think. "I guess on Thursday. She came to the office to see me about some new vision she had picked up concerning Jessica. She wasn't making much sense, actually. I was worried about her then. I kept thinking she was going off the deep end."

"Gwyn? Not in a million years!" Brent blurted out, then stopped, suddenly embarrassed. "I mean—hell, Adam, Gwyn is the most levelheaded woman I have ever met." He tried to recover. "What was her vision? Maybe it has something to do with her disappearance."

Adam looked past Brent out the car window, staring as a gust of wind sent leaves swirling up out of the gutter, scattering them across the front of his car. He remembered his last bitter words with his wife. "Just some absurdity about seeing Jessica by a silver rainbow, and how someone must be planting images in her mind because she was picking up strange visions."

"Strange how?"

"I don't know. Something about photos—or cardboard images. Like the people weren't real, just cutouts. As I said, she wasn't making much sense. I suggested she see a psychiatrist."

The sharp intake of Brent's breath was audible to Adam, and he was startled to see the fury in his friend's face and in his voice when he spoke. "What the hell is the matter with you, Adam? Your wife has undisputed psychic powers—*great* powers! Where the shit do you get off questioning what she sees? And how could you possibly tell her to see a psychiatrist? Christ! No wonder she didn't come to you with this new information!"

In all the years they had been friends, Adam had never seen Brent show any anger—certainly never with him. It puzzled him now. Had he been so wrong?

"Brent," he tried to explain. "The police questioned *us* because they suspect someone close to Gwyn took Jessica, and the same person committed the murders of those three women. They think this because of something Gwyn told them, and that burns the hell out of me! I don't appreciate my friends—or me—being dragged into the middle of a murder investigation. I just can't believe that the so-called serial killer is also the person who took Jessica. I'm telling you, it doesn't make any sense. Gwyn is mixed up in what she is seeing. That has to be the answer, and why the police are even *considering* such nonsense is beyond me!"

The color drained from Brent's fair complexion and his voice shook when he spoke. "I didn't know any of this. Are you telling me Gwyn saw something that ties in the murders to Jessica?"

"Yes. That's exactly what I'm telling you. Now do you see why I couldn't take what she said seriously?"

"No, Adam," Brent answered. "What I see is that we have left Gwyn vulnerable. She was in danger from this killer all along, but if Jessica is somehow involved, that triples the threat to her."

Adam's hands shook as he wiped a thin layer of perspiration from his face. Brent could see small tremors running through Adam's body and suddenly realized that he was just about at the end of his rope. "I'm sorry," he said. "I'm way out of line here, Adam. Of course you know more about this whole thing than I do." He placed his hand on Adam's shoulder and shook him lightly. "Come on, buddy. Don't fall apart on me now." He opened the car door and got out. "Let's go by your house and then talk to Karen. Who knows, maybe Gwyn has contacted her by now. I'll follow you in my car."

Gwyn lay on the bed watching as the attic room began to darken. She could hear low rumblings and occasionally see a splinter of lightning through the tiny window.

Her eyes returned to the floor, where Karen twisted and turned in a troubled sleep, whimpering and moaning. "No, Momma. Please. It hurts. Please, Momma. Not the brush."

When Gwyn thought she could stand it no more, Karen suddenly awakened, hurriedly dressed, and vanished down the stairs—ignoring Gwyn's efforts to get her attention.

Jessica pushed open the door to Manuel's bedroom and peered in. Manuel was rolling back and forth on the bed, emitting low moans. She went over to him and patted his shoulder. "Are you sick, Mannie?" she asked softly.

Manuel tried to focus his eyes on the little blond girl. "Yeah, kid," he groaned. "I feel bad. Real bad."

Jessica went into the bathroom, pushed her little step stool over to the sink, and ran cold water over a washrag. She twisted the cloth to remove the water, as she had seen Rosella do, then returned to Manuel's room.

She could see Mannie's body bathed in sweat as she climbed on the bed and began wiping his forehead with the cool cloth. "Don't worry, Mannie," the child—not yet three years old—said. "I'll take care of you."

She rubbed his head and neck with the cloth, then folded it neatly and placed it across his forehead. She leaned over and kissed him on the cheek. "Poor Mannie. Try to sleep now," she said as she curled up beside him, trying to fight off the tears that stung at her eyes.

There was no one left but Mannie. Auntie Karen had not been back in a long time. She reached in her pocket and removed the tattered picture of her mother. Why didn't she come for her? Auntie Karen had said her mommie would come when it was safe and that she mustn't forget her. But it had been so long. Had they both forgotten all about her? She studied the picture of her mother intently. Gwyn's beautiful face smiled at her frightened daughter from the worn photograph. Jessica held it tightly to her.

Please, Momma. Come get me!

The image slammed into Gwyn's brain with the force of a jackhammer. She saw her daughter on a bed next to a young man naked from the waist up. She heard Jessica as her child called to her.

Oh, no. Oh, God, no. Please don't let him harm my baby. Gwyn twisted, trying to remove the bindings, but discovered when she pulled, the knots tightened, pushing hard into her skin. If she pulled against the strips any more, she would cut off the circulation to her hands and feet.

She forced herself to remain still, her mind racing.

She had to get help. An address. She needed an address. She sent her mind searching.

Once again she picked up the image of Jessica on the bed with the young man. He didn't seem to be paying any attention to her child. For the moment, at least, maybe she was safe.

This time she tried to pan back, like pushing a button on a movie camera to get a wide angle. She had used this technique many times before, but to do it, she had to let go of the first image. Her mind had to be free, to explore.

She forced Jessica's face from her mind and concentrated on the room. It was a small bedroom—ordinary. A crucifix hung on the wall. She found the door and moved through it with her mind into a living room. The walls were covered with religious pictures and she could see several statues of the Virgin Mary.

Outside. She needed to be on the other side of the living-room door. She concentrated, forcing her mind deeper and deeper into the other realm.

She felt herself floating through the air to the other side of the door. She could see it now. She was in a hallway. The door below her had a number on it. 211. Apartment 211.

Not enough. She needed more. Again she could feel her body lift and float through the air. She was in an entryway. An apartment house entryway. Mailboxes. Rows and rows of mailboxes. There it was. 504 West Mill. She had it! She tried to hold on to the vision, to see more, but she was spent. Gradually she imagined her body returning from its journey. She was bathed in sweat and her head was pounding, but it made no difference to her. She had found her daughter! Jessica was alive!

CHAPTER
TWENTY-FOUR

Tucker accustomed his eyes to the dim lighting in Micky's Tavern and walked over to the bar. Micky Cahn nodded to him. "Well—what's the verdict, Officer? Was the dame knocked off in my alley?"

Tucker nodded. "No doubt about it. Everything checks. We even found a neat set of bloody fingerprints on the underneath side of the dumpster. Lucy Higgins must have grabbed the bottom of it before she died."

Cahn looked uncomfortable and rubbed the clean bar with a rag self-consciously. Tucker knew the signs. The man had probably known all along that Higgins had been in his bar the night of her death, but just hadn't reported it.

He plunged in. "What can you tell me about Miss Higgins? Was she a regular here?"

Cahn shook his head. "I wouldn't say a regular exactly. She came in once in a while."

"Do you remember her being here the night of her death?"

Cahn scratched his head and turned to straighten a row of bottles. "Might have been. Couldn't say for sure. Lots of people come and go. I can't be expected to remember all of them."

Tucker's piercing blue eyes seemed to look straight through Micky Cahn. "Well, maybe you can remember better at headquarters, Mr. Cahn. And maybe we'd better shut this tavern down until we complete our investigation. Come to think of it, we might need to dust this place for prints. Course the boys are pretty busy right now. Might not be able to get to it for a few days."

Cahn laid the rag aside and placed both hands on the bar in a gesture of surrender. "All right. All right. The broad was here that night. She came in early—about five—had a few drinks and tried to pick up a john. She was drunk when she got here, and none of my regulars would have anything to do with her. She had a bad reputation on the streets. Never had any repeat business, if you know what I mean."

"Why was that?"

"The word was that she lived in a pigsty, and didn't mind what she did in front of her kids. I heard once she had even offered the little girl to anyone who would pay her five hundred, but she never got any takers. Needless to say I didn't like the bitch. I tried to keep her out of here, but it wasn't always possible."

"Was it common knowledge on the streets that she abused her children?"

"Yeah. Pretty much. Like I said, she didn't have much repeat business. No one had much of a stomach for seeing the condition of her children. She always gave some cock-and-bull story about how the previous john had worked the kids over, but everyone knew she was the one who done it."

Tucker shook his head in amazement. "And didn't it ever occur to one of these kindhearted souls who couldn't stand to witness this abuse to call the police and report her?"

Cahn shifted uncomfortably. "I don't know. Maybe they didn't want to get involved."

"The night of the murder—did you notice her talking to any one person?"

"Naw. Not really. The men all ignored her . . . no . . . wait a minute. I remember now. She sat in a booth for a few minutes with some dame. I'd never seen her in here before. She didn't look like the kind of a broad who sat alone drinking in taverns. Sort of classy-looking, actually."

"Can you describe her?"

"Not really. I don't think I ever did get a good look at her face. She was a little thing, though. That much I remember. Couldn't have been much over a hundred pounds dripping wet."

"Do you remember what she was wearing or anything else about her?"

Cahn thought a minute. "Brown, I think. Seems like she was dressed all in brown. A suit of some sort. Brown slacks and a matching jacket—corduroy maybe."

Micky Cahn watched as the detective ducked his head against the increasing wind, made it to his car and drove away. He then went back to his bar and mixed himself a bourbon and water. He stood looking down at the drink for a few minutes, then dumped the contents down the drain. What the hell. He'd close up early and go home to his wife and kids.

He shook his head wearily. Who would have figured it? The very day he reported that bitch for child abuse, she gets herself offed in his alley! Wouldn't the police have a field day with *that* if they got wind of it! Damn good thing that hot line let the callers remain anonymous, or his ass would be in serious trouble!

Karen looked at the clock and realized she had lost two hours. Two valuable hours that she could have used searching for Gwyn. What was the matter with her lately? She kept taking these little catnaps, without realizing she was even sleeping. And more and more she was losing track of time. One minute she would be cleaning out a drawer, and the next minute she would be fixing supper. Odd. Really odd.

It had been like that for the last couple of years. She didn't feel in control of her life anymore. Actually, she felt a little like Olivia Henderson's clothing—just a mass of mixed-up parts that didn't fit together.

She had almost convinced herself the reason for seeing Dr. Beckman was Jessica's disappearance, but deep down she knew the real reason lay somewhere in her past. Somewhere there was an answer to these horrible scars on her body—scars that she had no memory of receiving.

She sometimes wondered if she wasn't getting Alzheimer's. That would certainly explain these gaps in her memory the last few years. How else could she explain waking up in clothing she had never seen before and did not remember buying?

She would have to ask Dr. Beckman about that on her next visit. The doctor seemed to think she was just overworked and worried about Jessica, but somehow she thought it was more.

She looked down at her charm bracelet and fingered the collection of religious medals that always gave her comfort when the going was rough. For the first time she noticed the empty clasp. Where had she lost her Saint Christopher medal? She hadn't even worn her bracelet in the last several days. Or had she?

CHAPTER
TWENTY-FIVE

Anderson looked up briefly from his desk as Tucker, Petterson, and Bozyk filed into his office. He stubbed out his cigarette, waving the men to seats. "Hell of a Sunday, isn't it?" he said, looking out the large double windows that were beginning to shake against the wind. "Looks like all hell's going to bust loose out there before long."

"All hell's busting loose in here, Captain," Tucker replied. "I just came from the tavern, and I don't know what to make out of what I learned."

"Which is—?"

"Micky Cahn finally admitted the Higgins woman was in his place the evening she died. About five o'clock. He said the only one he noticed her talking with for any time was a woman. A stranger to him. He had never seen her in his place before or since. He said she was sort of a classy-looking woman, nicely dressed—all in brown. Slacks and jacket, perhaps corduroy. He couldn't remember her face, but he said she was a tiny woman. Maybe about a hundred pounds."

Petterson interrupted, "The scrap of material we took from the fence at the duck pond! The lady from Children's World said it was part of their Junior line." He opened his notebook. "Yes. She said the largest size was a twenty-four-inch waist and a twenty-six inseam on the pants. I just assumed it must have come from some kid, but a small woman also buys clothes in a Junior size. My sister does all the time."

"So just what the hell are we saying here?" Anderson asked. "You're surely not trying to tell me our serial killer has a woman accomplice, are you? That the two of them worked together getting Higgins in that pond?"

"It could be, Captain," Petterson answered. "Remember the small prints in that rocky area outside the pond? We saw a number of prints that seemed new, but discarded them because of their size and the knowledge that children played in that location. But a small woman—with a shoe size of, say, a four or five—would leave a print that could easily be mistaken for a child's."

Bozyk cleared his throat and wished he had never gone into police work. Everything seemed perfectly clear to him now. If a woman was involved, he knew who it had to be.

"Karen Jackson," he finally said.

Tucker and Petterson turned and looked at him.

"Karen Jackson," Bozyk repeated. "She has to be the one." He stood up and walked to the front of the room. "First of all, she works at Children's World so would have access to the clothing. Secondly, she is no bigger than a minute. And most importantly, she is a friend of Mrs. Martin, which might account for those strange visions Gwyn was having. For all we know, she might have trashed her own house to throw us off." He shook his head. "It all fits, Captain. If a woman is somehow involved, I'd bet my next paycheck Karen Jackson is our baby!"

Anderson swore softly. "I just can't believe that. I've known Karen for years and never seen a hint of any mental problems—which she would certainly have to have to be a party to these grizzly murders."

Bozyk removed a small notebook from his pocket and flipped through a few pages. "Well, Captain, she *is* seeing a psychiatrist. A Dr. Beckman. Maybe I should check and see just what her problem is."

Anderson shook his head. "No. Don't bother trying. That's privileged information, and I've dealt with enough psychiatrists to know they won't even release a hint as to why a patient is seeing them."

"Captain," Tucker spoke up. "I agree with Leon. There is just too much evidence not to at least consider the possibility that Miss Jackson might be involved. Maybe we could get a photo and take it to Micky Cahn and see if he could identify her. At the very least, it might eliminate her as a suspect."

"All right then. Why don't you go back to Children's World and see if they have a photo of Karen. Take several other photos from our file and show them all to Cahn. If he can pick her out, then maybe we're on to something." He turned to Petterson. "I have a man stationed at the Jackson home. Get hold of him and see if he has anything to report. I want to know if Karen has gone anywhere in the last several hours. I also want to know the whereabouts of Brent Carlson. There's a man on him. Tell him absolutely not to lose him. If Jackson is involved, there's no telling but what Carlson might be also."

Tucker and Petterson left and Anderson sank down heavily in his chair. "Looks like you might be right about it all, Leon. You suspected Carlson was hiding something all along, didn't you?"

Leon shifted uncomfortably. "At first, yes, Jim," he said, reverting to a first-name basis now that they were alone. "But I don't think that anymore. I know now why Carlson was so concerned about Gwyn Martin."

"And why was that?"

"He's in love with her. And if I'm any judge of character, he would never do anything to hurt her in a million years."

"Well, shit!" Anderson exploded. "Who the hell does that leave, then? Our report on Karen showed no boyfriends—no family. Even Gwyn told me once that Karen rarely dated, and that she was her only close friend. It had to be someone she knows—but who?"

Karen stood at the window watching the storm. The first raindrops had just started and the force of the wind drove them against the windowpanes with a fury. Her house creaked and groaned under the pressure of the near-gale winds.

She had never felt so alone—so depressed. Her house was a shambles, as was her life. She looked at the damage the intruder had caused. Why? What had she ever done to deserve something like this?

And where was Gwyn? First Jessica, and now the only friend she had ever had! Gone!

She had always kept to herself until meeting Gwyn—but then little by little, Gwyn had drawn her out of her shell—opened her up to the world. She owed Gwyn so much. And yet both times when her friend needed her, she had been forced to sit on the sidelines, contributing nothing.

The sound of her doorbell startled her.

Gwyn! She ran to the door.

Anderson cupped one hand over the receiver and nodded to Bozyk. "It's the judge. Get Marlo in here."

"Yes, Operator, we'll accept charges. Please put the call through."

Judge McClure's booming voice came over the line. "Is this Captain Anderson? Jim Anderson?"

"Yes, Judge. Thank you for returning my call."

"No problem," the judge answered him. "I'm sorry about the delay, though. Been out on a boat all day, fishing. What's this about Karen Jackson?"

"You do remember her case, then, Judge?" Anderson asked.

"Remember? Hell yes, I remember it. A man doesn't soon forget something like that. I still occasionally have nightmares about that child."

"Judge McClure, you sealed Karen Jackson's records about twenty years ago, and I was wondering if you would consider opening them for us."

"What's the problem? Why do you need them? And I'll tell you right now, the reason better be good. I won't be a party to harming that woman in any way, and opening those records would not be in her best interests."

Anderson glanced up as Marlo and Leon entered the room.

"Judge McClure, I have a psychiatrist here with me.

Dr. Marlo Jacobs. Would you mind if I put you on the speaker, then she could hear and talk with you also?"

"No," McClure said. "I don't mind. I don't know that I'll be telling you anything, but go ahead. I've got to admit, though, that I'm curious as to what this is all about."

Anderson spoke swiftly as he switched the line over. "Your Honor, we have had a series of murders here in Omaha. In our investigation, we have done background checks on a number of people. We could not get information on Miss Jackson from Cook County because of the court order that sealed her records. Certain things have happened that now makes it even more important we know why her records were sealed."

Judge McClure grasped the situation quickly. "Is she a suspect in these murders, Captain, or are you just gathering background material?"

"When I first placed the call to you we were merely doing background checks," Anderson answered honestly. "But now we have discovered several things that point strongly to the possibility she might be involved in some way."

"Can you tell me a little bit more about the murders, Captain?" the judge asked. "Who was killed and why you think Karen might be involved?"

Anderson was beginning to get annoyed. It occurred to him that so far he had been the one answering all the questions. He tried to keep any hint of impatience out of his voice when he spoke. The last thing he wanted to do was irritate the judge. Then they would get nothing from him.

"Your Honor," he said, "three women have been

killed in the last few weeks. They were all stabbed, and placed in a body of water. So far, the only factor common to the women was that they were all involved in child abuse of one sort or another. Our psychiatrist believes strongly that the person responsible must have been an abused child."

For a few seconds there was silence on the line, then a long sigh as if Judge McClure was reaching a decision he disliked. "All right, I'll tell you everything I know, then I'll phone Chicago and have Miss Jackson's records faxed to you. You'll have them within the hour." He paused, then began again, choosing his words carefully.

"I sealed Karen Jackson's records because she stabbed her mother to death when she was eleven years old. And if there was ever a case of justifiable homicide, that was it. In all my years on the bench, I have never seen or heard of a child being systematically tortured the way the Jackson girl was.

"Her mother burned her with boiling water, scraped her skin with hot knives, and put harsh lye soap on a steel brush that she repeatedly used in the girl's vagina and anus. Karen was scarred so horribly inside that it took corrective surgery to even allow her to urinate properly. On top of that, the mother would hold the child under water in the bathtub for long periods of time. In the investigation that followed her death, it was discovered that on at least two occasions, when Karen was less than five years old, paramedics were called to revive the child. At the time, they had no reason to suspect the mother, and later Karen apparently learned to hold her breath long enough to survive the ordeals."

Marlo interrupted, "Judge McClure, was Karen given counseling after all this abuse was discovered?"

"Just briefly," he answered her. "During the time she was in the hospital. Then her great-grandmother from Missouri claimed her, and I had to release Karen into her care. However I made damn certain the woman was a competent guardian before I let her take Karen. As a matter of fact, at my own expense, I hired a private investigator to check on Karen for the first few months after the great-grandmother took her. I was just so appalled at what had happened to the child, I didn't want to take any chance on her future."

"And did she continue to get psychological help after she returned to Missouri?" Marlo asked.

"She was supposed to, yes. I know she did for at least a while. But from all the reports I heard, Karen had no memory of killing her mother. She blocked everything from her mind. The torture, the killing—everything."

"Did she even know her mother was dead?"

"Yes. But at first she kept saying her brother did it—even though when the police arrived, they had to pry the knife from Karen's hands. Then later she seemed to have no idea who killed her mother. The psychiatrist who worked with her wondered if she might have developed a multiple personality—but he could not establish that before she was sent to Missouri."

"*Did* Karen have a brother?" Anderson asked.

"No. Absolutely not. She was an only child. But during those first few days after the death of her mother, she kept calling herself by different names. She described everything that had been done to her, but she always talked as though it had been done to another sibling. 'She held *Carrie* under the water—she used a hot knife on *Amy*'—that sort of thing. Our psychiatrist thought he was really on to something, but after Karen was operated on, and came out from under the anesthesia, she never again referred to herself as anyone but Karen, and she had no memory of ever being abused by her mother. The psychiatrist would have liked to have continued working with her, but at that point he felt perhaps it was better for her sanity that she not remember. I do know he contacted someone in Missouri about his findings and suggested they might want to explore the possibility of a multiple."

"Is there anything else you can help us with, Judge?" Anderson asked, anxious now to discuss these developments with Marlo.

Judge McClure hesitated briefly. "I'm afraid I've told you all I can. But there *is* something you can do for me."

"Certainly," Anderson replied. "Just name it."

McClure's solemn voice filled Anderson's office. "If you find out Karen was responsible for your murders, handle her gently—and see to it she gets the best defense possible. If it would help her any, I'll even come and testify. I know this is going to sound strange, coming from a judge, but if there was ever a case where society owed someone a break, this has to be it."

Anderson nodded. "I agree with you there, Judge McClure. And you have my word on it."

CHAPTER
TWENTY-SIX

Manuel Garcia sat on the bathroom floor, both arms encircling the toilet as he dry-heaved, his slight body shaking from the exhaustive effort. In between the waves of tremors he laid his head down on the cool porcelain and wished he were dead.

Jessica stood beside him, bathing his forehead with a washrag. When his body began to shake violently, she ran into the bedroom and pulled the down comforter from her bed and dragged it into the bathroom. Her small arms pulled and tugged at the cumbersome piece, and gradually she managed to get it around Manuel's body. She tried to hold him, as she had seen Rosella do.

"Don't worry, Mannie," she said. "You'll be better soon." She laid her small blond head against him. "I love you, Mannie." She stood up and spread her arms wide. "This much! And when my mommie comes for me, you can come live with us! We'll take care of you always!"

Manuel raised his aching head and looked at the small ball of fluff trying to comfort him. Oh, God, how could he have even considered letting those filthy pigs get their hands on Jessica! He thought about what was in store for the girl, and retched into the bowl.

He reached around and pulled Jessica to him, sobbing. "I love you, too, kid," he said.

The phone. He had to get to the phone and call off the deal. For once in his life, he was going to do the right thing.

Karen opened the door, disappointed to find Brent and Adam instead of Gwyn. "Have you heard anything?" she said as soon as the two men were in out of the storm.

Adam shook his head. "No. We were hoping maybe you had."

"No," she answered bleakly. "Not a word. I've called everywhere I can think to call, but so far, nothing."

"Has Mike checked back with you lately?"

"It's been about an hour. He wasn't having any luck."

Brent took in Karen's shaking hands and unsteady voice. She, like Adam, was reaching the end of the line. He remembered the signs well from his childhood. Sometimes the mind could take only so much before it rebelled, and a feeling of helplessness in a situation caused the mind to break faster than anything else.

"I could use some coffee, Karen," he said. "And then let's make a list of all we know. Go back over every little detail of the last two days. Maybe if we all work together here, we'll come up with an idea."

"Certainly, Brent," Karen said, glad for something to do. "I have paper in the kitchen. It's also the only room in the house left presentable. Whoever wrecked my home was kind enough to leave me one room un-touched."

Adam looked around at the damage as if noticing it for the first time. "My God, Karen. What kind of a maniac would do something like this? I don't think you should be staying here. Why don't you go on back to our house when we're done."

Brent nodded his head. "I agree. In the first place, this has to be depressing for you."

"Depressing?" Karen answered wryly. "I'll tell you what's depressing," she said as they moved into the kitchen. "Depressing is when your only friend in the world is missing and you can't do anything to help." She sank down heavily on a kitchen chair. "Depressing isn't even the word for it. Maybe stark terror would be a more accurate description!"

"The coffee, Karen?" Brent prodded gently. "Why don't you get that started and then we'll get to work."

Karen rose quickly and crossed her large kitchen. "I'm sorry," she said as she began filling her coffee maker. "You'll have to forgive me. Every time I think about what might be happening to Gwyn, I lose all track of what I was doing." She shoved the top of her Mr. Coffee into place and switched the knob to brew. "I am just so scared. So damn scared!"

Gwyn had heard the faint sound of the doorbell over the storm. Now she was positive she could hear voices coming from the kitchen directly below the attic room. She made as much noise as she could through the tape covering her mouth, but against the wind and rain, she knew she would never be heard. She looked around the attic room. Somehow she had to make herself known to those below.

Her eyes kept returning to the train set. The on/off switch was only a few feet from her, if there was only some way to activate it. Anyone below would be certain to hear that loud piercing whistle.

An old memory resurfaced in her mind. Uri Geller using his incredible gift to bend a spoon. *"Ah, pretty one. So we are in the same business, you and I?"* he had said to her. Was he right? Could she use her powers as he had done? Only once had she ever been able to show any ability in the line of psychokinesis. The day she had moved that chair slightly. But then she had never really tried after that. The effort had left her sick and weak. *I vomited. What if that happened again? With the tape covering my mouth, I would choke!*

She would have to chance it.

Gwyn shifted slightly in the bed and glued her eyes to the switch on the train set. She forced all other thoughts from her mind, as she had been taught at Rhine. *"The mind is a powerful tool, Gwyn, but it must be used properly. The trick is to concentrate all those brain cells on one thing, and only one thing. If you allow any other thought to creep into your subconscious, it impedes the energy flow."*

Gwyn emptied her mind. All thoughts of her daughter vanished. All thoughts of the people so close in the room below flew from her memory. She had one goal in life. Moving that switch from off to on.

Soon the voices coming from the kitchen faded into nothingness. She could not hear the storm that raged outside the attic room. She was locked in a battle of wills with a small piece of metal, and it was a battle she was determined to win.

CHAPTER TWENTY-SEVEN

The three sat in stunned silence for a few seconds after the line went dead. Each was trying to digest the grizzly story Judge McClure had told them. Leon Bozyk seemed to sum up all their sentiments. "Son of a bitch!" he said.

Anderson shook his head slowly from side to side. "I still can't believe Karen Jackson killed those women. At least not without help. It would have been physically impossible for her to lift them, not to mention the fact that Jerry told us the knife thrusts were made by someone extremely strong."

Marlo spoke for the first time. "Jim, if I'm right, Karen did *not* do the killing. One of her other personalities did."

Anderson looked at her with skepticism. "Yes. I see what you're getting at, Marlo. But even if she is a multiple, she would still only be five feet tall and maybe a hundred fifteen pounds. Lucy Higgins weighed at least one-fifty. There's just no way Karen could have gotten her body over a six-foot fence without help."

"I agree," Leon said. "There had to be someone working with her. And if that's the case, it will go harder on her in court, that's for sure."

Marlo got up from her chair and paced around the room as she formulated her thoughts. "You're wrong, guys," she said. "Remember Judge McClure saying that Karen at first blamed her mother's death on a brother? Chances are, the same personality that killed the mother also killed our three women. Most multiples have a protector personality, and it is usually male. If this personality *perceives* himself as strong, then make no mistake, he *will* be strong! There are all kinds of documented cases to bear this out."

"And how do we know for certain that Karen really *does* have a multiple personality, and isn't just simply a psycho?" Leon asked.

"Everything fits," she answered him. "Everything. Almost all multiples develop because of extreme trauma in childhood. And this trauma is usually prolonged, horrible abuse that starts when the child is young, and lasts until about the age of twelve. The abuse is always sadistic and bizarre—which certainly is true in Karen's case. And then of course we have the psychiatrist suspecting it because Karen kept referring to herself as different people. Even her age now follows the pattern. Around the age of thirty, everything starts falling apart for a multiple. This is almost always the age they begin seeking psychiatric help." She shook her head. "No. I don't think there is the slightest doubt in the world but that Karen is a multiple."

"Do you think she is aware of it?" Anderson asked.

"Probably not." She turned to Leon. "How long has she been going to see Dr. Beckman?"

"I think she said about a month," he answered her.

"Well, I would be surprised if Dr. Beckman has made

the diagnosis yet. She likely has no idea what she is dealing with. It usually takes months and even years for a psychiatrist to realize a patient is a multiple. But I do think it would be a good idea to get Sheila—Dr. Beckman—to go with us when we pick her up. She might be able to convince Karen she needs help."

"There is still something else we need to discuss first," Anderson said. "Gwyn Martin was positive these killings were tied in somehow with her daughter's disappearance. And now Gwyn herself seems to have vanished. Could one of the personalities have harmed Jessica or Gwyn?"

Marlo shook her head. "I don't think so. From what you have told me, Karen was crazy about Gwyn's daughter. A multiple isn't totally insane in one personality, and kind and gentle in another. That makes for good fiction, but in real life, it doesn't happen that way."

Leon said the obvious, "Well, hell—we just established she probably knifed three women to death. That's pretty insane in my book!"

"No. It's different. Those three women were all guilty of extreme child abuse. To Karen—or one of her personalities—she saw it as saving the children. In her mind, she was doing the right thing to protect them."

"Then you don't think Karen would have harmed Jessica or Gwyn?" Anderson asked.

"No. I don't think so. She loved Jessica, and Gwyn is her best friend. I can't see any of the personalities doing serious harm to either of them. Now, quite often one of the personalities will do harm to the 'host'—in this case, Karen, but not to another person."

"What do you mean, the host?" Anderson asked.

"All multiples have a host," Marlo explained. "This is the personality the rest of us see. And the host doesn't usually know about the other selves. Probably, in this case, Karen is the host, although she might not be."

"What else can you tell us about multiples?" Anderson asked. "Is she likely to do something crazy when we pick her up? And how do we convince Karen that she has committed three murders?"

"That will depend a lot on the administrator, Jim. Every multiple has one personality who is in control of the whole person. This personality, called in psychiatric terms the internal administrator, decides who is allowed out, and when they are allowed out. If the administrator is skilled, she can keep the host from realizing anything is wrong for long periods of time—even years. She even decides which personalities have access to certain information and which personalities are allowed to remember various acts of abuse. Some personalities may know about the others—or some of the others—and different ones know none. I would be willing to bet when we pick Karen up, the administrator will call one of the personalities who knows about the killings. It could even be the administrator herself. She will probably not even let us talk to Karen."

"I'll be damned!" Bozyk said.

Marlo looked at him, and couldn't keep tears from filling her eyes as she continued, "You see, all of the personalities came into existence to protect Karen. When she was being burned or tortured in some horrid way, her mind couldn't take it—so a new person evolved. A stronger person. The object was to divide and conquer. And from what Judge McClure told us, I would imagine

Karen has several, perhaps dozens, of personalities living in her body. When the pain got to be too much, another personality was created. And these personalities will continue protecting her even when—or if—she is arrested."

"Well, she won't spend a night in jail if I can help it!" Anderson spoke adamantly. "Get Dr. Beckman on the phone, and then the two of you decide where we should take her. I want Karen placed in the best psychiatric unit available. We owe her that much at least."

The doorbell rang at apartment 211 on West Mill Street. Before Manuel could get from the bedroom, Jessica had opened the door to the two men. She stood looking up at them, aware now that she had done something wrong as she heard Manuel shout, "Don't open the door, Jessica!"

The short, plump man reached down to pick Jessica up, but she was too fast for him. She turned and ran back into the apartment and stood beside Manuel.

The tall man pushed the door closed behind him and walked nonchalantly into the room. "Hello, Garcia. What's this about changing your mind? We had a deal. Two thousand for the kid."

Manuel stood his ground. "I told Benny the deal was off. You can't have her. If you try and take her, I'll phone the police—I swear to God I will!"

"Now, Garcia, just think what you could do with two thousand big ones. Shit, you could stay high for a month on that." He pulled a cigarette out of his pocket and lit it, inhaling deeply. "And one way or another we're going to get the kid. You can make it easy on yourself, or hard. Ain't no difference to me."

The fat man walked over to Jessica. "She's a pretty one, all right. She'll photograph real good. And best of all, there won't be no one looking for her."

Jessica pulled away and ran into the bedroom, slamming the door behind her. She didn't know what was going on, but the two men frightened her.

Manuel knew he didn't stand a chance against the MacIver brothers. There were four of them, which meant the other two were probably waiting downstairs. They always traveled together, and ran the biggest child pornography ring in a three-state area.

Their method was simple. First they doped the children to avoid any initial hassle, then when they awoke, the brothers gave them ice cream, candy, toys—anything the kids wanted. They were kept isolated, and the only contact with adults was the brothers. In a few days, the kids began—grudgingly—to trust them, and gradually they were introduced into the life of pornography. When they were past the age to photograph—which came early because the children hardened—the girls were put on the streets to work for the MacIvers in other ways, and the boys were farmed off to high-paying men who liked the company of young boys. If the brothers thought there might be trouble from a rebellious youth, that youngster would mysteriously disappear. The kids learned fast to keep their mouths shut and do as they were told.

Manuel cursed the night he had met Benny MacIver and agreed to hand over Jessica. It was the night his mother had died, and he had gotten stoned out of his gourd. At some point in the evening, he had started shooting off his mouth about the kid, and Benny had approached him. If he hadn't been so spaced out, he would never have agreed. He had to believe that.

"What's it to be, Garcia?" the tall man said, grinding his cigarette out into the carpet. "Do you want to give the kid her sleeping powder, or does Mack there force it down her pretty little throat?" He pulled a gun from a shoulder holster. "And remember, you aren't in much of a bargaining position."

Sweat was dripping from Manuel's face, and his hands began to shake uncontrollably. "No. I'll do it," he finally said. "Maybe you're right. What the hell do I want with a snot-nosed kid screwing up my life?" He rubbed sweat from his face with his forearm. "Just tell me what you want me to do."

CHAPTER
TWENTY-EIGHT

The pain in Gwyn's head was searing, but she refused to acknowledge it. She kept her gaze locked on the switch, pushing it with her mind. Finally it moved slightly, teetered back and forth, then flipped over into the on position. The little train chugged into life. She had done it!

Directly below, the shrill sound of the train whistle caused the three people to jump.

Brent was on his feet immediately. "What the hell is that?" he said as he began running into the other room. He stopped when he realized the sound was fainter when he left the kitchen.

Adam yelled at him, "It seems to be coming from overhead." His eyes searched the beamed ceiling but failed to see the opening.

Both men turned their gaze on Karen. "Is there another level to this house? An attic, maybe?" Adam asked.

Karen shook her head back and forth, staring blankly. "No. Not that I know of, anyway."

"There has to be," Brent said as they continued to

listen to the shrieking of the train. "That sound is directly over our heads." He walked around the kitchen, carefully examining the structure of the ceiling.

"Come over here, Adam," he said as he pointed up to where the lines in the wood were separated slightly. "What is this?"

Adam looked up and knew exactly why the wood was seamed differently in this area. "It's a ceiling door that probably leads to an attic. I imagine that door will swing down, lowering a set of stairs. Many of the older houses were built that way." He pulled a chair over and climbed up to get a closer look. "The handle has been removed. I'll need a screwdriver or a knife to get it started."

Brent turned to ask Karen for the items, but she was gone. He rummaged through several drawers, found a hammer, and handed it up to Adam. "This should work. Use the claw end to force it down a little."

The Jake personality was back, and his instincts told him to run. Even if he could overpower the two big men in the kitchen, his only option would be to kill them, and this he couldn't do.

Karen's car was still parked in Gwyn's driveway. He would just get in it and go. Maybe he could get out of the city before they sorted it all out. He couldn't let them catch him. Karen would pay the price for his actions, and that wasn't fair.

He raced into the den, grabbed up the car keys and Karen's billfold, then ran for the front door. He opened it to find two uniformed police officers, Captain Anderson, Leon Bozyk, and two women. One of the women was familiar to him, the other was not.

Both officers tried to hold him as he came through the door, but he was too strong for them. He broke their grasp with a downward yank of his arms, then shoved one officer, sending him sprawling. The other officer made a lunge for him, but Jake stepped to the side and brought his powerful arm down across the back of the man's neck. He fell, out cold.

It was all happening so fast that Jake hadn't noticed Leon Bozyk slip around in back of him. Now the detective's massive arms wrapped around Jake, pinning his arms to his side. The detective lifted him up off the ground so there was no way to get leverage with his legs. He was trapped.

Anderson couldn't believe his eyes. Karen had succeeded in felling two of his officers, and would probably have gone through Leon if the detective hadn't grabbed her from behind. Thank God he had listened to Marlo and brought extra men along. He would never have believed the petite Karen could possess that kind of strength if he hadn't witnessed it firsthand.

"What do you want me to do with her, Captain?" Leon asked.

At his words, Karen suddenly quit struggling and slumped against his arms. "Just put me down, and I'll go with you into the house," she said. "We're all getting wet out here."

Dr. Beckman walked over. "Karen?" she asked tentatively.

"No. I'm Gloria, Dr. Beckman. Have you figured it out yet?"

The doctor nodded her head. "Yes. With a little help

from these people. I didn't know, though. I'm sorry I didn't realize about the rest of you."

"That's okay, Doc. We weren't ready for you to meet the others, yet," Gloria said. "But it's time now, isn't it?"

Dr. Beckman put her arms around Karen. "Yes, dear. All of us here want to help you. It's time."

They entered the house with Karen between Bozyk and Anderson. The two red-faced policemen followed after them, positive this was one incident they would be a long time living down.

Anderson did a double take when he saw Gwyn walk into the living room, propped up on both sides by Brent and Adam.

"Gwyn! Thank God you're all right! Where have you been? What happened?" He stumbled over his words, relief washing over him.

Adam let go of Gwyn when he saw Karen. "You little bitch!" he yelled at her. "All the time you had my wife tied up in your attic! What kind of a maniac are you, anyway?"

Karen shrank from his rage and Gwyn reached out toward her husband. "No, Adam— Don't. Leave her alone. She didn't know what she was doing."

Anderson motioned to the two officers. "Why don't you take Karen into one of the other rooms while we sort this all out." He looked at Dr. Beckman. "Maybe it would be a good idea if you went along."

Adam turned on his wife as soon as they had gone. "And Jessica? Did she take our daughter, also?"

Brent's arms were still around Gwyn, and he felt her body sag against him. She looked at him for help.

"Brent, I need a glass of water. My throat is dry—it's hard to talk."

Brent nodded his head toward Leon. "Could you get her water? The kitchen is in the back."

The room stayed strangely quiet until he returned. "I know where Jessica is, Adam," she said as soon as she finished drinking. "She's alive and safe. I have the address."

Everyone listened intently as Gwyn talked. She explained her vision, and the out-of-body experience that enabled her to see where Jessica was.

Adam's legs buckled under him at the realization his daughter was alive. He slumped into the nearest chair. *It's going to be all right. I'm going to get my family back!*

Anderson looked puzzled when Gwyn finished speaking. "I don't know a West Mill Street, do you, Leon?"

Leon shook his head. "I've worked every beat in this city, Jim, and I've never heard of it."

Gwyn seemed to dissolve before their eyes. "But there has to be. I saw it. It was an apartment building. Jessica was in 211, and the address above the mailbox was West Mill. I'm sure of it."

"Could it have been a different city, Gwyn?" Marlo asked.

"I—I don't know—yes—I suppose so. My God, I never thought of that." Gwyn extracted herself from Brent's grasp. "I have to talk with Karen. There's one personality, Aunt Sylvia, who knows where Jessica is. Maybe now she will tell me."

Gwyn went into the den and walked over to Karen. She took her hands. "Gloria? Gloria, listen to me. I have to talk with Aunt Sylvia. It's important. Won't you please let her come out?"

Gloria shook her head. "I told you, she doesn't listen to me anymore."

"But she has to! You told me you were the boss. You said it was up to you which personality came out. If you want her to, you could get her to come."

Gloria again shook her head stubbornly. "No. You can't talk to her. I can't get her to come out."

Suddenly a dramatic change came over Karen. She sat up straight in the chair, tossed her hair back, and sneered at the people surrounding her. "You bunch of assholes are pathetic, you know that?" she said. "Why don't you just leave us the hell alone?"

Gwyn recognized who she was speaking to. "Lily?"

"Bingo!" Lily taunted. "My—aren't we getting smart!"

"Listen carefully to me, Lily," Gwyn pleaded. "I need to know where Jessica is, and if you know, please won't you tell me?"

"I *don't* know—and even if I did, I wouldn't tell you. *Some* people mind their own business."

"But this *is* my business, Lily. Jessica is my little girl. She might be in trouble. I have to find her."

"Can't you get it through your head, dummy?" Lily mocked. "Gloria won't call Aunt Sylvia, and she is the only one who could help you."

Marlo spoke up from the doorway. "Why, Lily? Why won't Gloria let Aunt Sylvia talk to us?"

For a second Lily seemed confused. Then she tossed her head back haughtily and addressed her audience.

"How should *I* know? Maybe she thinks you're all a bunch of stupid jerks!"

They left Karen in the den and returned to the living room. Marlo put her arms around Gwyn. "I'm sorry. I wish there was something I could do."

"I just don't understand it," Gwyn said. "Why does she keep refusing to let me speak with Aunt Sylvia?"

"I don't understand it either," Marlo answered her. "I gather from what you said in there that Gloria is the administrator. She decides who comes out. She could let you talk with any personality she wanted to."

Adam interrupted, "Well, we aren't getting anywhere with Karen. The thing we need to do now is start calling different cities, give them the address, and see if we can track it down that way."

"I've already started the wheels rolling on that, Adam," Anderson said. "I called the station while you were in talking with Karen. My people are on it right now. The only trouble is, it could take a while. Mill is a common street name, and we don't even know if the city is in Nebraska. It could be anywhere."

"Is there anything else you can remember about the place, Gwyn?" Brent asked. "Anything at all?"

"No. Nothing," she answered.

"What was it you were telling Adam about a rainbow? When did you see that, and what exactly did it look like?"

"I had almost forgotten the rainbow!" Gwyn looked up expectantly. "It was a few days ago—in our yard. All at once I received an image of Jessica and she was sitting at the end of a big silver rainbow. I saw her clearly."

"Wait a minute," Bozyk said excitedly. "Karen was

raised in Missouri—a little town right out of St. Louis. Could your rainbow have been the silver arch in St. Louis?"

"Yes!" She nodded her head vigorously. "Yes! That has to be it!"

Brent's eyes were moist as he looked at Gwyn's radiant face. *Mary, Mother of God,* he prayed silently. *Please let them find Jessica safe!*

Adam was on his feet instantly. "We'll need to charter a plane." He went to the window and looked out at the storm. "I think it's let up a little. We should be able to get above it."

Anderson took control. "I'll phone the St. Louis police and give them the address. They can check it out while you're on the way. Go ahead and leave for Eppley Airfield now, if you want to. I'll phone ahead and have a plane waiting for you. As soon as I know anything, I'll contact your pilot and relay the information."

Adam went over to Gwyn and pulled her to him. His voice broke as he held his wife. "It's going to be all right, honey. Everything's going to be all right now."

They were ready to go in minutes. At the door, Gwyn turned to Brent. "Would you stay with Karen?" she asked him. "She needs a friend, now."

"Of course," he assured her. "Don't worry about it. I'll take care of her." He held out his hand to Adam. "Good luck. If there is anything we can do from here, let us know."

The three of them heard a shout, and watched as Mike Koerns rushed from his car. They waited in the shelter of the veranda for him to reach them.

"Gwyn! You're all right! What happened? Where were you?"

"It's a long story, Mike," she said. "It was Karen. She killed those women and took Jessica, too. I've been tied up in her attic for two days."

"Karen?" Mike exploded, dumbfounded. "Your friend Karen?"

"Yes—no—not exactly. I mean she didn't know what she was doing. The Karen we all know had no idea. She has a multiple personality, Mike."

Adam took hold of his wife's arm and started toward the steps. "Let's go. We're wasting time. You can tell him about it later."

"Go on in, Mike," Gwyn called as they raced off. "Brent can explain it all to you. Help him take care of Karen."

It was almost impossible to see. Rain pelted against the windshield of the car with such force, the wipers could barely keep up.

"I don't know, Adam," Gwyn said. "It looks to me like it's getting worse. I'll be surprised if a pilot will be willing to go up in this."

Adam kept his eyes glued to the road. "It just seems worse because of the speed of the car. A good pilot can take us up above the storm. I checked the forecast, and this is supposed to let up shortly, anyway."

"I just don't want to take any chances. We're too close now to risk something happening to us."

He took one hand from the wheel and pulled Gwyn to him. "I'm not going to let anything happen to you or Jessica again," he told her. "And that's a promise!"

* * *

A security guard met them as they entered the airport.
"Mr. and Mrs. Martin? Just follow me, please. Your
plane is waiting for you."

"What are the flight conditions?" Gwyn asked.

"A little rough because of the wind, but your pilot
shouldn't have any trouble. It's clearing to the southeast.
You will be out of the worst of it in ten or fifteen
minutes."

"You don't happen to have a message for us, do you?
From Captain Anderson?"

"Yes. I hope I got it right. He said to tell you the
address checked out, and officers are on the way. Does
that make sense to you?"

Gwyn breathed a sigh of relief. "Yes, sir! It makes
perfect sense." She felt like shouting.

They had been in the air for thirty minutes, and except
for a few wind gusts, the flight was going well. A
strange peace had come over Gwyn. Adam had been
correct. The weather was clearing, they were on their
way to get their daughter, and everything was going to be
all right.

She noticed the pilot begin talking into his headset,
then in a few minutes he turned around to them. "I have
a message for you. When the police arrived at the
address in St. Louis, there was no sign of your daughter.
They found two men shot to death in the apartment."

Adam's scream filled the small Cessna. "No! My
God, no! My daughter! What about my daughter?"

"I'm sorry, sir. The police are trying to sort out what
happened, but they don't know any more at this time."

Gwyn reached over and took her husband's hand. "It's all right, Adam," she said. "Jessica is safe. I know it. We'll find her, I promise you."

A rental car was waiting for them when they arrived at Lambert International in St. Louis. The young officer who met them was not encouraging. "I'm sorry to have to tell you this, but the bodies of the two men found in the apartment have been identified. They were brothers, and heavily involved in child pornography. We believe your child was taken by the two remaining brothers, and we are doing everything we can to find out where they have taken her."

Adam retched in the parking lot as the officer tried to steady him. When he could speak, he turned on his wife. "You told me Jessica was safe! Not to worry! My God! Pornographers have our child!" He began to sob hysterically. "She'll be ruined—my baby—my sweet innocent baby—you don't know—you don't know—"

"Adam! Listen to me!" Gwyn shouted, puzzled at her husband's choice of words. "They don't have her. I would know if she was in trouble. I'll find her!" She put her arms around him and held his shaking body to her tightly. She steadied her voice before speaking again. "Jessica is safe, Adam. Now let's go get our child."

"I'm sorry," he said to her as they drove, staying close behind the police car leading the way. "I don't know what's wrong with me lately. I—I seem to be losing it—falling apart."

She reached over and put her hand over his. "You aren't the only one, Adam. This whole thing has pushed all of us to the breaking point. I understand. Really I do."

Up ahead Gwyn could see the mammoth silver arch. "There it is, Adam," she shouted. "I know Jessica is close by. I can feel her."

The police car moved over to the exit ramp and Adam followed close behind. It was only a few minutes before the lead car pulled up in front of an apartment building and stopped.

Gwyn jumped from the car eagerly. "This is it! This is the same building I saw in my vision!"

The street was jammed with police cars and an ambulance was waiting as attendants carried out two bodies. The young officer came over to them. "Our men are just finishing here. Let me see if they've received any new information about your daughter." He left them and walked over to a cluster of uniformed men.

Gwyn stared at the building. "Jessica is here, Adam. She's in there somewhere."

The officer returned to them promptly. "I'm sorry, folks, but there is still no word on your daughter's whereabouts. She isn't in the apartment, but if you want to go look and see if you can find anything our officers overlooked, the captain said it would be all right."

They followed behind as he led the way. Adam had not spoken since they arrived, and seemed almost in a daze. Gwyn took his arm, trying to comfort him. "Don't worry, honey. She's here. It's going to be okay."

They took the elevator to the second floor. The door to apartment 211 was standing open, and more uniformed policemen met them. "I don't think you want to come in here, ma'am," one of them said. "It's still a mess."

Gwyn stood motionless staring into the room and the blood spill on the carpet. "No," she said. "We don't need to go in there." She turned and began walking down the hallway. She stopped in front of apartment 212 and looked at Adam. "Jessica is in here."

Adam tried the doorknob, but it was locked. He stepped back and with one hard kick the door flew open.

He saw Jessica at once. She was on the lap of a young Mexican boy, and her eyes were closed. He screamed with rage as he lunged for the young man. "What have you done to her? You son of a bitch! What have you done to my daughter?"

Gwyn grabbed for her husband and pulled him back. "Wait a minute, Adam. For God's sake, wait a minute!"

She knelt down beside her child and saw her even breathing. Tears filled her eyes as she gazed up at Manuel. "You saved her, didn't you?"

Manuel recognized the pretty lady from the picture Jessica always carried. He nodded. "They were going to take her—made me give her the sleeping powder—but I fooled them." He stopped talking and Gwyn for the first time noticed a small trickle of blood coming from his mouth. "Mama kept a gun in the nightstand—I got it—shot them. Had to come in here because of the others waiting downstairs. This was the other lady's apartment. The one who brought Jessica. They didn't know about it. I came in. Locked the door." His glassy eyes looked down at Jessica with love. "She's just sleeping—from the powder—I waited until then—so she wouldn't see me shoot them—had to protect her—had to—"

"Don't try to talk now," Gwyn said. "You're hurt." She looked over her shoulder at the officer who had followed them into the room. "Stop that ambulance. This man has been shot and needs help."

Adam reached down and picked his daughter up. Blood spurted from Manuel's slight chest when the pressure of the sleeping child was removed. Gwyn quickly shed her coat and tried to cover the open wound.

The room turned into chaos as several policemen rushed in, guns drawn. One of them knelt down by Gwyn and spoke harshly to Manuel. "Are you Garcia? Manuel Garcia?"

Manuel held his head up as high as he could manage. "Yeah, man," he said with a note of pride for the first time in his life. "I'm Manuel Garcia." He leaned over against Gwyn and the last thought to go through his mind before he passed out was how proud his mother would have been of him.

Gwyn held the frail boy against her and wept.

"We found the packet of sleeping powder Garcia gave her," an officer told them as they started downstairs. "I'm sure she'll be just fine as soon as she sleeps off the effects, but I would take her by the hospital to make certain."

Adam nodded his head. "Of course. We'll go there right now."

CHAPTER
TWENTY-NINE

Anderson took the call from the St. Louis police, then turned to the people assembled in his office. "She's all right! They found Jessica and she's fine!"

"Thank God!" Brent said. "And Gwyn? Is she okay?"

"Yes. Everyone is fine, except for a young man who was shot protecting Jessica."

Brent crossed over to Karen and took her hands. "Did you hear that, Karen? Jessica is safe!"

Karen looked around, startled. "Brent? What has happened? What am I doing here?"

Dr. Beckman walked over to her. "Karen?"

Karen looked at her with genuine alarm. "Dr. Beckman? What are you doing here? What's going on?"

None of them seemed to know how to explain it to her. They were not expecting Karen's own personality to return so quickly.

Brent spoke gently to her. "Listen to me, Karen. Gwyn found Jessica. She is alive and well! Isn't that good news?"

Relief played over Karen's face. "Jessica? And Gwyn? They're both all right? Oh, thank God. Thank

God." She looked around at Captain Anderson. "Is this true, Jim? Where are they? What happened?"

Anderson stood, trying to figure out what he could say to this woman, who had no idea of the damage she had done. "I don't have all the details yet, Karen. But they are both okay. Adam and Gwyn will be home with Jessica tomorrow."

At his words, Karen's shoulders hunched over and she emitted a long, strange scream. "No-o-o-! Oh, no!" Everyone watched as her hands began curling and she rose awkwardly from the chair. The voice that spoke was raspy and cracked like that of an old woman. "He'll harm them! Don't you see? I took Jessica to protect her from him, and now he has her again!"

They all watched in stunned silence, trying to figure out what was happening.

That voice! Mike thought. *I've heard it before. At the station. Warning me to stop someone! It was Karen!*

Marlo was the first to speak. "What are you talking about? Who will harm them?"

"Adam!" the voice spat at her in disgust. "Adam Martin! He is mad! Totally mad! I know—I know because I've lived with madness. I can see it in his face. In his eyes."

"Surely you are wro—" Brent started to say.

"No! I'm not wrong! There's something crazy inside him. Please!" She grabbed Brent's hand and began crying. "Please! You must believe me. I started to tell her—that night at Trini's. I called the station, but Gloria didn't let me stay out long enough."

Brent looked around at the others. "I know what she is talking about. On our date that night, Karen started talking with this same strange voice, then excused herself to make a phone call. I even noticed when she got up from the table, she seemed to be hunched over a bit, but figured she was just stiff from sitting so long. When she returned to the table, though, she seemed fine."

"I took her call," Mike spoke up. "She *did* sound as though she was trying to warn Gwyn about something. A man. She told me to stop him, and for Gwyn to watch out. She must have been talking about Adam!"

"Of course I'm talking about Adam!" Karen spoke with the same cracked voice. "Do you think I wouldn't know insanity when I see it? I lived with it for years!" She turned to Brent. "I know you love her, young man. And if you do, you'll listen to me. Adam Martin is crazy in the head, and getting worse every day. He'll kill them. I know he'll kill them!"

Before Brent could respond, Anderson's office door opened and Tucker rushed in. "Captain, see what you make of this. It just came in from New Jersey."

Anderson picked up the paper and scanned quickly through it. It was the police report covering major crimes committed in and around the Princeton area during the years Adam Martin was there. It was intended as a routine check to see if there were any crimes similar to the ones committed by their serial killer. And of course there was not. However, three young women had been raped and murdered in exactly the same manner as the coed and the attempted murder of Betty Crawford here in Omaha—the crimes that the pizza delivery boy had confessed to. Furthermore, one of the women killed was Nancy Colbert—daughter of Adam's old boss, Hank Colbert.

"Have you checked with the delivery boy?"

Tucker nodded. "He still insists he did it, but his parents arrived a few minutes ago from California. I talked with them just briefly, but they told me their son is disturbed and has been confessing to crimes for the last several years. He wasn't in with our list of habitual confessors because he only recently moved here."

The full implication of what was happening finally hit Anderson. Karen's fears—this report. He grabbed up the telephone. "Get me the St. Louis police," he said to the operator. "And make it fast!"

The personality that was Aunt Sylvia sat down, stunned. All of her planning, the pain she had caused the Martin woman, were going to be for nothing. He had them again.

She could not remember just when she had begun to suspect him. Long ago. Before the birth of their darling child.

She had watched him closely over the years, slowly recognizing the signs he was able to hide from the others. Whatever spark of human decency that had ever existed in Adam had been beaten out of him long ago. Just as with Karen's mother. The only difference was that Adam's brilliant mind helped him hide it. He had learned to play the game of life well. And perhaps along the way his playacting had become blurred. Probably by now, he himself did not know a true feeling from one invented to fit the occasion.

In the weeks before she took Jessica, she had watched the restlessness return. The nervous energy. He had worked in the yard at a feverish pitch—repairing fences that did not need it, trimming trees, pulling weeds. In the house, Gwyn had laughed about Adam "spring cleaning" in the fall. She had not noticed the slight tremor in his hands as he worked—his obsession that every little item in their home be placed in a particular place. Just so. But *she* had noticed—and remembered. Another time, another place. All the signs.

Then on the day of the picnic, she had watched from Karen's window as Adam played with Jessica alone in the yard. He had started by tossing her in the air and catching her, a favorite game of theirs. But as she watched, he began throwing Jessica higher and higher. She could see the fear on the child's face, and hear Adam's sick laughter through the open window. Then he threw his daughter higher still—so high he almost couldn't catch her. Adam seemed to snap back to reality as he lunged for her. She saw him cuddle the child in his arms, wiping tears from his eyes.

She knew then she had to save the little girl. Whatever it took. It would be only a matter of time before he harmed her.

Later in the afternoon, she saw her chance. Jessica was sound asleep, and hardly stirred as she lifted her from the swing and carried her to the bed in the attic room. Jessica would not be frightened in this room where she had spent many hours playing with her "friends."

Throughout the long evening, several of the "others" had emerged briefly to entertain the child and keep her contented. The activity level at the Martin house was so high, no one noticed when Karen disappeared for short periods of time.

After midnight, she had bundled Jessica up and headed for St. Louis and the one woman she knew she could trust with the little girl—Rosella Garcia.

Rosella had lived next door to Karen and her great-grandmother for ten years. In those years, she had treated Karen as a daughter, and Karen had seen first-hand what a difference a truly loving person could make in the lives of children. Rosella always had at least ten young ones in her charge at any given time—yet each child was given his or her fill of love and attention.

She knew Rosella was the one person who could keep Jessica happy and safe until she figured out what to do about Adam. If she was correct, it wouldn't be long before he cracked wide open. Then her plan was, of course, to return the child to Gwyn.

She told Rosella little concerning her reasons for placing Jessica in her care. She only said the child was in terrible danger at the present time and must be protected. Rosella had accepted her word unconditionally.

The Gloria personality had realized the danger this action posed to the others—so she chose to ignore it—allowing only the child personalities access to this information. But gradually over the weeks and months, all the personalities became aware of what Aunt Sylvia had done, and formed an unspoken bond of loyalty toward her. Though they didn't know *why* the child had been taken, they were unswerving in their support of the one personality they trusted above all the others—Aunt Sylvia.

And now she had let them down. By her deeds, they were now all in jeopardy—not to mention the child and her mother. Adam was at the breaking point. She was positive of that. He would never return with them.

Her mind couldn't stand the pain.

Up ahead, Gwyn saw the hospital sign. "This is it, Adam. Better get over in the right-hand lane—it's the next exit."

"I have something else I want to do first," he told her. "It will only take a minute."

Gwyn looked at him, puzzled. "Adam, I don't think we should take any chances here. We need to make sure Jessie wasn't given too much of that sleeping powder. Let's go by the hospital first."

His hands tightened on the steering wheel. "No, Gwyn. This is important. Don't worry. Jessica will be just fine." He drove past the exit.

Anderson's stomach was knotted in fear, but he tried to reassure the others. "Now let's don't get too worked up here," he said. "After all, Adam doesn't know we have anything on him. There is no reason to assume he will harm Gwyn or Jessica at this particular time. And the St. Louis police are dispatching cars to all hospitals in the area. Adam told them he would take Jessica for a checkup, and I'm positive they'll find him."

"I blame myself for part of this," Marlo said. "I knew from his records he was the most likely one to exhibit abnormal adult behavior because of his childhood."

Bozyk went over and put his arm around her shoulder. "But he wasn't the one we were looking for, remember? He had nothing at all to do with the crimes we were investigating. There was no way you could have known about all the rest of this."

Marlo slid her arm comfortably around Leon's waist, thanking him silently for his support. "There is an old medical saying, 'If you hear hoofbeats, think horses, not zebras.' Simply put, that means you go for the obvious—the logical answer."

Anderson nodded his head. "I've heard that same quote in referring to police work. The only trouble is, in this case when we heard hoofbeats, it was *both* horses and zebras."

Marlo looked at Karen huddled in a ball on the couch, sucking her thumb. "Yes," she said. "I see what you mean."

Adam had left the interstate and was driving now on a winding country road. Presently he pulled off and followed a muddy bicycle path that led down close to the Missouri River. Gwyn could see a large riverboat going by, filled with people. Something made her want to scream at them for help.

Adam had not spoken a word to her since leaving the main road. She had no choice but to sit there quietly, waiting to see what he had in mind.

He braked to a stop and killed the motor. When he turned to her, his eyes were filled with tears. Without saying a word he reached into his overcoat and pulled out a small gun. He had gambled correctly they wouldn't check him at Eppley—that they would be rushed right through to the private plane.

Gwyn shrank back against the door.

"Adam! What are you doing? Why do you have a gun? I don't understand."

"It's very simple," he said. "We are a family, and

nothing is ever going to change that again. We are all going to die here, together, as a family."

Gwyn's mind spun in a dozen directions. "But why, Adam? We can be a family again. We have Jessica with us now, and everything is going to be all right. You just need a little rest, that's all."

"No," he said quietly. "It's all falling apart. I knew it would. It was only a matter of time."

Gwyn's hand moved up slowly behind her, trying to reach the handle of the door. Adam saw the slight movement. "Don't try it, Gwyn," he said. "Even if you made it, you would be leaving Jessica with me. And you wouldn't do that, would you?"

She knew he was right. There was no way she could escape and get Jessica from the backseat. No way at all.

Time. She needed time to think. She had to keep him talking.

"What did you mean when you said it's all falling apart?" she said. "*What* is falling apart?"

"My life, Gwyn. I thought you could stop me, but you never did. I wanted you to, you know. At least at first."

"Stop you, Adam? From what?"

"From killing," he answered simply. "I heard all about you at Princeton. Remember that new wing built at the parapsychology lab? It was mine. I designed it. Everyone always talked about what a gifted psychic they had studying there. You, Gwyn. They were talking about you."

"But I never met you when I was at Princeton, Adam. What are you trying to say?"

"I followed you! That's what I'm saying! After I killed Nancy Colbert I wanted to be caught! I needed someone to stop me. I thought if you were such a great damn psychic, you would be able to." He stopped talking as another flood of tears cascaded down his face. "But instead, I fell in love with you, and you never picked up on my problem. So I thought maybe I could leave the past behind. Get a fresh start. Begin over again."

"But you can, Adam." Gwyn spoke earnestly, cajoling, hoping she could convince him. "I don't care about the past," she lied. "We can be a family again—just like it was before."

Slowly Adam shook his head from side to side. "No. I've started again. In Omaha. Three girls. Like before. But the second girl—somehow she lived. She will be able to identify me. It's over."

Betty Crawford! Oh, God, it was Adam in my vision. He was the black cloud. My mind must have rebelled at seeing Adam rape and try to murder that poor girl. It refused to accept such a terrible concept.

And the laughter—the spine-chilling mad laughter—came from my husband!

She realized Adam was still speaking and tried to concentrate on what he was saying.

"They haven't even found the last body, yet. I killed her the night you disappeared." He laughed mirthlessly. "They questioned me about you! And my alibi was that I was off killing someone else and couldn't possibly have harmed my wife! Isn't that funny, Gwyn?"

He was insane. Totally, completely insane. Why hadn't she seen it? Why hadn't any of them seen it?

Suddenly it occurred to her that perhaps one person had. The Aunt Sylvia personality. That must have been why she took Jessica. To save her from Adam! That was why Gloria refused to let her come out. Deep down, she knew Jessica was still in trouble! Probably all along, subconsciously, she herself was picking up threads of these thoughts. Her psychic mind was protecting Jessica by not allowing her to find her child.

And the nightmares! They weren't psychic impulses, but ordinary subconscious thoughts working themselves out in her dreams! The friendly black dog that turned on Jessica. Adam! *Oh, God. Why didn't I see it!*

"It's better this way, Gwyn," Adam said as he turned and looked at his sleeping daughter. "Jessica will be better off dead, anyway. Who knows what might have happened to her in the last nine months? Or what might be in store for her in the future."

"She's just a baby, Adam!" Gwyn pleaded. "She has her whole life ahead of her. You don't really want to hurt her! I know you don't!"

"Terrible things happen to kids, Gwyn. Awful, horrible things. I know. They happened to me. And I won't let my daughter go through them!"

"What happened to you, Adam?" Gwyn spoke softly, stalling for time. "Tell me about it."

Adam brushed his hand over his eyes, not wanting to remember. "Everything," he finally said. "Just about everything. Sexual abuse, pornography, beatings—hell, I was being photographed having sex with prostitutes when I was five years old. I hated those bitches! God, how I hated them!"

Gwyn looked at him strangely. "You told me you came from a good home—that you lived in Brooklyn with your parents until their death when you were seventeen."

He snorted. "Yeah, well, I lied. I don't even remember my parents. But they were probably assholes like all the rest of the people who took care of me. No one ever cared."

"I care, Adam. And your friends in Omaha care."

"It's too late, Gwyn!" he shouted at her. "Can't you get that through your head? I'm over the line! I *like* killing, now! But even more, I like the feeling of a family—of belonging. We would have died together days ago if Karen hadn't stayed so late at our house. I had been following you. The police station. Saint Michael's. Through the grounds at the university. Waiting for the right time—the perfect moment. I was there at our house later that night, after you returned from your drive. Watching. I saw Karen leave—she went out to the sidewalk and I was afraid she would see me parked across the street in a rental car. But she didn't, and then just as I started to get out of the car, you came running out and Brent showed up. I left. Thank God I left." He smiled at her calmly. "Now it's perfect. Now Jessica is here and we're together again. We belong together. The three of us. For eternity. It's the only way!"

Gwyn could see there was no use trying to reason with him. He was way beyond the point of reasoning. What was she going to do? Dear God, what was she going to do?

There was no way she could use her psychic powers. It had taken every ounce of her energy to move that tiny switch. There wasn't a chance on earth that she could do something to his gun.

Suddenly she had another thought. Wolf Messing—clouding men's minds—a bank teller who saw something that wasn't there—guards who believed they were talking to someone else—

She looked at Adam and began to concentrate. *You do not want to harm us, Adam. You love us. We are your family. You will not shoot Jessica. You will not shoot me.*

Adam put his hand to his temple and began rubbing. He turned and looked at Jessica asleep in the backseat. He brought the gun up and aimed it at her. "I don't want to kill you, baby, but I must. I must."

"Adam, wait!" Gwyn spoke rapidly. "Maybe you are right. Maybe it is better this way. We'll go together—all three together. But give me a minute. I want to say a prayer for us. Please, Adam—just a minute."

He lowered the gun and looked at her. "All right. But don't try anything."

Gwyn closed her eyes. It was their only chance. If Wolf Messing could make someone believe something that wasn't there, then perhaps she could, too.

Don't wake up now, Jessica! Please God, don't let her wake up now!

Gwyn began concentrating. She forced her thoughts into Adam's head. *You are hearing a gun go off, Adam. Listen to it. The noise is loud. Look at your daughter. There is blood on her dress. You have done it! You have pulled the trigger! Look at Jessica. She is dead. The blood is red. It's spilling out all over. You have done it!*

Gwyn opened her eyes slowly. Adam was crying. "I'm sorry, my Jessie! I'm sorry I had to do that. But it's better this way." He turned the gun on Gwyn.

Again Gwyn closed her eyes and forced the idea into her husband's mind. *You are hearing the gun again, Adam. The noise is loud. It fills the car and hurts your ears. You can smell the gunpowder. It is strong. Look at me, Adam. My shirt is red from the blood. You are done, Adam. You have killed your wife and child. It is over!*

Gwyn stayed quiet, trying not to breathe. *Please, Jessica. Don't wake up now, baby! Don't move!*

Adam's voice filled the car. "I'm sorry! God forgive me, I'm sorry!"

The sound of the gun going off was real this time.

EPILOGUE

The small assemblage at Saint Michael's sat in the wooden pews, talking softly, waiting for the wedding march to begin.

"Did you see the story in *People* magazine?" Marlo asked the now retired captain. "They did an in-depth feature on Karen and everything she had been subjected to as a child."

Jim nodded his head. "Yes. It might help next week when her hearing comes up—although I don't anticipate any problems. That hospital in Dallas did wonders for her."

"I knew they would," Marlo answered. "It's a new approach for multiples. Instead of trying to 'kill off' the personalities, they integrate them all into one whole person. That way the 'others' don't fight it so much. They know they will still be a part of Karen."

Leon reached over and took his wife's hand. "Don't underplay your part in all this! You and Gwyn made so many trips to Dallas this last year, I considered buying stock in the airlines!"

Marlo squeezed his hand. "And you were a doll to put

up with it! A fine thing to do to a new husband, wasn't it? Leaving you alone like that?"

Leon leaned over and kissed his wife on the cheek. "And damned if it wasn't well worth the wait!"

Anderson watched the two, happy for them both. It had been an amazing year. He had retired, and Gordon Tucker had taken over the reins. In fact, he hardly missed his job, and that surprised him. He had other things to occupy his time now—like taking Jessica to the zoo, and once in a while fishing. He liked his role as surrogate grandpa to the little girl. He had even gone through Molly's things, giving Gwyn many items to save for Jessica until she was older. Somehow he was certain Molly would have approved.

Though he still missed Molly deeply, he was contented with his life. He had always liked this city of his, but after everything came out about Karen, and her reasons for doing what she did, he was even more impressed. The people of Omaha came down solidly behind Karen. There had been an outpouring of sympathy and support for the woman who had been through so much. No one seemed to care that she had killed three women. In their eyes, she was a hero for saving the children.

The hearing was strictly a formality. Even Judge McClure was coming to testify on her behalf. Karen had been released from the hospital last week—in time for the wedding—and as soon as the hearing was over, she could begin to start putting her life back in order. Even her job at Children's World was waiting. Obviously, the corporate heads heeded public sentiment.

Karen looked up as Mike Koerns slid into the pew

next to her. "Well, hello, Mike." She smiled at him. "Are you here officially or as a guest?"

He laughed, taking in Karen's delicate beauty. "Only a guest, I assure you. Engineers don't report the news!"

"How have you been?" she asked him.

"Hanging in there," he replied rhetorically. "And yourself?"

Karen laughed impishly. "The same—only a few times over the last months I've been hanging by my fingertips!"

"I know," he said openly, honestly. "Gwyn always kept us up-to-date on your progress. I'm so glad you're all right, now."

"Me, too," she said simply.

"Say," Mike stumbled slightly over the words. "Would you like to get something to eat after we're done here? Or do you have other plans?"

Karen took a deep breath and looked down at her hands, suddenly shy. When she glanced up, Mike was gazing at her, waiting patiently for an answer. For the first time, she was aware of his kind, gentle eyes.

"Yes," she said softly. "Yes, Mike. I think I'd like that."

In a small room at the back of the church, Gwyn adjusted her blue suit, and checked her appearance in the mirror one last time. In about fifteen minutes she was going to become Mrs. Brent Carlson—and she had never been happier. What had started as deep friendship had evolved into love during the last year. And what a year it had been—getting reacquainted with her daughter, helping Manuel get the drugs out of his system, the trips to Dallas for Karen—and through it all, Brent had been there for her, helping make arrangements, counseling Manuel, caring for Jessica. What a wonderful man she was marrying.

With their help, Manuel had turned his life around. After he recovered from his wounds, he testified against the two remaining MacIver brothers, breaking up one of the largest child pornography rings in the country. He was finishing high school now, here in Omaha, living with her and Jessica. It could have been no other way. One of the first things her daughter had said to her when she finally awakened that night was "Get Mannie, Mama! I promised him he could live with us!"

The door opened and Jessica entered, dressed in blue gingham and carrying a basket filled with rose petals.

"Should I get Grandpa Jim now?" she asked.

Gwyn knelt down and gave her daughter a kiss. "Yes, honey. Tell him it's time."

She stood and looked into the church, at the people assembled there. Her coworkers, friends, Brent's family, and even the Crawfords—all three of them! When the news had broken about Adam, they had come to her— offering their support and showing her they did not hold any animosity toward her for what Adam had done. It was a most unselfish act, and Gwyn had cried at their compassion and understanding. Betty Crawford had recovered fully, and even the emotional scars had faded slightly when she learned the terrible history of the man who had attacked her.

Gwyn still ached for the small boy who had been exposed to so much abuse. Adam—Karen—both victims of sick, twisted adults. Yet in the end, Karen had succeeded in saving a lot of children—including Gwyn's own. And there was another person she felt indebted to—Rosella Garcia. Not only for the care she had given Jessica, but also for being a good mother to Manuel. When all was said and done, he drew from her love, nearly sacrificing his life for her child.

The organ began playing and Gwyn heard Father Morland ask Karen and Manuel to take their places at the front. She watched as Brent entered through a door by the altar to stand beside Manuel, his best man. He looked nervous, uncomfortable—wonderful.

Jim took her arm and they watched as Jessica began walking down the aisle, dropping rose petals along the way. It was a new beginning for them all.

**From the *New York Times* bestselling
author of *Kramer Vs. Kramer***

"A timely, intelligent book." — <u>Houston Chronicle</u>

"Corman makes you feel the moral outrage at
the heart of this book." — <u>Los Angeles Times</u>

AVERY CORMAN
PRIZED POSSESSIONS

*He called it a misunderstanding. She called it rape.
Her family called it an unforgivable crime.*

Elizabeth Mason is a pretty and talented college freshman. At a
campus party, she meets a handsome, athletic senior. But that
night, everything happens too quickly. Elizabeth is raped. At
first, she tells no one. But when she finally breaks the silence
of her secret, her family faces the tragedy that has changed
their daughter's life forever — and the shattering injustice that
threatens to tear them apart...

A Berkley Paperback on Sale in May 1992